*Nothing ever happened
in Friendship, Missouri*

Its citizens were proud of its peaceful respectability, its decency.

They respected the wealthiest man in town and his lovely, public-spirited wife.

They admired the town's most beautiful and glamorous woman, who had traveled so widely and done so many interesting things.

They thought that the chief of its tiny police force was an unnecessary luxury, especially since he hailed from distant and disreputable New York.

They thought that their town was safe from scandal and immune to disaster.

And now all of their illusions were about to be ripped to bloody shreds. . . .

———

"Well-written . . . compassionate"—*The New York Times*

D0958238

Also by Jon Cleary and
available from Popular Library:

HIGH ROAD TO CHINA
04335-0   $1.95

# *VORTEX*

by Jon Cleary

POPULAR LIBRARY - TORONTO

*VORTEX*

Published by Popular Library, a unit of CBS Publications,
the Consumer Publishing Division of CBS Inc., by
arrangement with William Morrow and Company, Inc.

Copyright © 1977 by Sundowner Productions Pty Ltd

ISBN: 0-445-04446-2

Printed in Canada

10   9   8   7   6   5   4   3   2   1

**For Natascia**

# *VORTEX*

———

# Chapter One

The weather began to look ominous late Saturday.

It was not unusual for that time of year. From time immemorial as winter grudgingly gave way to spring, the same shifting, threatening patterns had begun to form in the skies above the North American continent. The first people, whose ancestors had come out of Asia over the land bridge of the Bering Strait, inched their way south through the Keewatin Ice Field 20,000 years ago; they came down out of Alaska into Alberta, Montana, Wyoming and finally on to the Great Plains; there they met the weather and were assailed by it. Their descendants, the Indian tribes, knew the terrible power of the storms and saw them as spirits wreaking vengeance for evils done by the tribes; the medicine men stood in the open and waved their arms for the storms to pass on. Which the storms frequently did, taking the medicine men with them, arms still waving.

The landscape changed, the faces and customs of the men changed. The Spaniards, led by Coronado, came up from the south, bringing with them a new God, who still produced the same terrible weather. The French, traders and trappers, filtered down from the north, bringing no God or gods but only the worship of money, and the

9

wind and the rain and the hail showed them no favouritism. Finally the Americans, convinced then as now that God was on their side, came out of the east and learned the same lesson: the weather was an element of hell. The spring storms had many faces, but their threat never changed: they came with the regularity of a fifth season. They had many names, but eventually the Spanish name for them became universal: tornadoes.

They are born in thunderstorms, the rumbling, crumbling cities of cumulo-nimbus clouds that mock horizons, tower into the stratosphere, turn day into night as they challenge the sun. Columns of air begin to rotate in the thunderstorms, increasing in violence and velocity; a funnel of cloud drops down from the mass, spinning in a counter-clockwise direction, and within the funnel are winds whirling at up to 300 miles an hour; some scientists claim the force of winds is greater than that. Close to a thousand tornadoes occur in any given year and on one day, Palm Sunday, 1965, 37 separate tornadoes hit 5 Mid-West states, killing 266 people, injuring 3300 and levelling more than 10,000 buildings.

Hurricanes and cyclones, other great wind storms, have names, usually those of women, since most meteorologists are men and male spite has its own expression. But tornadoes are never given names, though they are often called them, usually in language unprintable in a weather bulletin. This may be because even the most chauvinistic of meteorologists can't bring himself to hang a female name on such a living hell.

A great swathe of territory, extending from the Gulf of Mexico to the Canadian border and beyond, is know as Tornado Alley. The people who live in it are terrified of the storms and yet, paradoxically, careless of them. Because the paths of tornadoes are narrow, sometimes only a hundred yards, rarely more than half a mile, wide, the people live by the optimistic philosophy that the twisters will strike in the other fellow's yard. That some tornadoes, such as the one that hit Missouri, Illinois and Indiana on 18 March 1925, can stay on the ground for over 200 miles is something they prefer not to think about. They build storm cellars to retreat to, listen to warnings on the radio and television, keep an eye on the darkening sky. But, by and large, right up till the moment when they hear the express train roar of the wind and see the whirling funnel bearing down on them, the great majority of people believe "it won't happen here". They are only like the rest of mankind who have been misreading signs, ignoring warnings, turning blind eyes ever since the Serpent spoke to Eve.

Late on this particular Saturday a severe low-pressure system, a concentration of cold dry air, was developing on the eastern slopes of the Rocky Mountains, spreading from Montana down into Wyoming. Fifteen hundred miles to the south floods of warm moist air were merging and pushing up out of the Gulf of Mexico. The two fronts, armies of the elements, were moving inexorably towards each other. The battlefield would be a vast one, west of the Mississippi to the Rockies, north from the Gulf to the Canadian border. The cold dry air slid down the mountain slopes, crossing Colorado; the wet warm air moved north over Louisiana and Texas.

In Kansas City, Missouri, in the offices of the National Severe Storms Forecast Center, the weather men watched their radar screens, scanned the satellite photographs, listened to the telephone reports, and knew a classic situation was building for the development of an epidemic of tornadoes. At midnight on Saturday the Center issued its first Storm Watch, the initial step in alerting an area that it may be in for severe thunderstorms.

The message was received in the communications section of the Police Department of the town of Friendship, south-west Missouri, at 12.01 on Sunday morning. It was routinely recorded and the despatcher on duty, Officer Jack Atcheson, made a note to inform the local radio station when it came on the air at six o'clock in the morning. Then he went back to his science fiction magazine and life on another planet where the crime rate was nil and policemen were as obsolete as lamplighters.

The two weather fronts continued to march towards each other. Several small twisters, like probing scouts, touched down, then lifted, doing no damage but scaring those people who, awake or in their dreams, heard the roaring in the darkness. Friendship, a quiet town, slept peacefully and woke to a dark dawn.

# I

"Headquarters? This is PD-Four, out on Route 86. I got one on the ground here, about a mile west."

Jim McKechnie, cruising alone along Forest View Drive, cut in: "This is Chief McKechnie, Roley. Is it a big 'un?"

"Naw, chief, ain't nothing to worry about." Roley Trubauer, despite his German name, was an ex-Arkansas hill-billy; he still whittled wood when sitting around doing nothing and his drawl ran no quicker than cold molasses. He would report a minor accident or Armageddon with the same slow, unexcited voice; he sometimes drove McKechnie to distraction, but there was no other officer in the eight-man department who was more reliable. If the Second Deluge was happening out west of Route 86, Roley Trubauer wouldn't panic. "I'll just keep an eye on it."

"Keep reporting in, Roley, but don't go chasing it."

"You think I want to get this little old heap of mine more dented than it is, chief?"

That was one of the few sore points in the Friendship Police Department. For two years McKechnie had been asking for new squad cars, but the answer had always

12

been that the city had no money to spare. Two months ago an appropriation had finally come through: enough to buy one squad car. It had embarrassed McKechnie that the accompanying instructions had specified that the new car should be for his own use.

"Just don't get yourself dented, Roley."

He made a note on his pad, put it back on the clipboard on top of the two *Wanted* notices. The wanted men were a white and a black, their mug shots showing their defiance of the camera and, behind the camera, the law that had brought them in on their last offences. This time, teamed up, they had killed a cop and robbed a bank and the notices, put out after an earlier, bungled hold-up in Arkansas, said they were dangerous. Friday they had held up the bank in Columbus, Kansas, killed the cop and got away. Saturday McKechnie had had extra copies of the fliers run off and now each squad car carried one fastened to its clipboard. McKechnie privately hoped the killers were a long way from Friendship.

He continued on along Forest View, occasionally looking west between the houses to see if he could catch a glimpse of the twister. The sky there was dark, but he could not see any sign of the tell-tale funnel. He was tempted to switch on his loudhailer, warn the residents to get out and down to their cellars, but if the twister was only a small one and didn't come any closer the people wouldn't thank him for hauling them out of bed so early on a Sunday morning.

He switched on his microphone: "PD-Four? You there, Roley? What's happening now?"

"She's lifted, chief, just disappeared the way they do. Don't think we got anything to worry about. I'm heading over that way. Looks like she might of passed close to Clint Blamey's place. I'll go see he's okay."

"Don't get too far under that black stuff." McKechnie had pulled up at the end of Forest View where it dipped

13

in a curve down to the main part of town. Rain spattered the windshield like a handful of thrown glass stones, but was gone at once; the sky suddenly seemed to lighten. "Looks like it's by-passing us, heading north. You there, Despatch? Jack? Better get on to Joplin, tell 'em it's heading their way."

"You coming in now, chief?" Jack Atcheson asked.

"In a while." McKechnie, in his driving mirror, saw Dr Stenhouse coming down the sidewalk behind him, collar of his raincoat turned up against the wind, checked golf cap pulled low over his brow. "Make some fresh coffee, Jack."

Officer Atcheson, whose father had been a moonshiner, had the weird notion that coffee was like whisky: the longer you kept it, the better it got. "Any time you say, chief."

McKechnie got out of the car, glad to stretch his legs. He was a tall man, lean and flat-bellied, in good condition for a man who spent most of his working day behind a desk or riding around in a squad car. That was another of the sore points in the Police Department: when he had become chief three years ago he had insisted that everyone on the staff, including the despatchers, had to do something about their physical condition. Roley Trubauer had lost thirty pounds and ever since he had been insisting that he never felt comfortable, that his ass was now just all bones and not worth sitting on.

The wind whipped at McKechnie, but it wasn't cold and it blew some of the night's cobwebs out of his face. "You're up early, doc."

"Morning, chief. I was up late, too. There was a dance out at the country club. You should've been there."

McKechnie had never been a member of the country club. When he had been a patrolman he could not afford it and when he had made chief he had decided, reluctantly, not to apply for membership. He would have enjoyed the facilities of the club, the golf, the tennis and the swimming, but he knew that eventually there would be extra dues he would be expected to pay. Some time, on a distant tee or in a quiet corner of the bar, he would be asked by some member for a favour: the dropping of a drunk-driving charge against an errant son, the hushing-up of some woman's death from an illegal abortion. For that same reason he never socialized with any of his staff, only putting in a token appearance at birthday parties or wedding anniversaries but never accepting an invitation to supper or even a drink. In a small town he had decided that neutrality was the safest philosophy for the chief of police.

"Saturday is not my night for loosening up." Saturday, drunken drivers' night, and Wednesday, church night, were the two busiest shifts of the week. Normally he kept in touch wherever he was, at the movies or at Lee's house, then went home to bed at midnight. But last night, alerted by the Storm Watch from Kansas City, aware of the rising wind, sensing in his bones that something might happen he had been unable to sleep and he had got up at three o'clock and gone out cruising in his car. "Why are you up so early?"

Stenhouse nodded towards the big house that stood at the end of the bluff where the street dipped down into the town. "I'm on my way in there."

"How is Miss Rose?"

"She won't see the end of the day. I had to tell the family that last night."

"How did they take it?"

"They've been expecting it."

Russell Stenhouse was the town's leading doctor. He had come down from Illinois as a young man during the war, liked Friendship and its surroundings and stayed on; he and McKechnie were the only two outsiders who had ever made it to the top of their respective trees in the town.

He was a dapper little man in his late fifties, with a trim white moustache, a careful stare and an honest contempt for anyone who thought medicine was anything but a business. His bedside manner was a mixture of St. Luke and Price, Waterhouse and he didn't care if some patients thought the latter image prevailed. He was easily the town's best doctor and he knew it. He was married with two grown children who had married and moved away from the town and though he and his wife were known to be unhappy together they put up a front and were leaders of the country club set.

"It'll be a relief for the Farquhars, I guess," he said. "After all, she's been away from them for twenty-five years. When she came home a month ago to die, I'm not sure she was too welcome."

McKechnie looked towards the big frame house with the green copper cupola on the tower that jutted above its two storeys. Two big maples, their winter-bare branches moving restlessly in the wind, half-hid it from the street. In all his time in the town, ten years, he had never been inside the Farquhar house; but there was no reason why he should have been. The Farquhars, despite the fact that their fortunes had declined over the past couple of decades, were still *the* family in Friendship. Only a select few were invited to the big old house, and policemen never.

"What's she like? Miss Rose, I mean."

"You mean to look at? A skeleton now—the cancer's eaten away at her like a bunch of maggots." He looked down at the red bricks beneath his feet. There weren't many streets left in the town with these old pavements, but the people on Forest View Drive, the old money and the new, had resisted the invasion of concrete. "But I remember her when I first came here. Best-looking girl in town in those days."

"How old would she be now?"

16

"Forty-six, that's all. A crying shame, she's got to go so young and such a way."

"Where's she been all the time she's been away?"

"Don't know. The family never talked about her, least of all her brother Gil, and he's the only one of them has ever been my patient. The others, Mrs Farquhar and Gil's wife, they used to go up to Joplin. Mrs Farquhar was a big city woman and I guess she never trusted small town doctors. It never took any skin off my nose, but some of the other doctors thought it was a bit snooty."

"Were you surprised they called you in when Miss Rose came home?"

"Gil did that. Adele Farquhar has accepted me socially for years. She finally got around to accepting me medically."

"I saw Gil Farquhar driving down Dogwood about twenty minutes ago."

"Gil? You sure? This early?"

"Who else drives a twelve-year-old Cadillac? No, it was him all right."

Stenhouse looked up towards the house, shook his head, flapped his cap peak up and down with one hand. "Hope nothing's wrong in there. I mean I hope Rose hasn't already gone."

"Will it make any difference what end of the day she goes? This morning or this evening?"

"No, I guess not. Wasn't thinking about that, as a matter of fact." But he didn't elaborate. "Well, I better get in there."

"Let me know when she dies, doc."

"Why?" He was turning away, but stopped and looked back over his shoulder. "Let her die and be buried without any fuss, chief."

"I wasn't intending any fuss. I just like to know who's alive and who's dead in town, that's all. Sometimes I have

17

trouble telling the difference, but a certificate from you helps."

Stenhouse nodded, reserving his opinion of the town. Then he went on up the gravel driveway, flat-footed, deliberate-paced. McKechnie had never seen him hurry, as if he knew that, no matter what he did for his patients, he would always eventually lose them to death. A gust of rain came down the street like a silver wind, swept on out over the main section of the town. McKechnie looked east where a thin line of light showed in the grey clouds like a Judas smile. Suddenly pessimistic, he felt that no signs should be trusted today.

He got back into his car and drove on down the winding street into the business section. He had come to Friendship ten years ago from New York after the sudden, totally unexpected death of his wife. He had been looking for a haven and he had found it in this small town which, though the effort sometimes showed, tried to live up to the name it had been given 140 years ago. The first settlers had come from Tennessee and Kentucky, complaining of being crowded out by the settlers from further east who were turning the Wilderness Road into a turnpike. The Farquhars had been among them, their name now the only one left of the original twelve families who had founded the town; the others, feeling crowded again as the town grew, had moved on further west, to Oklahoma, Texas, or, in some cases, just to the cemetery on the edge of town. But though Friendship had expanded, it had never developed into a city, either in size or in attitude. It was a conservative short-back-and-sides community; there were no men's hairdressers, but two barber's shops. Some of the men who had been away to college wore button-down shirts but they didn't, couldn't, buy them at any of the town's stores. The smartest women's store called itself The Boutique, but everyone else called it Alice Brown's after its owner. There were twenty-five

18

churches and two bars in town, reversing the proportion of the New York neighborhood where McKechnie had begun on the beat; McKechnie was not convinced that more people went to heaven from Friendship, though their livers were probably in better condition to go on to ambrosia. It was a town unconcerned with the whims and wars of the outside world, smug, friendly and with its normal quota of human frailties. Its population today was 7018 and, give or take a few bodies, it had been the same when McKechnie had first come here.

When he had arrived there had been a vacancy in the Police Department. The then police chief, Ralph Henry, had had all a small town policeman's suspicion of a New York cop; but he had been a practical man and he had appreciated that only a bigoted fool would turn down an applicant who had been on the verge of getting the gold shield of a big city detective. The first year or two had not been easy for McKechnie and several times he had felt like resigning and going back to New York; but a vacation trip to see his parents and a visit to his old precinct had been enough to convince him that he wanted no more of big city living. Three years ago he had made chief when Ralph Henry had retired and it had been a measure of the other officers' acceptance of him that there had been no evident resentment of his appointment. Now he earned $950 a month, less than a New York cop on the beat took home; but he had hunting and fishing right on his doorstep and, the big city cop's impossible dream, the respect of his fellow citizens. And, as from a year ago, he also had Lee Barron.

He passed the *News* plant, nodding affectionately at it as if he were nodding at its editor and publisher. Lee's great-grandfather had started the newspaper; the Barrons were the only ones in town who might have challenged the Farquhars as *the* family. Lee, home from college and then a year on the *St Louis Post-Despatch,* had inherited

19

the newspaper and printing plant from her widowed father and within three months of taking over had started to shake up the paper and the town. She had contributed to the shaking up by falling in love with the chief of police. McKechnie winked at the building, which took up the south-west corner of the town square, diagonally across from police headquarters. If he had stayed on in New York would he have finished up getting engaged to the editor and publisher of the *New York Times,* supposing a woman had achieved that position? The pay was better, but New York cops usually married into their own class.

He went round the square, heading east. He passed the iron statue of the Confederate soldier who, through an error on the part of a surveyor brought in for the job, had been put up facing north-west, a direction largely undisturbed during the War between the States. The sculptor had not been very talented and the soldier's expression, which was meant to be determined, had turned out bewildered. Which, perhaps, had been more appropriate because, though the town had opted for the Confederate side, most of its men had headed north and joined the Union army. It had been the one major schizophrenic split of the town and since then the citizens had done their successful best to keep the peace among themselves. The statue had remained, a reminder, rather than a memorial, of what could happen when the town's leaders misjudged the sentiments of its citizens.

McKechnie switched on the local radio station and heard the high nasal voice of Derry Brass, the junior announcer, saying a Tornado Watch had just come in and that a small twister had been sighted for two minutes out on Route 86. Then he went back to playing the gospel music that made up the station's programme from 6 a.m till noon. The Florida Boys went through "Just a Little Talk With Jesus" and McKechnie, a so-so Catholic who

20

had never been particularly chummy with Jesus, switched back to the police band. He guessed that those who had heard the Tornado Watch had probably looked out their windows, shrugged and gone back to their breakfasts, their love-making or whatever else occupied them at seven o'clock on Sunday morning.

He drove into a squall of rain and when he came out of it saw the old blue Cadillac coming down the middle of the street straight ahead of him. He banged his horn, swinging sharply to his right, and saw the startled face of Gil Farquhar as the Cadillac went past only a foot from him. In his mirror he saw the other car's brake-lights come on, but he just waved an arm out of his window and drove on. He wasn't going to back up and get out in the rain just to tell Gilbert Farquhar to keep his wits about him when he was driving. He thought maybe the man in dark glasses sitting beside Farquhar was already doing that. But he wondered why Gil Farquhar, normally the most careful of drivers, should have been driving so inattentively.

He drove out along Airport Road, past the ragged edge of town where the few blacks lived. Despite its small population, Friendship was a spread-out place, a relic of its early days when its settlers had not wanted to be crowded; it had fought against encroachment by the county and, despite rising costs and some complaints from taxpayers, had maintained its original boundaries. But the territorial imperative, thought McKechnie, who surprised even himself sometimes with his random choice of reading, would eventually be beaten by taxes. The jungle beasts and birds of Africa, fighting to keep their own patch of territory, didn't know how easy their battle was compared to that of *Homo* so-called *sapiens*.

The wind had dropped and the rain had eased. As he approached the airport, one concrete runway and two small hangars, he saw the plane parked outside the locked

21

doors of one of the hangars. He turned in the gates of the airport and drove down to the gravel parking strip outside the hangars. He got out, putting on his cap and squeezing it down on his head in case the wind came up again. He walked across to the plane, a six-seater Learjet.

A man in tan dungarees and a smart-looking flying jacket with an emblem on the pocket opened the door of the aircraft, but didn't get out. "Hi, looks a trifle stormy."

McKechnie glanced to the west, where the sky looked as if last night had abruptly decided not to continue any further, was going to defy the sun, the clock and the calendar. "That's what the radio has been telling me. You heard the warnings? There's a Tornado Watch just been issued for this area."

"I heard it." The pilot was a man in his mid-forties with narrow eyes and the air of a man who had been flying all his life and forgotten where he had started from. Or where he was going to: any destination would do. "But I can't take off yet. Much as I'd like to."

He's no fool, McKechnie thought, he's a professional. "You waiting for someone?"

"My boss."

"A local man?"

"No, I just brought him in. He's visiting someone in town."

McKechnie glanced to the west again. "I think you ought to get out of here." The wind came up again and the plane's wing shook. "Maybe I can take a message in to your boss. You know where he is?"

The pilot shook his head, but all of a sudden McKechnie sensed the man was either lying or hedging. Either way, he had closed up, shutting the door of himself if not of the plane.

"Mind if I look at your registration papers?" said McKechnie.

"Are you entitled to do that? This is an airport, there's

no law as far as I know says I have to check in with the local police—"

"You don't know us local police. We make our own laws, hasn't Hollywood told you that? May I see your papers, please? Your licence and the plane's papers."

The pilot hesitated, then reached back behind him and drew out a small satchel. He took out some papers and handed them to McKechnie. The wind tore at them, as if all at once on the pilot's side, and McKechnie had to turn his back and hold the papers close to him. The pilot's name did not concern him, but he looked up when he saw the name on the plane's registration.

"The Vanderhorn Corporation? *The* Vanderhorn?"

The pilot hesitated again, then nodded as McKechnie gave him back the papers. "Yeah. I brought down the—one of the vice-presidents."

"They don't have any plants around here. They thinking of moving down here?"

"I don't know. I guess so."

"Someone meet him here?"

"A guy in an old blue Cadillac."

Then McKechnie heard his car radio calling him. There were other questions he wanted to ask the pilot, but he had the feeling the man wouldn't know the answers to them. The radio insisted, crackling with static, sounding like a metal-voiced shrew. He went across to his car, called in.

"Chief?" Jack Atcheson sounded excited, gulping his words. "Roley Trubauer's just called in. He thinks you better get out to the Blamey place. The twister hit it and there's a dead woman there. Molly Farquhar, Gil Farquhar's wife!"

## II

The Blamey farmhouse was set back about two hundred

yards from the road and a long straight driveway led up to it. The twister had followed the driveway as if a course had been set for it. It had demolished the avenue of red cedars lining the gravel track, uprooting at least half of them and leaving the rest as jagged stumps, the freshly-exposed wood bright as blood-tinged bone in the grey light. McKechnie remembered a common name for the red cedar, the graveyard tree, so-called because it was planted so often as an ornamental in cemeteries. It was well-named this morning: beyond the avenue the flattened farmhouse promised nothing but tragedy.

Trees and branches lay across the drive and McKechnie pulled off into the field on one side and followed the tracks of Roley Trubauer's car up to the house. He rounded the barn and a smaller shed, both reduced to a rubbish dump of timber, and pulled up in the muddy yard. In the fields beyond, following the track of the tornado, he could see three or four dead cattle and, still further on, the stripped trees of the Blamey orchard. A power line had been brought down and lay in the mud, crackling spitefully and spitting sparks.

Trubauer, tall and baggy-fleshed, all seams and tuck-pointing where his wife had taken in his uniform, got out of his car. "She's in there, chief. Where the front bedroom was."

"You sure it's Molly Farquhar?"

"Shit, Jim—" Trubauer swallowed, started again. McKechnie had no ear or tongue for four-letter words and he had told his men so. "I *know* her, Jim. It's her all right, but she's a real mess. Looks like the goddam twister tried to tear her apart."

From a long way off there came the sound of the ambulance siren; at such a distance it sounded more like a keening than a warning. That'll be Zeke Norval, McKechnie thought. Zeke always drove like that, with the siren wailing, whether it was peak-hour Friday or early morning Sunday, a serious accident case or an old woman being taken for her quarterly check-up. You got your money's worth with him, he never wanted you to confuse his ambulance with a taxicab.

"Anyone else in the house?"

"Not far's I can see. But that don't say there's no one there."

"You look in the storm cellar?"

"It's empty. There ain't no one else here, Jim, 'less he's buried under all that wreckage. No sign of Clint Blamey at all. At all." Trubauer had a habit of occasionally repeating himself. as if his tongue had stuck in a groove. "That's danged funny, you reckon? I mean, what the hell was she doing out here on her own?"

"We'll start being detectives later, Roley. We'll get her out of here first."

The ambulance came into sight, siren still wailing. It swung in from the road, came bouncing up the tracks of the police cars, the siren dying away. Zeke Norval, thin, bald at twenty-five, fell out of the driving cabin as if his legs were springs and he had just been released.

"Christ!" He wiped both hands down the front of his white tunic, stared at the wreckage of the house. "Sure make a mess, don't they!"

The frame house, once two storeys high, was now only shoulder-high to McKechnie. The walls had collapsed, folding inwards, and were now nothing but a pile of splintered lumber. The roof had settled down over the lot, like an iron pie crust. Pieces of furniture showed under the wreckage: a bent iron bedstead, a shattered mirror, a torn and damp green curtain like a defeated flag. Clint Blamey. wherever he was, was homeless.

McKechnie went round the house, checking that the broken power line had made no part of the wreckage live and dangerous. Then he came back and the three men lifted the body of Molly Farquhar out from what had once

25

been the front bedroom and put it on a stretcher. A framed photograph, the glass broken, making the face of the woman in the photo look shattered, lay close to the body. McKechnie recognized the woman as Blamey's dead wife.

Zeke Norval went to get a blanket and McKechnie, trying to make his eye as cold and unfeeling as possible, looked down at the dead Molly Farquhar. He had seen her often around town, spoken to her frequently; but he had never really known her. He had always thought of her as an addicted committee woman; she had belonged to every organization in town bar Alcoholics Anonymous. She had been a feverish woman: his image of her was that she was always in mid-stride, never at rest: but she was at rest now, forever. But her face was smashed and there was no way of telling whether she was at peace.

Zeke Norval came back, put a blanket over her and a minute later he was bouncing down the track again, rushing back to be available for more tragedy. The siren began to wail again as he got out on to the road.

"Shoot," said Trubauer with great restraint, "I wish he'd blow up that goddam si-reen."

McKechnie looked once more at the wrecked house. "You think Clint is somewhere under there?"

"He could be, but I don't reckon so. His car ain't in the barn, either. Molly Farquhar's car ain't here. So how'd she get out here?"

McKechnie had no answer to that. He was turning away when he saw something sticking out from beneath the sodden green curtain. He stepped back into the wreckage, picked up the object. It was a woman's handbag, made of expensive brown leather that was dark now with water. He opened it, took out a chequebook and some other papers: the name on all of them was Molly S. Farquhar. It was a large handbag, the sort a woman carried over her shoulder on a long strap, and there was a rear pocket to

26

it, closed by a zipper. The pocket bulged and when Mc-Kechnie pulled on the zipper it stuck on something. He pressed down with his fingernail, got the zipper fully open. The pocket of the handbag was full of $20 bills held together by a rubber band. He put the bag under his arm and counted the bills.

"Twenty-two hundred dollars." He looked at Roley Trubauer. "Do women usually carry that much money around with them?"

"Not my missus. She had that much money, I'd never let her outa the house."

McKechnie looked at the chequebook. The last butt showed a withdrawal of $2200, dated two days ago. "Did you ever see her and Clint together?"

"Only nodding to each other at church socials, things like that."

McKechnie put the money and the chequebook and papers back into the handbag. "Well, we better be getting back to town. When are you supposed to go off duty?"

"Pretty soon. Eight o'clock."

"I think you're going to be working overtime. I can't afford to keep you staking out this place all the time, but stay on patrol out this way, try and get by here every ten minutes or so. Make out your report and bring it in later. I'll go see Gil Farquhar, give him the bed news. He'll have to go down to the hospital, identify the body."

The radios were squawking in the cars behind them, but neither of them took any notice. "What we going to do, Jim?"

"Meaning?"

"What was she *doing* out here? A nice respectable woman like her. When I file my report where I found her, it's going to be all over town. You know what this place is like. Gossip goes through it quicker'n a twister."

"Just as devastating too, I guess. But we're in the business of crime prevention, not gossip prevention. I don't

27

know why the hell she was out here, but I got more to do than protect the Farquhars' good name, if that's what you're thinking." He looked up at the sky, slitting his eyes against the wind. "We got that to worry about, for one thing. That weather could be full of twisters. You hear Jack's latest bulletin? They've had two over in Oklahoma this morning already, down there in Wagoner County."

Trubauer cocked a baggy eye at the sky. "I seen dozens of them twisters at a distance, but that's all. Wonder when your luck runs out?"

"You'll survive, Roley. Ever I've seen a survivor, you're one." He looked at the power line still sizzling in the mud. "Better get the power company out here as soon as they can, shut off that power before someone gets himself electrocuted."

Going back to town McKechnie turned on the local radio station again. The Blackwood Brothers were telling the Lord how great He was. It had taken McKechnie some time, when he had first come down here to Bible Belt country, to accustom himself to the seriousness with which the local people took their religion. He went to Mass irregularly; said a prayer occasionally, usually when he wanted something or had had a narrow escape; wore his religion with a sceptic's casualness, like an old Sunday sweater. But the people here in Friendship, members of twenty-five churches, wore their religion as if it were a reversible garment, one side cashmere, the other hair. They alternated between showing it off and being afraid of it. They loved the gospel singers who were both their spokesmen and their comforters. McKechnie hated the hymns, but they were no more banal than the hymns the nuns and priests had taught him back home in New York. He sometimes wondered if the Lord turned a deaf ear to some of the music that was supposed to praise Him.

The Blackwood Brothers finished and Derry Brass came on. "We got a Tornado Warning, folks, from the

Weather Service over in Springfield. This is it: A Tornado Warning is in effect until 10 a.m. Central Standard Time for persons in Vista, Hooten and Raeburn Counties. A tornado was reported by the public six miles north of Colt, Oklahoma, at 6.50 a.m. Central Daylight Time and is moving north-east at forty miles per hour. That's the warning, folks, but I better mention we had a little one, a twister, I mean, just outside town a little while ago. We'll give you details as we get them. So take care, you hear? Get down in your storm cellars, take your little old radios with you and listen to Wendy Bagwell as she sings—"

McKechnie turned off the radio. The tornado reported north of Colt still had another hour to travel before it would reach the vicinity of Friendship; but the chances were that it would have petered out long before then. It had not been reported as a major twister and the small ones usually proved local. But he still felt a sense of unease. As he came into town he saw several men on their front porches, their just-delivered Sunday newspapers in their hands, squinting up at the grey sky. He wanted to go on the loud-hailer, tell them to get their families down into their storm cellars right away, but he resisted the temptation. Every year he had been in Friendship there had been Tornado Warnings; there had been several last spring and summer. But none had ever hit closer than the one that had hit the Blamey farm this morning and he couldn't expect the men to take any notice of him if he shouted at them that he felt in his bones that today would be different. A couple of the men waved to him, then went back into their houses, already opening their newspapers to get the important news: what was the Kansas City Royals' line-up for today's game against the Yankees, what was going to happen with the new state highway Jefferson City was talking about.

The sky looked lighter and the clouds actually seemed to have lifted by the time McKechnie pulled up outside headquarters. He went into the one-storey brick building, telling himself his bones were wrong. But knowing that even so early they had been right: today was different already. Molly Farquhar was dead in circumstances that might need a lot of explaining.

He met Jack Atcheson coming out on his way home. "Fresh coffee in there, chief. I told Lucy to let it simmer a while."

Atcheson was a short wiry man with a flat-planed bony face and a dark crew-cut, the same sort of hair-style he had been wearing when he had joined the force twenty years ago. He suffered from arthritis in one leg and spent most of his time now as a despatcher. But in an emergency McKechnie sometimes called him back to drive a squad car and he came back willingly, as if wanting to prove that he was not finished as a cop.

"Bad news about Molly Farquhar, eh? What was she doing—?"

"I don't know, Jack. Don't spread the news around yet, okay? I still got to tell the Farquhars."

"Won't even tell the missus." But he would; Jack Atcheson told his wife everything. As if that was the first law in every policeman's book. "Enjoy the coffee. Don't forget, let it simmer a while."

"Right till I've boiled away every grain. Stick by your phone, Jack. Just in case I have to call you back."

"The missus won't like it. But okay, chief."

Lucy Chapley, the weekend part-time despatcher, was at the communications console. She was a widow with two teenage boys who had been well on the way to being delinquents when McKechnie, trying some oblique psychology, had brought the mother into the Police Department. He had no idea what arguments there had been in the Chapley home, but ever since Lucy had come to work here there had been no more trouble with her boys. Or maybe they now went up to Joplin and raised hell there.

30

Lucy pressed down some keys and looked up at him. "I heard you tell Officer Atcheson not to broadcast the terrible news about Mrs Farquhar." She was 'a plump pretty woman who took her job and herself seriously, had an old-fashioned formality about her that made her call Jack Atcheson *Officer*. "What do I tell the radio station if they hear about it? They've been calling in about the twister out at the Blamey place."

"Tell them the house was demolished, but don't tell 'em any more than that. Not till I come back from the Farquhars'. Get on the phone and tell the officers off-duty and the volunteers that I want them on stand-by."

Bud Grierson, in charge of Records and Identification, came in, held out a cup of coffee. "Better grab this, chief, before it's ruined. Jack's had it bubbling like he was thinning molasses. How's it outside?"

McKechnie took the coffee. "Mixed. It's still pretty black over to the west. The twister made a helluva mess of Clint Blamey's place. Put out a call on him, Lucy. Give it to the cars, just our fellers, not the sheriff's or the Highway Patrol guys. Tell 'em to keep an eye out for him. Also, get on to Derry Brass down at the radio station. Ask him to put out a message for Blamey to get in touch with me."

"He was here in town last night, I saw him."

Bud Grierson was in his mid-fifties, twenty years older than McKechnie, and he would have been promoted to chief if the town had not decided that it wanted someone younger, someone with more years of service left in him. He was a short, grey-haired man with a long, defeated-looking face, as if being passed over had scarred him; but McKechnie always remembered that Grierson had looked the same way ten years ago, as if early in life he had already become resigned to being too late for everything: promotion, ambition, even happiness. McKechnie did not know if Grierson resented him and was always careful never to bring up the subject of his own promotion.

31

"You speak to him?"

"No. He was in Wayman's bar, having a drink. Looked like he was filling in time, waiting for someone. He kept looking towards the door every time it opened."

"I'm sure he wasn't waiting for Mrs Farquhar," Lucy Chapley said primly. "Not in a bar."

"I didn't say that, did I? All I'm saying he was in town last night and that ain't usual." Grierson had a high scratchy voice that could irritate when he was irritated. "Saturday nights he usually goes up to Joplin. Since his wife died a year ago, he's done that regular. Mebbe he's got a girl-friend or something up there. Mebbe he was waiting for *her*."

"Well, we'll ask him when we find him," said McKechnie. "I'm going up to the Farquhars' now. Like I said, no information to anyone till I've seen the family. Roley will be in soon with his report, Bud. Sit on it."

When he got outside the sky had lightened still further, though there was still no break in the clouds. The wind was still strong, snatching at the redbud blossoms on each of the four corners of the square and fanning a dull fire of them across the spring grass. On the far side of the square the neon sign above Tom's Café flickered fitfully like orange lightning; a man got out of a pick-up truck and went in under the sign, holding his hand above his head as if afraid of being struck. From up on the hill there came the sound of the Catholic church bell, calling the faithful and the not-so-faithful-but-habit-ridden to the first Mass. Only Father Indelli tested the faith of his congregation so early. The other pastors slept in, grateful that their flocks preferred the later service.

McKechnie drove back up to Forest View Drive. He took the police car in off the street, parked it in the curved driveway. The Farquhars, ten years ago, had still had eighteen acres of land surrounding their house; it had been the last big estate, except for farms, left in the county. But now they had only three acres and the rest had been sold off to lawyers, doctors and auto franchise dealers who had built houses designed to show how much their owners had paid for the land, which hadn't been cheap. The Farquhar house stood among the ranch houses and haciendas and Tudor log cabins like a memorial.

He rang the front-door bell, an old-fashioned bell that tinkled inside the hall like an echo from the past. There was the sound of footsteps, then the door was opened by Wilma Mae, the black woman who had lived in the house since her birth. No one else on Forest View had help who lived in; you could buy an $80,000 house but you couldn't buy live-in help any more. Wilma Mae Roberry, if nothing else, distinguished the Farquhars from everyone else in the street.

"Morning, Wilma Mae. I'd like to see Mr Farquhar."

"He busy, chief. This ain't a happy house this morning. Maybe you come back some other time?"

"I'm afraid not, Wilma Mae. It's important I see him now."

"Who is it, Wilma Mae?" McKechnie recognized the voice from inside the house: no one else in Friendship had a voice like it.

"It's Chief McKechnie from the police, Miz Farquhar. He wanna see Mr Gilbert, he say it important." She swung open the door and McKechnie saw the tall grey-haired figure standing at the bottom of the wide stairs in the hall. "I told him now ain't the time—"

"Come in, Mr McKechnie. We'll go into the drawing-room."

McKechnie tucked his cap under his arm, wiped his boots carefully on the porch mat and stepped into the wide hall. There was no wall-to-wall carpet here: polished wood gleamed like brown marble. The large rug in the middle of the floor might be worn, but it had come from Darghazin, Persia, not Dalton, Georgia. The mahogany

33

balustrade of the curved staircase shone with the same lustre as the floor, a gentle curve of highlights climbing to the floor above. Pictures hung on the wall: a Homer, a Wyeth, a Benton, some early American prints. McKechnie, who recognized the value of neither the rug nor the paintings, still knew he was in the midst of money. He suddenly realized that the twelve-year-old Cadillac outside meant nothing.

"You are a discreet man, Mr McKechnie, so I know you have not come here without good reason." Adele Farquhar closed the heavy mahogany doors of the drawing-room, shutting them in; this was a rare home in today's world, one where privacy still counted. "Please sit down. There, facing the light, so that I can see you clearly. My eyes are not what they used to be and I am too vain to wear spectacles in front of gentlemen."

She didn't smile as she said it. It was not a coy remark but a statement of the fact that, no matter if her eyesight was failing, she saw herself clearly. She was seventy years old and still beautiful, tall and as straight-backed as McKechnie himself. She had been born in Mississippi to a family with more prestige and less money than the family she had married into; she had gone to New York in the Twenties and gone on the stage. She had never been a star but she might have been one had she not married Senator Robert Farquhar and retired from Broadway. There were still people in New York who remembered her and her voice, the most beautiful, they claimed, ever heard in the American theatre. McKechnie, a man with a delicate ear, listened to it as if to music.

McKechnie looked around, then sat down on a green velvet couch. "I have bad news, Mrs Farquhar. Maybe I should see your son."

She looked at him steadily. "He is upstairs with his sister. Tell me your news."

McKechnie told her, trying not to sound blunt yet keeping his words to a minimum. She closed her eyes and for just a moment her back wilted. Then, her voice firm as ever: "Where is my daughter-in-law?"

"Down at the hospital, ma'am. She'll have to be taken over to the county morgue later, but she is down there for the time being. The county coroner is coming over from Vista. He's probably on his way now, seeing who she is."

Adele Farquhar nodded, as if it were only right that a Farquhar should get preferential treatment, even in death. But she said, "Can't Dr Stenhouse handle it? Do we have to have outsiders?"

"In accident cases like this, yes. It's only a formality."

"Have you told the newspaper people about it?"

He shook his head. "I don't run the Police Department for the media, Mrs Farquhar."

She gave him a small apologetic nod. "I should not have asked that question. I said you are a discreet man and I meant it."

"I didn't think you'd ever noticed. We haven't met that many times."

"I'm observant, Mr McKechnie. It was part of my training as an actress. I was one of the old school who were taught to look out, not in. And I *know* about you— I've made enquiries. The town holds you in very high regard."

"Thank you. But discreet as I'm supposed to be, I'm going to have to ask some questions. Maybe tomorrow—" He looked up at the moulded metal ceiling above them: they didn't make them like that any more. The floorboards above the ceiling creaked: someone was walking around in the room up there.

"You mean when my daughter is—is also dead? Dr Stenhouse told me he had given you the news about her."

"It's a terrible day, Mrs Farquhar." The wind, like a reminder, whipped the branches of the maples against

35

the front of the house. "I don't mean the weather. I mean in here, for you and everybody else in the house."

She was silent a moment, sitting up straight in the straight-backed chair, hands at rest on the walnut arms of it. For the first time McKechnie noticed the portrait on the wall behind her: Robert Farquhar, silver-haired and handsome, the stock model of a Senator, looking down with pride and love on his wife. He had been twenty years older than his bride and he had died thirty years ago and, McKechnie had been told, was still mourned by her.

At last she said, "You are a kind man, too, Mr McKechnie. I don't envy you your profession—not this side of it. Do they give you citations for sympathy as well as bravery?"

"No, ma'am. I don't think I'd agree with it if they did. It's no effort to be sympathetic."

"It is for some people."

He knew that as well as she did, but he wasn't going to go into it. He stood up. "I'll have to come back tomorrow, I'm afraid. Even if—"

"Oh, Rose will be dead." She closed her eyes again, but only for a moment. Then she stood up, put out her hand. He took it gently, but her grip was firm. "Thank you for coming yourself, Mr McKechnie, instead of sending another officer. But I'd like to ask you a question. Do you know why my daughter-in-law was out at the Blamey place?"

The way she put the question puzzled him, but he could read nothing in her face. "I don't know. That's something I hope your son will be able to answer."

"Be gentle with him when you do question him. I don't know how he—" Then her voice broke. He waited apprehensively for her to break down, not quite sure how he would handle the situation; she was not the sort of woman he could put his arm round, comfort her as he had done other embattled women. But she recovered,

36

opened the doors for him. "Come tomorrow morning. But please keep the newspaper people away from us today. I understand you are friendly with Miss Barron. Explain that we need our privacy today. Of all days."

They walked out into the hall just as two men, Gilbert Farquhar and a stranger, came down the stairs. McKechnie looked at the stranger, recognized him, and recognized too why the Farquhars, today of all days, needed their privacy.

"Mr Vanderhorn?" he said. "I saw your pilot out at the airport. I warned him he'd better take off, get away from this weather, otherwise you're likely to lose your aeroplane."

Gilbert Farquhar looked at the man beside him at the bottom of the stairs, then at his mother. She raised her chin a little, mistress of the situation.

"Mr Vanderhorn, this is our chief of police, a man of great discretion," she said. "Mr McKechnie, this is the Vice-President of the United States."

## Chapter Two

The weather that Sunday across the United States was varied. In the north-west there was rain blanketing Washington State, Oregon and Idaho. In California, Nevada and Arizona the sun shone out of cloudless skies as if reflecting the smugness of the people who had chosen to live there. The Rocky Mountain states, the Gulf states and the Mid West crouched under the tumultuous skies above them. The eastern seaboard, from Florida north to Maine, had slight cloud, sunshine and rising winds. In Washington, DC, the biggest cloud was in the White House.

The President of the United States, an irascible man even in good weather and a good press climate, was angry. "He called me at three o'clock this morning," he told the First Lady, a woman who had long ago learned the first lesson of a politician's wife: strive for an infinity of patience. "Said he was going down to see that woman of his! Three o'clock in the goddam morning!"

"I'm sure he didn't call her *that woman*." They were in her bedroom on the second floor of East Wing and she was having breakfast in bed, her one self-indulgence of the week. "And you're not annoyed that he called you in the middle of the night—you've been called at that hour before."

"Not by *him*! He's out of his goddam mind. All right, so he loves the woman. But he ought to give a thought to his position!"

"He's been doing that for the past three and a half years. Longer. Fifteen or twenty years, isn't it? How long have they been friends?"

"They're more than friends, you know that. She's been his mistress all that time."

"All right. Lovers. Or is that a dirty word?"

"It is in a politician's lexicon, especially this year. Jesus, you're no comfort at all. You sound as if you agree with what he's done."

"I do. I think it's gallant and courageous and wholly admirable. I just wish for Rose Farquhar's sake that he had been all those things twenty years ago. She's never been his doxy, like some women we've had in this town. I'm glad he's gone down to stand by her. Better late than never, as they say in the politician's lexicon."

"You never heard any politician say that," said the President. "Only a fool would admit that something he had done hadn't happened at exactly the right time."

"I'll ask Willis when he gets back," she said. "One thing he's not, he's no fool."

The President, standing at the bedroom window, shook his head at the clouds that seemed to be thickening overhead. Down in the White House grounds the wind appeared to be growing stronger. Cherry blossom blew across the lawns like discarded ballot papers.

# I

Willis Vanderhorn had been used to hatred all his life. It seemed to be a corollary to his wealth and position, like privilege and luxury. He remembered, as a child, riding with his grandfather down Market Street, San Francisco, when their big grey Packard had been stoned by some men his grandfather had described as Bolsheviks. It was only years later that he had come to recognize that his grandfather had been out of date, that the Bolsheviks had belonged to an earlier decade; it was only then he had recognized that his grandfather had been out of date on many things. There had been other haters though they hadn't thrown stones as had the men in San Francisco. At Exeter where he had gone east to school; at Stanford; on Wall Street; it had taken him some time to appreciate that, though the haters were now of his own class, their feeling was no less virulent. Still later when he had gone into politics he had discovered the enmity towards him and his family stretched across the nation, a web that no amount of attempted goodwill could break. The Vanderhorn Foundation, the mild liberalism in his politics, none of it took the opprobrium from the Vanderhorn name. His native state had told him he would never be elected to the Senate by its voters and he had had to move east to a more conservative state where the citizens would vote for anyone so long as he was a Republican, not black not a Catholic and could finance his own campaign. Grandfather had left more than a fortune to his heirs he had left the yoke of a name.

Yet Willis Vanderhorn had been surprised at the hatred displayed by this man who sat opposite him, whom he had met for the first time this morning. When her brother had come east to Maryland a month ago, Rose had pleaded with Vanderhorn not to be there; he had been puzzled by her request but he had agreed to it. Since they had met this morning out at the airport Gilbert Farquhar had said nothing that could be termed anything but polite. But Vanderhorn recognized an enemy when he saw one.

"I am sorry about your wife."

"You said that Mr Vice-President."

"I don't think we need to be too formal in here, do we? Yes, I did say it. But I thought you hadn't heard me."

40

Gilbert Farquhar sat slumped in the chair his mother had sat in when she had been in this room with McKechnie. He was a tall man but did not have his mother's carriage and so looked shorter than he was. He was still handsome but erosion had set in early and, if he lived so long, he would not be a handsome old man. Frustrated ambition and self-pity had blotched him, softened the bone in him to Plasticine. He had wanted to be a politician, perhaps take over his father's Senate seat, but he had never been able to make his mark with any of the state's party bosses. He had practised law for a while, but he had not been successful at that. Gradually he had retreated did nothing now but watch the family investments. It irked him that, ironically, so much of the family money was invested in corporations that, over the years, had become part of the Vanderhorn empire. It was he who had broken up the estate ten years ago and he had been almost spitefully meticulous in seeing that none of the money gained had been invested in anything remotely connected with Willis Vanderhorn. But his mother had never allowed him to sell off those stocks they had already held. So the man opposite, however indirectly, still supplied him with the bulk of his income.

"I know I'm not welcome here, Farquhar—especially now. I'll be gone as soon as—" He didn't finish, but he didn't have to.

Farquhar stirred himself, sat up. "Mr Vanderhorn—" His voice was good, almost an echo of his mother's; and he had something of her no-longer-fashionable courtesy. "You aren't helping my mother by staying on. Nor my sister," he added tentatively.

Vanderhorn got up and walked to the window. Net curtains hung between the heavy green drapes and no passer-by in the street would be able to distinguish him properly. He was a man of medium height and, though still athletic at fifty-five, was bottom-heavy. He had a broad open face and a shock of thick dark hair that no amount of expensive barbering had been able to train. He was not handsome or even good-looking, but women had always found him attractive. Even those who found his wealth unattractive.

"That policeman is still outside in his car."

"I guess he's waiting for me." Farquhar stood up, was tall for a moment as he straightened his back. He seemed to be searching for strength he had lost years ago. "I have to go down to the hospital."

"I think I better have a word with him. Will you ask him to come in?" Then Vanderhorn made an apologetic gesture. "Sorry. I'm accustomed to having things done for me."

"So Rose told me. On our way back from Maryland."

"How much more did she tell you about me?"

"Very little. You had been living together for six years before we even found out about it."

"We never *lived together*—though I wish now that we had. But thanks for putting it so delicately." He looked up at the portrait on the wall. "She used to joke with me about what your father would have said. Her being the mistress of a Republican."

"That would be the least of your sins in my father's eyes," said Gilbert Farquhar and went out of the room.

Vanderhorn looked up at the portrait again, said quietly, "You had better forgive me, Senator. Your daughter already has."

A few moments later McKechnie was ushered into the drawing-room. "I'll go and get my coat," said Farquhar and left the two men, the policeman and the Vice-President, alone.

"I think your warning to my pilot was good sense, chief. Would you mind going out to the airport and telling him to take off for somewhere where the weather is not so unsettled? I tried phoning the airport, but the office there seems unattended."

"It always is Sunday mornings, sir. We don't get much traffic in there weekends, just the occasional private plane. I'll go out and tell him. Where will I tell him to head for?"

Vanderhorn looked out the window again. "How far out of town was the tornado that killed Mrs Farquhar? Three or four miles? Are we likely to get another hereabouts?"

"Could be, sir. I never attempt to guess the weather, not down here. We're on the edge of the Great Plains and they say the weather down here changes as soon as you turn your back."

"Sounds like Washington."

"The difference is, down here we can't do anything about it." But McKechnie smiled and added, "Sir."

He's a Democrat, Vanderhorn thought, or I'm a Norman Thomas Socialist. But at least the man had smiled when he had said it. "Where do you suggest my pilot should head for?"

"You staying over, sir? I mean, are you leaving here today?"

"That depends, chief. But, unfortunately, I think I shall be. Leaving, I mean."

"Then if he heads for Springfield, he should be okay. The Tornado Warnings are for areas mostly west of here, we're just on the fringe. You can drive over there and meet him. Or, if things clear, he can come back and pick you up. Sir?"

"Yes?"

"Are you alone? I mean, do you have any aide with you, or Secret Service men?"

"No, chief, I'm alone. Very much so." McKechnie sensed another meaning to what he said, but Vanderhorn didn't underline it. "Why do you ask?"

43

"I'm not trying to butt in here, sir. But I feel like I'm, well, responsible for you. I mean your safety."

"You mean because I'm the Vice-President?" Vanderhorn nodded, shoved his hands into his pockets and went to the window again. "You step into a position like mine, chief, and you become two men. Yourself and whatever the office calls you, Vice-President, Secretary of State, whatever. Is it like that as chief of police?"

"In a town this size?" McKechnie smiled again. "Not to the same degree, sir."

Vanderhorn's famous smile showed both top and bottom rows of teeth: the Friendly Shark, he had once been called by a fellow Senator. Overseas commentators had remarked upon the proliferation of teeth among America's politicians, as if they were one giant advertisement for dentifrice or perhaps lobbyists for the American Dental Association. Molar politics, the Washington correspondent of Tass had called it, but he had never been known to smile anyway.

"Chief, come back and see me after you have taken Mr Farquhar down to the hospital. Oh, and after you've seen my pilot. Until then, I'd appreciate it if you told no one, and I mean *no one,* that I'm here in Friendship."

"Does Washington know you're here?"

"Nobody knows but the President. You're in privileged company. May we keep it that way?"

Gilbert Farquhar came to the door, raincoat buttoned to his neck, an old tweed hat pulled low down on his head. He looked ready for the elements, of any kind. "When you are ready, chief." He glanced at Vanderhorn. "Have you explained the situation to him?"

"No. I don't think Chief McKechnie wants to be burdened with too much information."

McKechnie stood outside the conversation, aware of the tension between the two men. He was curious as to what had brought the Vice-President to this house on this particular day: did it have something to do with the dying woman upstairs? But maybe Vanderhorn was right: he shouldn't be burdened with too much information. He went out to the hall, leaving the two men to their antagonism and their secret.

"Perhaps you *should* tell him," Farquhar kept his voice low. "We may need him to keep people away from here later. Now that my wife is dead. She was very popular in the town."

"I appreciate your concern for my position—"

"I wasn't thinking of you, Mr Vice-President. I was thinking of my sister."

Vanderhorn uttered something like a sigh, then nodded. "I've asked him to come back. If he is to be told, I'll do it myself."

"Whatever you say. I just want Rose to die in peace, that's all."

"At least we have that in common."

Farquhar left then, turning quickly on his heel and going out of the room. A moment later Vanderhorn, standing at the window, saw him and McKechnie going down the front steps to the police car and the Cadillac in the driveway. A third car was standing there, a yellow station wagon that must have just arrived. He couldn't see who was in it, but it didn't interest him. He was not really interested in anyone in this town but the dying woman in the bedroom on the floor above. And she, she had told him, had turned her back on the town almost twenty-five years ago.

"She is sleeping." Adele Farquhar had come into the room. "We can leave her for a while."

"Do you think we should get a nurse?"

"I can look after my daughter, Mr Vanderhorn—I and Wilma Mae. We nursed her through all her childhood ailments, some of them serious. Not as serious as today's,

45

but then not as hopeless, either. The fewer outsiders we have in the house, the better. I haven't had my breakfast —I presume you haven't had time for any, either. Would you care to join me?"

They went down the hall to a small rear room that looked out on to a garden where dogwood, redbud and azaleas struggled to hold their buds against the threshing of the wind. Beyond the wide deep lawn at the back of the house there was a thick wood where oak and hickory grew. Vanderhorn wondered if Adele Farquhar usually breakfasted like this or whether the table had been set for company. The glasses holding the orange juice were crystal, the toast-rack was silver, there were fine lace mats under the thin china plates.

Adele Farquhar saw his observant eye. "Wilma Mae has a sense of occasion, Mr Vanderhorn. We once had Vice-President John Garner stay here on his way home to Texas. He and my husband were very good friends."

"I know. Rose has told me all about you and her father. I wish I had met the Senator. I often wanted to meet you too, you know."

"As the Senator's wife, Rose's mother or in my own right? Toast? I noticed the way you put that, Mr Vanderhorn. *You too*. Is that the way your wife is referred to?"

"I'm not quite sure what you mean," he said warily. He did not want Carolyn mentioned today: on this one day his wife did not belong in his life. There was the screech of tyres on the road below the garden, an echo: Carolyn always drove like that. "Thank you, Wilma Mae. Those eggs are just the way I like them."

Wilma Mae had come in from the kitchen, placed eggs and bacon in front of them both. "I read 'bout what you like, Mr Vice-President. They was a article in *Ladies Home Journal* by your wife. She wrote what you like and what you didn't like. I cut it out and showed it to Miz Farquhar. Ain't that right?"

"Wilma Mae has quite a file on you," said Adele Farquhar.

"Sometimes she call me Wilma CIA. I hopes you like your eggs, sir."

She went back to her kitchen and Vanderhorn said, "What did you mean by *you too*? You sounded offended."

"When my husband was alive, people always made him the centre of attention. They would invite him to speak, to preside at some function, to be the guest of honour, and then as an after-thought they would turn to me and say, *And of course you, too, Mrs Farquhar*. Several of us Washington wives formed a You Too Club. It doesn't, of course, happen only to politicians' wives. The women of all public men suffer from it, I'm sure."

"Not Rose."

"No. But then it was no compliment to her that she didn't."

"I did ask my wife for a divorce. Fifteen years ago. But she is a believer in marriage, a devout one. She also enjoys the Vanderhorn name. If in name only, as they say."

"Don't let us malign her, Mr Vanderhorn. I am not a woman who believes that marriage is necessarily a holy institution—there is too much hell in many of them for that—but if your marriage broke up I am sure not all the blame was on your wife's side."

"No," Vanderhorn admitted. He pushed his eggs away, suddenly finding them tasteless. Or perhaps he found it tasteless to be eating, to be going through his daily routine, while his love, his only true love, was dying upstairs. "But I should like you to know that Rose did not break up my marriage. My wife and I were already going our separate ways before I met Rose."

"That is a comfort then, even if a small one. You like your coffee black, don't you?"

"The Wilma CIA file? Yes, please."

47

"I should like you to know something, Mr Vanderhorn. It was I who had my son get in touch with you last night to tell you that Rose had only twenty-four hours to live. He was very much against the idea. I think Rose would have been, too, had she known."

"Why did you do it?"

"I felt you owed it to Rose. To be with her when she died."

"We agree on that, Mrs Farquhar. I was preparing to come down here anyway. You never answered the phone when I called each day after Rose came home—"

"My son always spoke to you."

"He gave me the barest bulletins. Just that Rose was still alive—never any more than that. Your daughter-in-law came to the phone on Friday when I called. She said if I valued Rose's good name I should come down here. She didn't explain, just hung up at once. That was when I made up my mind to come down this weekend. I had to wait till the weekend to get away from Washington without anyone's knowing. Then your son called last night to say—well, to tell me the worst. I didn't get the chance to ask your daughter-in-law what she meant about Rose's good name. I never met her."

Adele Farquhar had never been one to avoid a person's eye: she looked directly at him. "And now you'll never have the chance to ask her. I think it is better that way, Mr Vanderhorn."

"If Rose is going to be hurt—"

"Rose has been hurt enough. Just let it rest and don't ask any more questions. We'll bury her and she won't ever be hurt again. I depend upon you for that, to see that her name is never connected with yours. You have managed to keep it out of the gossip columns for twenty years. I don't want someone defaming her after she is dead."

"I can only protect her while I'm still alive. And I'll do

48

that. But when one is dead biographers tend to feel they are falling down on the job if they don't tell all."

"Do you think you will merit a biography, Mr Vanderhorn?"

He smiled, but it was a wry smile and only a few of the famous teeth showed. "Vice-Presidents usually do, Mrs Farquhar. Even the failed ones."

## II

When McKechnie got outside with Gilbert Farquhar he saw Lee Barron's yellow station wagon parked at the end of the driveway.

"Excuse me a minute, Mr Farquhar." He walked down the driveway, put up a restraining hand as Lee went to get out of the station wagon. "Stay there, honey. What are you doing here?"

"What do you think? I heard about Molly Farquhar being killed."

"Where did you hear that?" Who was the blabbermouth in the Police Department? He'd hammer him into the ground as soon as he found out.

"Down at the hospital. I heard the ambulance siren right after I heard the radio warning about the twister. I went down to the hospital and Zeke Norval told me what had happened."

"Good old Zeke." But he might have guessed it and he cursed himself for not having tried to put a clamp on Zeke's mouth. "Well, you can't go in there now. Mrs Farquhar has asked me to keep everyone away, at least until tomorrow."

"Who's in there now? I saw a man standing at that front window behind the curtains."

"He's—he's a friend of the family, I guess. I didn't meet him." He wondered how he could lie to her so easily; but wondered if she believed him. Already he felt the

49

weight of the day beginning to increase. "Go home, honey. They've got enough trouble."

"Maybe I could just have a word with Gil." She nodded up the driveway to where Gilbert Farquhar sat waiting in the Cadillac. "A sympathetic word."

"Tomorrow." He put his hand on the door of the station wagon as she tried to open it. "Your sympathetic word would just somehow turn into a few questions."

She looked out at him, puzzled but not yet angry. "Are you putting up the barricades on me or something? I'm not just your girl-friend, darling. I'm here as a newspaper-woman—"

"Don't give me any of that bull about the freedom of the press. Please go home. All I'm doing is protecting a citizen's right to his privacy. They're entitled to ask for that."

She stared at him, still puzzled but a little angry now. He had always been co-operative with her and her reporters, even if sometimes reluctantly so, but this morning she sensed there was going to be active opposition to her. He was no radical, but it was unlike him to suddenly start defending the town's leading family as entitled to privileges.

He read her thoughts: "You don't think they're entitled to privacy, right?"

"I didn't say that."

She was not a beautiful girl, but she would always attract most men's attention before a conventional beauty would. Her eyes were a trifle too large and her cheekbones too wide; black-haired and always looking tanned, even in winter, her looks aroused suspicion in some people that perhaps an Indian or a light-skinned black had paused for a night or two in some earlier generation. There was no truth to the suspicions, but, perversely, Lee encouraged them with a secret smile whenever she heard of them. It would not have worried McKechnie if she had had mixed

50

blood, nor would it have worried her. She wrote editorials trying to form the opinions of her readers, but never cared two hoots for anyone's opinion but her own. Except, occasionally, his.

"You must have your reasons," she said, and he could see she was trying to be even-tempered. "But I hope you're not suddenly concerned about people's right to privacy just because they are the Farquhars."

"Your tongue matches your typewriter sometimes," he said. "Real mean."

"Up yours, chief," she said angrily and started the engine of the station wagon. "Watch your feet!"

She backed out of the driveway in a snarl of gravel, swung the station wagon round and went off down the curve of the hill in a screech of tyres. McKechnie stared after her, turned his face away as a shower of rain hit him like pellets, and went back up the driveway. Gilbert Farquhar was still sitting patiently in the Cadillac, gazing straight ahead with the abstract expression of a man who no longer placed any importance on time.

"I told Miss Barron to come see you tomorrow. If that's okay?"

"I'm not interested in seeing anyone." Farquhar turned his head slowly, as if his stare were a heavy weight that had to be lifted physically. "Tomorrow or any day. That includes your Miss Barron."

"I'll tell her. But she's not *my* Miss Barron. Not when she puts on her newspaper hat."

It started to rain steadily as the police car led the Cadillac down through the town to the hospital. The sky was still almost black over in the west; it was easy to imagine that the world stopped dead just across the Oklahoma line. Lightning scratched frightening graffiti on the black wall and thunder rolled like a thousand distant battles. He wondered what towns lay under the barrage and switched on his radio.

Lucy Chapley, prim and almost pious, as if she were reading God's Word over at the Second Baptist on Cedar Street, was halfway through another Tornado Warning: "—reported by Highway Patrol 6 miles north of Miami, Oklahoma, at 7.50 a.m. Central Standard Time but has now lifted."

McKechnie called in: "This is PD-One, Lucy. I'm on my way down to the hospital with Mr Farquhar. Any word yet on Clint Blamey?"

"No report as yet, PD-One." Lucy Chapley stuck strictly to the manual: there was no informality with her. Give some people a uniform, McKechnie thought, and they become generals. You gave Lucy a switchboard and she thought she was running a moon-shot.

He switched off without signing off. His department was tightly run and he had a firm respect for procedure, but sometimes Lucy Chapley got on his nerves. He had enough to keep him on edge today and he wanted no small irritations added to it.

The hospital was a one-storey building that had begun as a ten-bed facility and had been added to over the years. It was owned and run by the town's seven doctors and McKechnie sometimes wondered if they ever paused to look at it whole as they drove up to it in their cars. Wings and annexes had been added to it till it sprawled like a bad accident. The morgue was a timber-walled room stuck on the back end of the main building, a storeroom for the dead.

Dr Stenhouse was waiting in the tiny hall that connected the morgue to the main building. "You want me to come in with you, Gil?"

Farquhar shook his head, drew himself up straight and went into the morgue without a word. Stenhouse said, "How did he take it?"

"Quietly," said McKechnie. "I gave the news to Mrs Farquhar and she told him."

"What about their visitor?"

"You met him?"

"He arrived while I was there. First time I ever thought I might have to treat myself for shock. You instructed to keep your mouth shut, too?"

"He didn't have to issue me any orders. Hell, I don't want the responsibility of him. The sooner he gets out of here, the better." McKechnie looked at the closed door behind them, wondering how Farquhar was reacting to the sight of his dead wife. "Has the coroner arrived yet?"

"He's been delayed by the storm over in Vista. I didn't examine her, I'll leave that to him. I—" He ran the ball of his thumb against the bristle of his moustache, then smoothed it back with his fingers. "Maybe I'd better go in and see Gil. He's not accustomed to sights like that."

But then the door opened and Farquhar, pale and strained-looking, came out. He was still wearing his hat, but now he pulled it off and put a hand on the door, as if about to go back and pay his proper respects to his dead wife. Stenhouse took his arm and turned him back.

"Once is enough, Gil. Leave her now."

They went out to their cars. The rain had stopped again, but clouds scudded low overhead, like the underside of an avalanche. Two nurses ran along a path like gulls before the wind. There was still the rumble of thunder over to the west, but McKechnie could see no lightning now. He closed the door of Farquhar's car as the latter got in, then leaned on it.

"We found your wife's handbag near her body. There was 2200 dollars in it. Did she usually carry that much money around with her?"

Farquhar did not seem to be paying attention. "What? No. No. Why would she?"

"I don't know. Unless she was going somewhere. There were no credit cards in her bag."

"We don't believe in them. We always pay cash or by

cheque." He had been staring straight ahead, but now he looked out and up at McKechnie. "I insisted on that."

McKechnie wondered what else he had insisted on and how Molly Farquhar had responded; but he would ask those questions another time. "Did you have a joint account?"

"We each had our own." Then he said bluntly, "I'm going home. Good morning. chief."

"I have to come back and see the Vice-President. Do you want to talk to me further today or should we leave it till tomorrow?"

"I told you, I'm not interested in talking to anyone."

McKechnie had learned to be patient: often it was a better weapon than a gun. "I understand how you feel. But I still have to know what your wife was doing out at Clint Blamey's place."

"Does it matter?" Farquhar sounded as if it didn't matter to him. He didn't sound callously indifferent but more like a man who had just given up. "My wife is dead. Isn't that final enough?"

"For her, yes. If I can find Clint Blamey and he can explain satisfactorily what your wife was doing out there, maybe I won't have to trouble you. But if I don't—"

He had to step back as Farquhar. who had started the Cadillac's engine. suddenly took off. The car rolled drunkenly as it was swung between two other cars. then it went out of the hospital parking lot, bounced as it hit the gutter, and went speeding down the street. McKechnie noticed that it was not headed back up towards Forest View Drive, towards home. It was going in the opposite direction, out of town towards the Blamey place.

He debated whether to follow Farquhar, then heard his radio calling him. "PD-One, PD-Four is calling you." Lucy Chapley sounded excited. "Come in, PD-Four."

Roley Trubauer came on the air, drawl as unhurried

54

as ever. "I just seen Clint Blamey, chief. Passed me out on Razorback heading south. I gave him the signal to pull up, but when he saw me he took off like a cut cat."

"You go after him?" McKechnie wondered if Lucy was turning a deaf ear to Trubauer's phrase: *like a cut cat* wouldn't be in her manual of police description.

"I was heading the wrong way, chief. You know how narrow Razorback is—by the time I turned around he was to hell and gone. Shoot, chief—"

"Okay, Roley. Keep looking for him."

"We already have an APB out on him, PD-One," said Lucy.

"Ten-four," said McKechnie and wondered if he had smeared the sarcasm thickly enough on his tongue.

What the hell was Clint Blamey up to? He was a loner, a widower in his late thirties, but he had never caused the Police Department any trouble. He was a hard worker, running a Jersey herd on part of his farm and growing apples and peaches; the region was a marginal area for peaches and it was a measure of Blamey's determination that he would take the risk on such a crop. He had a reputation for paying his bills on time to local storekeepers, but McKechnie had no idea how he stood at either of the town's two banks. He was a regular church-goer, keeping to himself at the services, but four or five times a year he would appear at a First Baptist get-together and be welcome. He came into town once a week to do his shopping, had a few drinks at Wayman's bar, was polite and friendly to anyone who spoke to him, and went home, still minding his own business. If he ever got on a bender or wanted sex, McKechnie guessed he went up to Joplin. But he was a quietly religious man and maybe he wanted neither.

Dr Stenhouse was sitting in his car as if waiting on McKechnie to come across and make some comment on

Farquhar's abrupt departure. McKechnie went over to him, but made no remark about Farquhar. "Doc, did you examine Mrs Farquhar? I mean thoroughly?"

"No. That'll be Dr Main's job when he gets here. Why?"

"Was there any sign she'd been assaulted? Raped?"

"I didn't even look. I noticed she was wearing a trouser suit. The pants were still buttoned at the waist." Stenhouse frowned, shook his head. "It never crossed my mind, chief. I guess I *am* in a state of shock. I'll go have a look at her."

"Can you give her a thorough examination, I mean just short of an autopsy?"

"I'm stepping into the coroner's territory."

"I'm always stepping into other people's territory, doc. Sometimes it's the only way to get things done."

"What's on your mind?"

"Clint Blamey. Roley Trubauer tried to flag him down out on Razorback and he took off, as Roley said, like a cut cat."

"The hell he did!" Stenhouse shook his head again, but in negation this time, not in wonder. "Blamey isn't a rapist, I won't buy that."

"Just take a look at Molly Farquhar, doc. Every guy's got it in him to be a rapist, if he can get his cock up."

"When did you join Women's Lib?"

Then a young nurse came running towards them as Stenhouse got out of his car. "Oh, Dr Stenhouse, Reception said they'd seen you here. Could you come back and see Mrs Ness? She's playing up again, telling us she's going to walk out and go home."

"Goddam old women," said Stenhouse. "Don't you ever grow old, nurse, or I'll refuse to treat you. This will take a little time, chief. I'll call you about that other matter as soon as I can get around to it."

"Thanks. doc. Tell Mrs Ness if she walks out of the hospital I'll arrest her for disturbing the peace. I'm just in the mood for it."

"You're welcome to her down at the jail any time you like. Bad-tempered old bitch. Lead on, nurse. You're seeing the law and medicine in their true colours this morning."

"I never had any illusions, doctor," said the nurse, young, pretty and already wise in the ways of men whatever their profession.

"Another Mrs Ness in the making," McKechnie said to Stenhouse.

"And they wonder at the mayhem among the sexes," said Stenhouse and followed the young nurse into the hospital.

McKechnie went back to headquarters. There was some traffic in town now, people coming home from Mass, some Sunday workers stopping off at Tom's Café for breakfast. In the square the Confederate soldier held his finger up to the wind but he was facing north-west and the wind was coming from behind him. Gusts of rain occasionally blew across the streets like shreds of curtain. But the sky to the west had lightened a little, though the clouds there were still as thick as mountains.

As he entered headquarters he paused by the glassed-in section where Lucy Chapley sat. "Anything on the storms from the Community people?" There was a Community Warning Center over in Vista. the county seat.

"A hailstorm down near Pea Ridge, that's all. You have a visitor. chief. I told her to go into your office."

From Lucy's expression he guessed who his visitor was: she did not approve of Lee Barron. He went into his office, closed the door.

"That's twice you've met me this morning and you haven't kissed me yet." Lee said.

He leaned down, kissed her forehead, then went round

57

and sat down behind his desk. "Okay, that's the passion bit out of the way. What do you want this time?"

"Information. The same as I wanted up at the Farquhars' house. Look, darling, I'm trying not to be a gate-crashing reporter. But the wife of one of the town's leading men was killed this morning. Is it too much to ask for all the facts so that I can get the story straight?"

"You've got all the facts from Zeke Norval."

"He didn't know why Molly was out at the Clint Blamey place. Do you? And where's Clint Blamey? I heard Roley Trubauer report in that he tried to pick up Clint and he took off. I think he said like a cut cat."

"How long have you been here in my office?"

"Long enough. With the door open you can hear everything that comes in on the radio."

"God-*damn*!" He rocked back and forth in his chair, staring at her, wondering why she could so easily get under his skin when she put on her newspaper hat. He had already begun to wonder if their two roles would prove incompatible when they married. "Look, I don't know any more than you do. I've seen Gil Farquhar, but I didn't ask him any questions. I'm leaving it till tomorrow. When his sister will be dead, too."

"You're trying to make me sound like some sort of ghoul."

"I just know how the Farquhars would feel, that's all."

He had never told her how *he* had felt when the newspapermen and the television interviewers had besieged him after his wife's death. He, about to go to work, had been kissing Paddy goodbye at their apartment door when the vengeful junkie had tried to shoot him. Paddy, seeing the aimed gun, had flung herself in front of McKechnie and taken the bullet in her heart. There had been a department enquiry into why he had shot the junkie five times, as if grief and anger were no excuse for the wasteful

58

expenditure of bullets; and every day, almost every hour it had seemed. the reporters had been at him, asking their own questions, demanding their right to know. There had been times when he had felt like killing *them*.

"Are you trying to hide something?" Lee said. "You know how I feel about that, especially by a public official."

He knew, all right: you only had to read her editorials. She was forever attacking any sort of cover-up, from town level up through county and state to national level. Currently she was attacking the Administration in Washington for being less than frank about its farm policy. editorials that made her popular in a Democratic farm community such as Friendship and Vista County. McKechnie wondered what she would say if he told her that half a mile from where they sat the Vice-President of the Republican Administration, a man of many words and few disclosures, had virtually ordered him to offer no information to anyone at all.

"Let's say I'm being sympathetic to someone else's grief. If that's a crime, go ahead and expose me."

She looked at him carefully, softening her attitude. "All right, forget I'm here from my paper. I *know* you. Even if you aren't hiding something. you've got something on your mind that's worrying you. Can I help?"

He wanted to say, *Yes—if you weren't a newspaper-woman*. He loved her as much as he had loved Paddy. A naturally affectionate man, he felt the need to love and be loved: he sometimes wondered how he had gone for so long denying that need. Sex had never been any trouble. He had had his first woman twelve months after Paddy's death and up until he had met Lee he had taken regular trips to resorts where he wouldn't be recognized and where there were always women looking for men with no commitment on either side. With Lee there had been no difficulty: she liked going to bed as much as he did. But she gave him more than sex and since meeting her, even though their relationship was not always placid, he had found more peace and contentment than at any time since Paddy had died.

"I've got some problems," he admitted; he knew it was useless trying to lie too brazenly to her. "I'll tell you about them when I retire."

"You're a son-of-a-bitch," she said. "I don't know why the hell I fell in love with you."

Then his phone rang. Lucy Chapley said, "Dr Stenhouse is on the line, chief."

McKechnie put his hand over the phone. "I'll see you later, honey. This is police business."

Le's mouth tightened, but she stood up, leaned across the desk and kissed him. Then she went out of the office without a word, slamming the door behind her. McKechnie gazed at it for a moment, then he took his hand away from the mouthpiece. "Put the doc on, Lucy."

"Chief?" It was either a bad line or Stenhouse was having difficulty with his voice. "Dr Main, the county coroner, is here with me. We've had a look at Molly Farquhar. There was no sign of sexual assault. But—" The line crackled, then was silent.

"You still there, doc?"

"Still here. Chief, she was dead before the twister hit her. She'd been shot."

## III

"She was also pregnant," said Stenhouse, lighting his pipe and sitting back in the front seat of his car. He drove a Rover 3500, the only British, indeed the only foreign, car in town. "About three months, I'd say."

"How old was she?"

"Forty, forty-one. She wasn't my patient, remember?"

"Is it unusual for a woman to become pregnant for the first time at that age?"

60

"No, it happens. It's only unusual when the woman's husband is impotent, has been ever since they got married."

McKechnie, who didn't smoke, wound down the window on his side and let some of the fresh air blow in on him. The coroner had already gone back to Vista, and McKechnie and Stenhouse were now sitting in the latter's car in the hospital parking lot. The wind had dropped and the clouds, like rock sculpture, stood still overhead. But McKechnie knew the wind hadn't died, was only resting.

"Doc, I'm beginning to feel I'm in the middle of a twister. Right in the eye of it. Any minute now all hell is going to bust loose."

"First thing you better do is get that feller up at Farquhars' to hightail it back to Washington. We're going to have enough headlines in our own newspaper, without getting us into the big city ones."

"You thinking of him? I know you're a Republican, about the only one in town."

"I'll pretend I never heard that. I'm thinking of Adele Farquhar, that's who I'm thinking of."

"Okay, I'm sorry about the Republican bit. But if he goes, it will be because he's thinking of the political angle." The wind sprang up again, hurling a handful of rain into the car; McKechnie wound up the window. "I was going to soft-pedal Molly Farquhar's death as much as I could. But it's a whole new ball game now. For a start I've got to bring every man I've got back on duty, try to pick up Clint Blamey before he gets too far away. It also means I've got to put a call through to the Sheriff's Department and the Highway Patrol."

"Can you keep them away from the Farquhar house?"

"That's no problem. The shooting took place within the town limits, just, so it's still in our jurisdiction. We'll be doing the investigating. All the sheriff and the Highway Patrol will be doing is help us pick up Blamey."

"You think he shot her?"

"I don't know. But he's my Number One suspect. You going back to the Farquhars'?"

"You want me to? I have a couple of other calls I have to make."

"Leave the family to me, then. I've got to call in to headquarters, then I'll go up and see them." Then he remembered something: "When Gil Farquhar left here, he wasn't heading home. He went west. He could've been going out to the Blamey place. I wonder what he's going to say when I tell him maybe Clint Blamey shot his wife?"

"It need not have been Clint. I don't think he's any more a murderer than he is a rapist."

McKechnie looked out the window, the view fractured into an abstract pattern by the dribbling rain on the glass. "Christ, whatever happened to yesterday?"

"Yesterday?"

"A quiet day. The report sheet was practically blank. Not even a drunk arrest." He got out of Stenhouse's car, looked up at the clouds, which had started to move again. "The sun was shining yesterday morning, remember?"

"I never take any notice of the weather, unless it spoils my golf. My patients give me all the goddam climate I can handle."

McKechnie smiled, glad that he could manage such an expression. His face had the feeling of frozen rubber. "Were you always bad-tempered, doc? Even as a kid?"

"I was St Francis of Assisi when I was a kid. I was going to be a veterinarian. I should've stuck to animals. All they do is bite, they never complain. You can trust 'em more, too."

"Not all of them. You ever made friends with a copper-head?"

"Vets don't treat snakes. Or anyway this one wouldn't have. Though sometimes I feel I'm treating 'em now."

He drove off. McKechnie went across to his own car,

called Lucy Chapley and told her to call in the off-duty men, then he contacted Roley Trubauer.

"I'm back at the Blamey place, chief. Gil Farquhar's out here, just sitting in that old Caddie of his. I been across to see him, but he said all he wants is to be alone. Alone."

"Tell him I'd like to see him back at his house in twenty minutes. Roley, Molly Farquhar was shot, but don't tell him yet—"

"Shit!" Trubauer forgot to be restrained. "You sure, chief?"

"Sure," said McKechnie patiently. "But like I said, don't tell Farquhar. I'll give him the bad news when I see him. In the meantime I want Clint Blamey picked up. Go carefully with him—he could be carrying a gun."

"You think he shot her? Jesus God Almighty—"

"I'll see you at headquarters the end of your shift, Roley. How's the weather out there?"

"Pissing with rain. But that's the least of our problems, right?"

Each of them signed off, but then Lucy Chapley came on the air. "PD-One, could you speak to PD-Four about his language? There is no need—"

"Okay, Lucy. I'll speak to him."

*That* was the least of their problems. He might be swearing himself by the end of the day.

Five minutes after he got back to headquarters Jack Atcheson and the three other off-duty men had reported in. They were young men, all three of them farm boys who had opted for the glamour and excitement of a policeman's job only to find that it could be as dull and routine as working on a farm. Even to having to work on Sunday.

"The wife's sour on you, chief. We were gonna go visit with her folks—"

"I was gonna spend the day with my girl, down in her storm cellar—"

63

"She'd be safer with a twister than you. Hey, chief, what's going on?"

Bud Grierson came in and he and Atcheson, by right of age, took the two chairs opposite McKechnie's desk. The three young men stood lounging against the walls. The office was not large and it was packed with uniforms, badges gleaming, guns prominent. McKechnie looked at the men and wondered how much he would eventually have to tell them. Several teletypes lay on his desk, put there by Lucy: there had been four more minor twisters reported within a radius of 100 miles of Friendship. He picked up the teletypes, abruptly glad of them.

"There's these for a start. If a twister hits us, I don't want any of you down some cellar with your girl. Or even your wife."

"We had these warnings before, chief," said Grierson. "What else is worrying you?"

McKechnie hesitated, then told them fully about Molly Farquhar. He knew there was no police reason why he should have hesitated to tell them; but he felt like a man on the edge of a pond holding a stone ready to be thrown. The ripples might burst a dam. "There was a .38 slug in her skull. Gone in through the right temple, but hadn't come out the other side. It was old ammunition, soft lead, so it was probably one of the older model guns. If it had been the new stuff, it would have gone right through."

"Suicide or murder?" Atcheson was holding a cup of coffee, looking at it as if to check whether it had aged enough. "It wasn't no accident, right?"

"It could've been suicide." McKechnie was surprised the thought had not occurred to him. He supposed the Farquhars, even one by marriage, were as capable of that as anyone. "We'll leave that open for the moment. In the meantime I want Clint Blamey picked up. He's got away from Roley once already this morning, so take him carefully. Better go in pairs. When Roley comes in, Bud, you better go with him."

"You want someone to ride with you, chief?" said Atcheson.

"I've got to go up to the Farquhars'. I can do that on my own. That's it. Check in with Lucy every ten minutes."

As he drove back up towards Forest View he wondered why he had not told Atcheson and the others about Molly Farquhar's being pregnant. It would be on the coroner's report and even if the officers didn't read the report they would soon hear about what was in it. Then he realized he had become, almost without knowing it, the family's protector: Lee had been right. Or, by projection, was he really only trying to protect Vice-President Vanderhorn?

Once again it was Adele Farquhar to whom he had to give the news. But this time Willis Vanderhorn was in the drawing-room with her. "She had been dead several hours, Mrs Farquhar. Have you any idea what time she left the house last night?"

Adele Farquhar did not seem to have heard him. He was about to repeat the question, when she turned her head slightly and looked directly at him. "She left here last night about eleven o'clock. Just after my son had called Mr Vanderhorn."

"Was there any connection? I mean between the phone call to the Vice-President and her leaving all of a sudden like that?"

"You will have to ask my son that, Mr McKechnie. They were man and wife. Their relationship was none of my affair."

McKechnie didn't believe that. Gilbert and Molly Farquhar had lived all their married life in this house: Adele Farquhar, whether she admitted it or not, had been part of their marriage. "Did you know your daughter-in-law was pregnant?"

The old woman's hands tightened on the arms of her

chair; he saw the liver spots stand out on the white skin. "I presume you're certain of that fact, Mr McKechnie?"

"Dr Stenhouse is. And the county coroner."

She pondered the evidence, then said firmly, "No, I did not know."

"Do you have to continue with these questions?" said Vanderhorn. "Mrs Farquhar has enough to bear as it is."

"Mr Vice-President, I have what could be a murder on my hands."

Vanderhorn nodded. "I'm sorry. Of course. But perhaps you could spare Mrs Farquhar the questions and leave them for her son."

"Thank you, Mr Vanderhorn." Adele Farquhar stood up. She swayed just a little but recovered before either of the men could rise and go to her. "No, please. I am all right. Will you excuse me, Mr McKechnie?"

She went out of the room, tall and straight-backed as ever; but McKechnie had the feeling that suddenly all her years had at last caught up with her. She was an old woman who had finally admitted there was no future. Though he hardly knew her, somehow he guessed that it was an admission she had been fighting against for years, possibly ever since her husband had died.

"She is a remarkable woman," said Vanderhorn.

"I'm just beginning to recognize it." McKechnie put away his notebook; he remarked with surprise that he had made no notes at all in it. "I haven't been out to the airport yet, sir. Are you still intending to stay on?"

Vanderhorn got up and moved to the window, gazing out through the rain-marbled glass at the nervous branches of the maples. "Are you married, chief?"

"My wife is dead, sir. She died just over ten years ago."

"I'm sorry to hear that. She must have been a young woman?"

"Twenty-two."

Vanderhorn nodded sympathetically, but did not pursue the subject. He was a sensitive man whose sensitivity was not always apparent behind the façade of political bonhomie. "I suppose you are wondering what brings me here to Friendship? The truth is, chief, Miss Farquhar and I have been very good friends for almost twenty years. Do I have to spell out what I mean by that?"

"No, sir."

He had begun to suspect something of what Vanderhorn was telling him. The Vice-President was not the first public man who had had a secret private life. History, he guessed, was peopled by the shadows of women who had been kept in the background.

"It was not easy for me to get down here. I had to steal out of my house in the middle of the night to avoid the Secret Service men who are supposed never to let me out of their sight. It used to be said that a man had no secrets from his valet. Now it's his bodyguard."

"I've never had any trouble from either."

Vanderhorn turned back into the room, smiled. "Are you your own man, chief? I think you are."

"I try to be, sir."

"I wish I were." One of the half-dozen richest men in America: McKechnie found it hard to believe in Vanderhorn's bondage. But the Vice-President had not spoken as if looking for sympathy: he would never be so bankrupt as that. "I have to be back in Washington tonight. There'll be some panic this morning, but a certain person knows where I am and he'll cool the Secret Service. But if I am still missing tomorrow morning the media are sure to start asking questions. They allow me some privacy at the weekend, but only because they want a private life of their own for a day or two. And because Vice-Presidents are not really news, not seven days a week." Did I catch a note of bitterness there? McKechnie won-

67

dered. Like everyone else in the country, he knew where Vanderhorn's ambition really lay. "But Monday they're back on the job."

"Do any of them know about Miss Rose?"

"Some of them, I'm sure. But they have never made capital out of it, just as they never made capital out of President Roosevelt's relationship with Lucy Mercer. The majority of newspapermen are decent men when it comes to respecting a decent woman. And Miss Farquhar, or Miss Rose as you call her, was all of that. Though down here in the Bible belt, in her own territory, perhaps some people might not think so. If my, er, mistress had been a tramp, I'm sure the media would have shown me no mercy."

"Why would they change their attitude now?"

"A number of factors. Fear of being scooped—though I don't think that word is used any more—being scooped by some of their less ethical rivals when the latter find out. It's an election year and, God and the GOP forgive me for saying it, we are not favourites to win. The Vice-President sneaking out of Washington and flying halfway across the country to be with his dying sweetheart, a woman not his wife, would be too good a story to be passed up. Especially by those White House correspondents who are Democrats."

It was McKechnie's turn to look out the window: to gain time, to put his own attitude into shape. He did not appreciate the Vice-President's having confided so much in him: he was being burdened by more than a man in his position should be asked to bear. The sky had darkened, the clouds were suffocatingly low. "I think you should go back to Washington now, sir. You can't really help by staying here. I mean, help Miss Rose."

Vanderhorn was silent, hands stuck in the pocket of his jacket, his shoulders hunched as if against the wind rattling the windows. It was a characteristic pose that cartoonists had made famous. "I *can* help her. She didn't want me to come down here. But this morning she asked me to stay. I owe her that, to be here at the end. If you loved your wife at the moment she died, Mr McKechnie, you will understand what I mean."

McKechnie's cap crumpled a little under the pressure of his big hands. He felt the weight of Paddy's ghost in his arms. He nodded, then stood up.

"There may be some callers here this morning. The word's already around town that Molly Farquhar's dead. So far they don't know she was shot, but they soon will. You best stay upstairs, sir. I'll go out now and tell your pilot to hop over to Springfield."

"I'm grateful, chief. For your concern and for your efforts."

"I've never been responsible for just an individual before. Only a town." He smiled. "Somehow, sir, you weigh much heavier."

They had just walked into the hall when they heard the key in the front door. Gilbert Farquhar came in, pushed in by the wind. He closed the door, took off his tweed hat, then stood stockstill as he saw McKechnie and Vanderhorn. As if we were enemies, McKechnie thought.

"Officer Trubauer said you wanted to see me." Farquhar's voice was hoarse, as if his throat had closed up.

"I'll go upstairs," said Vanderhorn. "Will you be back, chief?"

"I think so, sir." McKechnie waited till the Vice-President had gone upstairs, then he turned back to Farquhar.

The latter was staring up at the disappearing figure. "Has he taken over this house?" All his politeness had gone; he sounded angry and churlish. "Are you working for him?"

"Take it easy, Mr Farquhar. I'm working for nobody— well, I'm working for the town. I came here to see you,

69

not the Vice-President. I have more bad news about your wife."

Farquhar didn't move while McKechnie, as briefly and gently as he could, told him about the shooting of his wife. The house creaked and tapped as the wind and rain besieged it, but the hallway, despite McKechnie's voice, seemed still and silent. I'm in a morgue, he thought, I'm cutting up a dead man.

"There was one other thing, Mr Farquhar—" He paused, wondering how many cuts with the knife were necessary. But the law demanded its pound of flesh in the interests of justice, even from the innocent. So he had learned and had felt the incisions himself. "Your wife was pregnant. Did you know that?"

Farquhar at last moved. He took off his coat and hung it and his hat carefully on the heavy, old-fashioned rack against one wall. He looked at himself in the mirror of the rack, but showed no expression: he could have been looking at a stranger, someone in whom he had no interest.

At last, turning to face McKechnie squarely, he said, "Yes, I knew that. I learned it two nights ago." He frowned as if trying to remember what today was. "Friday night."

"Was that before or after your wife had called Mr Vanderhorn?"

"I don't know. Does it matter? Mr Vanderhorn hadn't made her pregnant," he said with bitter humour.

It was a tasteless remark that surprised McKechnie: you expected better in these surroundings. He knew Adele Farquhar would never have made such a comment. "Did she intend having the baby?"

"I don't know. She didn't seem to know, herself." Suddenly he said, "Who killed her? Clint Blamey?"

"We're looking for him, but I don't know if he killed her. Was she a friend of his?"

"Apparently, though I only found that out, too, on

70

Friday night. My wife seems to have achieved the impossible—kept a secret in a small town."

Only for a while, McKechnie thought: the town's going to know all about it sooner or later. "When did you last see your wife?"

Farquhar gestured helplessly. "I'm not sure. Ten, ten-thirty. I was sitting with my sister all evening. My wife said good night and went to her room."

"You didn't share the same room?"

"No. Do you have to take all this down in that damned notebook?" There was no politeness at all about him now.

McKechnie ignored the question. "Your wife's car—is it out in the garage?"

Farquhar blinked, having trouble being attentive. "No. Isn't it out at Blamey's place?"

"You were out there, you'd have seen it if it was. Who was your wife's doctor?"

Farquhar blinked again. "Doctor? Oh. Dr Stanton, up in Joplin."

"Can I call him?"

Farquhar blinked yet again; he seemed to be suffering from a delayed reaction to the news McKechnie had given him. "What? Yes, if you must. Down there in the study. There's a pad with numbers on it beside the phone."

He waved a vague hand, didn't move as McKechnie left him and went down the hall. McKechnie tried the wrong door, found the second one that opened into the study. Deliberately he did not look around him as he went to the phone on the big leather-topped desk. He was intruding here more than he wanted to; fifteen years as a policeman had still left him with a respect for other people's privacy. Even in New York, when a place had to be broken into, he had always stood back and let his partner break down the door. There were some cops, he knew, who got a kick out of peeling the skin off other people's lives.

71

He flipped open the phone pad, found the doctor's name and number. "Dr Stanton?" He introduced himself, told the doctor about Molly Farquhar's death. "This is confidential, doc. Mrs Farquhar was pregnant. Had she been to see you about it?"

"I haven't seen Molly Farquhar in, oh, almost a year. She was always a pretty healthy woman. A little high-strung, but very healthy. If there's anything I can do to help—"

McKechnie thanked him, hung up and went back down the hall to Farquhar. He closed his notebook as he did so. He still had filled only half a page; he had taken more notes on a simple auto accident. Was he still trying to protect this house and everyone in it, trying to make the record as bland and brief as possible?

"I'll keep my report as brief and impersonal as possible," he heard himself say. "That's all I can promise."

Farquhar looked at him, puzzled; and McKechnie realized the man had made no such request of him. Then Farquhar said, "What about him upstairs? Will he be mentioned in your report?"

"I don't see any necessity for it," said McKechnie, remarking again the bitterness in Farquhar's voice when he mentioned Vanderhorn. "I'll probably have to come back. You'll still be here?"

"Where do I have to go?" said Farquhar, but he was looking at the stranger in the mirror, asking him the question.

McKechnie put on his cap, turned up the collar of his jacket and stepped out into the wind and the rain as Cliff Fryger, the mayor, came up on to the porch. Fryger was the town's florist and mortician, a combination that gave him his own scent, a mixture of roses and formaldehyde. He was naturally a cheerful man, but this morning he was trying to be appropriately dignified and shocked.

"I heard the dreadful news about Molly Farquhar,

72

being killed by that twister. I've come to see what I can do, Gil being a member of the town board and all—"

"There's nothing, Cliff. I've just seen him. He asked me to tell everyone to stay away, leastways for today." He led the way down off the porch. "They don't expect Miss Rose to last out the day—"

"Oh my God! Some people get it all at once, don't they? Trouble, I mean."

"You'd know, Cliff. Are you here as mayor or mortician?"

"Both, I guess." Fryger never took offence; or never seemed to. "You have to intrude, I mean the dead have got to be buried."

"Come back tomorrow. You'll probably have to arrange a double funeral. Hello, here's your partner."

"My partner? I don't have a—Oh, Charlie."

The Reverend Charles Arber got out of his car and came up the driveway to them. He was a small man with a blank thin face made blanker by his glasses; he was always turning his head away so that the glasses caught the light and became opaque. His church, the Episcopalian, did the poorest business in town and his only claim to status was that the Farquhars were his main parishioners.

"I thought I'd nip up here before services, see what I could do to help." He had a flat dull voice and he had a listless air about him, but he was always using verbs like *nip* and *run* as if they might suggest he was not as defeated as he and everyone else knew he was. "A prayer or two at a time like this—"

"Not this morning, Reverend," said McKechnie and explained the situation about Rose Farquhar. "If they're going to do any praying, I think they'd rather do it alone."

"People need a shoulder to lean on—" But Arber, narrow-shouldered and needing support himself, did not press the point. "I'll call them this evening, run up here if they want me to."

"I'll be back first thing in the morning," said Fryger, then looked up at the clouds building above them like an avalanche. "That weather worries me. You hear about the twisters down there in Oklahoma? Maybe that one out by Clint Blamey's place won't be the last we'll have today."

"We'll just have to pray," said Reverend Arber, who had no other defences against anything at all.

"Where is Clint, by the way?" said Fryger. "Nobody mentioned him."

"We're looking out for him." McKechnie got into his car, trying to close the topic before it got too far.

But Fryger wouldn't let it go: "If he wasn't out at his place, what was Molly Farquhar doing out there?"

"Now don't let's start any gossip," said Reverend Arber, but turned his face and glasses full on to Mc-Kechnie; he shone with curiosity. "We mustn't jump to conclusions."

"Why not?" said Fryger; he suddenly looked his usual cheerful self. "Everybody else will."

"Let it lay," said McKechnie curtly.

Both men looked at him, brought up short by his tone. He left them and went across to his car. They stared at him, said something to each other, then went down to their own cars. He waited till they had driven away, then he called headquarters.

"Lucy, this is Chief McKechnie. Tell Jack Atcheson to come up here to the Farquhars' on his own. I'll wait for him."

"Will you be coming back here, PD-One?"

"Not unless it's urgent. I haven't had breakfast yet." He also had to make a quick trip out to the airport.

"Where will you be for breakfast in case you are needed?"

"At Miss Barron's house." Make what you like of that, Lucy. "I'm always there for breakfast Sundays. You know that."

Indeed she did, but her voice was as primly formal as ever. "Just checking, PD-One."

He sat in the car, the windows rolled up against the intermittent rain, and waited for Jack Atcheson. He felt suddenly worn out and, warmed by the muggy interior of the car, he was ready to fall asleep. But his mind, if not alert, was too restless. He looked out through the melting windshield at the house, the fort of which, unwillingly, he had just become the defender. He owed the people inside nothing: they had no right to ask him to assume the role they had burdened him with. As police chief it was not his duty to protect reputations or even ensure a citizen's right to private grief. As for Vice-President Vanderhorn he owed the man even less and had no time for what he stood for: his politics, his vast inherited wealth, the power that he and his family before him had bought as other people bought life insurance. All at once he was angry, was tempted to drive away and leave them to defend themselves. Then he sat back, shaking his head at himself. He had never attempted to define duty, but he had always felt that it went beyond the bounds of the police manual. If it did not, then it left a man no will to sacrifice. And he could never forget how Paddy had sacrificed herself.

Jack Atcheson pulled into the driveway behind him. He got out and went back to him. "Nobody, and I mean *nobody*, Jack, is to go into the house. Except Doc Stenhouse."

"Do I let anyone go out? Gil Farquhar, for instance?"

"Why him in particular?"

"Jim, I didn't want to mention it back down at headquarters. I could see you had something on your mind besides what you were telling us. Last night when I was

75

coming on duty, about 11.45, 11.50, I guess it was, I saw Gil Farquhar. I was driving in from my place and he passed me in his Cadillac, heading out along Route 86. Looked like there was two people in the car. Going out towards Clint Blamey's place."

"You sure it was him?"

Atcheson repeated almost his, McKechnie's, words of an hour or so earlier. "Who else drives an old Caddie like that? No, it was him all right."

# *Chapter Three*

The National Severe Storms Forecast Center in Kansas City watched the growing family of tornadoes moving up from the Gulf of Mexico. By 9 a.m. Sunday, six had already been reported in Texas and Oklahoma, all of them moving north-east.

The biggest, christened Daddy by the watchers, was first sighted near the town of Ardmore just north of the Texas border at 6.50 a.m. It killed three people and injured 20 others and demolished 60 mobile homes and 20 houses. An hour later it touched down again east of Ada, where it killed a family of five people by picking up a freight car from a railroad siding nearby and dropping it on their home. At 8.55, having intermittently lifted and then plunged down again, gouging the countryside like a runaway rotary hoe, it swept on to a hamlet of seven houses and a school north of Wetumka, levelling them all and tearing up the adjacent railroad tracks and twisting them into steel pretzels. It was moving at 45 miles an hour and the winds at its centre were estimated to exceed 250 miles an hour. It lifted again, but it had been on the ground for 60 per cent of its 2½-hour track. If it stayed on its present course and didn't wear itself out the watchers in Kansas City reckoned it would pass between Tulsa and

Muskogee and would enter Missouri somewhere just north of Vista County. Accordingly the center sent out another Tornado Warning and Lucy Chapley, in Friendship, duly recorded it and at once got in touch with Derry Brass at the radio station. Derry Brass broadcast the warning and the news of what damage the tornado had already done and wondered if he should change the next record: the Associated Banjo Clubs of Arkansas playing "Nearer My God to Thee".

In the White House the President, who never listened to weather bulletins except on Election Day, stood at the window of the Oval Office in the West Wing and looked down towards the Washington Monument. George Washington, he thought, had had his troubles with *his* Vice-President. Ben Franklin had once described John Adams as "in some things, absolutely out of his senses." But Adams, temperamental, stubborn, inclined to vicious envy, often necessarily separated for long intervals from his wife Abigail, had never consoled himself with a mistress. He had had too much respect for the position he occupied.

The President's assistant personal secretary knocked on the door and came into the study. Mondays through Saturdays he saw her only occasionally; those days he was at the mercy of his personal secretary of twenty-five years, Miss Polk, who had come all the way with him from his days as a Congressman. Miss Polk was a dragon; sometimes, like all dragons, hard to live with but invaluable in guarding the drawbridge. Sundays the President looked forward to dealing with Miss Delamaide, who was thirty years younger than both Miss Polk and himself and was capable of charming any male dragon out of his armour-plating. Which was why Miss Polk, who sometimes tired of her own reputation, had hired her.

"Mr President, I've finished typing those notes you wanted to give the Vice-President for his speech at the United Nations tomorrow. Shall I send them over to his home?" Miss Delamaide had gone to a Philadelphia Main Line school and always used *shall* instead of *will*. It annoyed the President, who had gone to a small public school and a small college in Nebraska, but he never showed his annoyance with her. As he did with Miss Polk, who shared his background.

"Hold them a while, Natalie. Put them on my desk." She went close by him towards the desk and he smelled her perfume. "That's a nice perfume. What is it?"

"I wonder sometimes if it's a bit heavy for the daytime, especially a Sunday. The Saudi Arabian ambassador gave it to me."

"Are we friendly with the Saudis?"

She smiled, relaxing a moment with him. She was a good-looking redhead with a figure that must have impressed the Saudi Arabian ambassador, a notorious woman's man. Is this how a man starts to stray? the President wondered. Your nose caught by a perfume a bit heavy for the daytime, especially a Sunday (when she worked for him); your eye hooked on a bosom . . . But Willis had never told him how or where he had met the Farquhar woman.

"Not too friendly, Mr. President. I try to stay neutral."

"What does the Israeli ambassador bring you?"

"Just news of his wife and children. He's very much a family man." She smiled again, standing at ease with him, one hip just slightly out of line. Goddam it, he thought, I guess it can start like this. He wondered what his wife thought of Miss Delamaide. But he wouldn't ask her. You had to be more diplomatic with wives than with ambassadors. "Like you, sir."

She'll have to go, he thought suddenly. He knew he would never stray, but Sunday was supposed to be a day of rest, not temptation. "That'll be all, Natalie. I'm not to be interrupted for the next ten or fifteen minutes. I want to make a phone call."

"What number, sir? I'll get it for you."

"No, I'll get it. Just see that the switchboard gives me a line."

A minute later the phone rang in the house in southwest Missouri. The line he had, though coming through the switchboard over in the Executive Office Building, could not be listened to by the operators. He said, "May I speak to Mr Vanderhorn?"

"Who calling, please?" said Wilma Mae.

"A colleague," said the President of the United States. "He'll know who it is."


# I


"Billy Greb called me," said Lee, putting a plate of hotcakes on the table. "He said he saw a police car going out to the airport about half an hour ago. Then just after that he saw a Learjet taking off. It flew right over his house."

Billy Greb was the *News*'s staff photographer, a boy wonder who boasted of having a camera eye that could take in detail as clearly as his camera. If the Learjet had been half-obscured by the low clouds, he'd still have recognized it.

"Nobody around here owns a Learjet." Lee sat down, passed the spiced sausages that she had sent down specially each week from St. Louis. "Who was it?"

McKechnie savoured a mouthful of sausage if not the question.

"Some pilot who'd lost his way. He'd put down to ask where he was, but there was no one on duty out there."

"The name of the town is painted on the roof of the hangars. All he'd have to do is check his map. What's the matter with you? You're starting to act like some politicians I've met up in Jefferson City. Why did you just happen to be out at the airport when he put down?"

He chewed on the sausage, which was suddenly tasteless. "Why can't we just have a quiet Sunday breakfast like we always do?"

"Because every other Sunday nothing's going on. This morning something is. Look, darling, I know some police work has to be kept under wraps for a while. But what's happened with the Farquhars? And who did that Learjet belong to, even if, as you say, the pilot was lost? Which I don't for a moment believe."

He sighed, put down his fork. "You'll just have to be patient. I could tell you nothing's going on, but you wouldn't believe me——"

"You never said a truer word."

"——because you must be one of the most disbelieving bitches I ever met. I don't think you even believe that I love you——"

"Oh, I believe that. I'm not the sort of girl who takes a man to bed who doesn't love her."

"I wish you were as old-fashioned in other ways. Like minding your own business when a man, and a cop at that, tells you to."

"Chief, in a pig's eye, if I may be blunt. Or would you like me to be blunter?"

But she smiled, knowing what she classed as his prim attitude to four-letter words. She sometimes fondly accused him of hypocrisy, having heard the obscenities that poured out of him when he was making love to her, but she actually admired him for his restrained language in public. She knew, as no one else did, that it was part of a greater control of himself in general. Only she knew the fury that was latent in him, that had erupted when he had pumped the extra bullets into the already dead junkie in New York. He had told her all that lying in bed beside her the second night they had made love. She knew that most people used obscenities because they thought it trendy or because they had an otherwise limited vocabulary; she herself occasionally used them as a means of letting off steam. The day she heard McKechnie use a four-letter word it would be because the fury had finally broken out of him. She sometimes wondered how terrible that fury would be, whether it would be just before he killed another man.

"Darling, I'm not going to sit back just because you tell me to. I think you're probably trying to hide something that most people in this town know anyway. You know what they say about a small town like this. Everybody knows what everybody else is doing—they only buy the newspaper to find out who's been caught. Am I right?"

"Not this time." But that was all he admitted and he knew he had made a mistake in saying even that much when he saw her big eyes narrow.

"I think if you told me what's going on it might save a lot of heartburn. I'm going to find out anyway and I'd rather not hurt anyone if I can avoid it."

"For Christ's sake—" For a moment he looked as if he might lose his temper; but he drew in his breath, then relaxed. He said more evenly, "Why do you have to know everything that's going on? If you think someone might get hurt, why persist?"

Lee was not given to glib explanations of herself or her conduct. Her father, an uncomplicated man, would have answered such a question as McKechnie had put with the justification that a newspaperman, being just that, *had* to persist. But Lee had more of her mother in her, a woman gay in public and serious in private, who had left her daughter the legacy of the need for self-examination.

"I'm not sure," she said. "Maybe it's because I don't like gossip and gossip feeds on half-truths. If there is some scandal connected with the Farquhars isn't it better—" Then she stopped.

"Go on," he said, afraid that she already knew more than she admitted to.

"I just can't believe there would be any scandal—with them, I mean. Everybody's known that Gil and Molly haven't been happy together for years, but that's no scandal. That's the way it is with half the married couples in town. And Mrs Farquhar is beyond reproach." She looked at him squarely: "Is it Rose?"

"Can I have another cup of coffee?" He pushed the sausages and hotcakes away from him, leaned his elbows on the table and looked across at her. He knew now that he was going to have to tell her *something*. It would only be half the truth, but it wouldn't be a half-truth. "Will you accept something off the record? At least till tomorrow morning."

She gazed at him a while, looking for the truth in his face: and found it. He had made a decision and she recognized he would not lie to her. "All right. But only till tomorrow morning."

"Molly Farquhar wasn't killed by that twister out at the Blamey place. She was already dead—she'd been shot."

Her eyes widened a little, but otherwise she remained unmoving. "By Clint Blamey?"

"I don't know."

"There's more to it than what you've told me. I'd have found out about her being shot just by going back to the hospital morgue. And I was going to do that anyway as soon as you'd had breakfast. What else is there?"

It was his turn to examine her, wondering how much he could trust her. Then: "This is very much off the record. She was pregnant—three months gone, according to Doc Stenhouse. The only trouble is, Gil Farquhar is impotent, has been for years."

She was silent for a while, then she said, "So she could have been pregnant to Clint Blamey and Gil found out and shot her? Is that what you're trying to hide till tomorrow morning?"

83

It was an out and he was tempted to take it. But couldn't. The belligerent day rushed at the house again, rattled the windows, warned him that tomorrow the truth, like a debt, would be due. Unless, of course, what Lee had said *was* the truth. He thought of Gil Farquhar driving out into the countryside at midnight: alone? But Jack Atcheson had said there had been two people in the old blue Cadillac. Had Molly, already dead, been riding in the car with him? He suddenly realized he had overlooked a most important clue. Where was Molly's car? It hadn't been out at the Blamey place; or at least he hadn't seen it. But then neither he nor Roley Trubauer had looked for it; even if the twister had picked it up and demolished it, they still should have seen it. He was a hell of a detective, ten years' inaction had dulled him, made him careless. You did not look for clues as a small town police chief. Or not in Friendship. Crime here had always been straightforward, like the gospel sermons you heard in the pulpits or on the radio. He tried to remember the major crimes in his time here: two murders, two suicides, three rapes, burglaries, an attempted hold-up of a supermarket. Clues had not been part of the coin, they had not been needed. The crimes had been solved without benefit of them; there had always been witnesses who had done the Police Department's job for it. Unlike in New York, the witnesses in a small town were not afraid to help the police. But he could do without witnesses now, at least till tomorrow morning. Then they could come to him in hordes.

"I don't have any proof," he hedged. "You can print what you suspect, if you like. But you could have a libel suit slapped on you. Nothing in this is straightforward."

"Is that a police cliché or are you telling me something?"

"Jesus!" He stood up, took his gunbelt from the back of the kitchen chair and buckled it on. "Some day, when you've got nothing better to do, you can write an editorial about when the press took over the third degree from the police."

She got up, came round the table and put her arms round his neck. "All right, no more questions till tomorrow morning. But I want the whole truth then and nothing but the truth. Just do me a favour—don't give the story, whatever it is, to anyone else."

"Who else? You think I'm going to call the *New York Times*?"

"You might. I think you're still a big city boy at heart."

"You're wrong. I'm small town now right down to my socks." But if ever the full story of what was going on today got out, it would be a *New York Times* story. And every other goddam newspaper in the country, not to mention the television and radio news channels.

They walked through the house, their arms round each other. He never came in or went out the back door; she had insisted on that and he had seen her point. Their relationship had to be out in the open, for the good of both of them. When they married, and they knew now it would be soon, he would be moving into this house. Neither of them wanted it whispered behind the curtains of the neighbouring windows that he had sneaked into it through the back door.

The Barron home was at the opposite end of Forest View Drive from that of the Farquhar house; at one time it had been next door to the Farquhars before they had sold off most of their land. It was an old house, built from local stone, standing in two acres of garden in which grew dogwood, azaleas and a magnificent elm that was McKechnie's particular favourite. He joked that he looked forward to sitting in its shade in the summers of his old age. The interior of the house was comfortable, not as elegant as that of the Farquhars, but still suggesting a spaciousness from the past; the rooms, too, were admired by McKechnie who had grown up between walls that had always seemed within arms' reach. The furniture was solid, built by men who had had time to put some of themselves into their work; and books were on shelves in every room, invitations to the enquiring mind. McKechnie knew he would be happy in the house when the time came to move in with Lee.

They kissed under the pediment of the front door, the one ornate feature of the otherwise plain façade. The rain had eased again, but the wind blew along the porch, rocking the old swing. There was a feverishness to it, a warning that McKechnie heeded. The wind blew against his face, slapping up his collar, but it was in his bones that he felt its message. He had a sudden chilling fear that this house might be destroyed before the day was out.

"Will you be working the rest of the day?" Lee said.

"I guess so. I've called all the fellers back on duty." To ward off any further remarks about the Farquhars he said, "Just in case those Tornado Warnings turn out to be right."

"I think you'd like that. Just to bury whatever's on your mind on the back page."

She was too smart: married life might not be so hot with her. "Assuming we get through the day, tonight for supper?"

"Seven o'clock. I love you, you know that? You're an aggravating son-of-a-bitch at times, but I love you."

"Likewise." He grinned, kissed her on the cheek. "Take care."

"Why? What's going to happen?"

"Nothing," he said. "Unless we get that twister."

"I'll run when I see it." Even the intelligent can be so dumb and careless, he thought. "But every spring and summer of my life I've seen days like this. So have you, since you came here."

He nodded, agreeing with her; but his bones were stiff and convinced otherwise. "Seven o'clock. Bud Grierson brought me in a jack salmon yesterday. I'll bring it along and we'll have that. I'll cook it."

She was a terrible cook and Mondays through Fridays had a woman come in to keep house and cook for her. Weekends she and McKechnie ate out or he did the cooking. "Mrs Pitt left an apple pie in the freezer. I'll see if I can warm it up without spoiling it."

The moment of domesticity comforted him; they parted on a good note. He went out to his car, aware of the trembling curtain in the house across the road. That would be Eleanor Milly, wife of the town's leading lawyer, a woman who missed nothing of what went on in the street and, through her husband's practice, little of what went on in the town. Enjoy yourself, Mrs Milly, he said silently, and resisted the temptation to jerk his finger at her. He wondered if he would really feel at home here on Forest View Drive, if he was really a small town boy after all. But there was no point in thinking about those things today.

He got into his car, put a call through to Roley Trubauer. "Roly, is Bud with you?"

"Just got together, chief. We're heading out towards Razorback again, case Clint Blamey comes back that way."

"Do that later. Go out to Clint Blamey's place and check around there, down in the woods behind it, everywhere, see if Molly Farquhar's car is there. She has—had a fawn Chevvy, I think."

There was some murmuring and crackling, then Trubauer said, "Bud says it was a Buick and it was cream, she just never bothered to get it washed."

He was learning more and more about Molly Farquhar: he had always thought her one of the neatest and smartest-looking women in town. He would have to start looking more closely at what people drove around in: maybe there was some hint to their character there. Come to think of it, he couldn't remember Gil Farquhar's old blue Cadillac ever showing any hint of having been washed or polished.

"Anyhow, I want to know how she got out to Clint's place last night."

He switched off, drove slowly along the street, puzzled at his reluctance to approach the Farquhar house again. He had never shirked his job before; but he had never before been caught in a web like this. For the first time he realized his importance in the town. He had never had any conceit about being chief of police; coming from New York, still imbued with the values he had grown up with, he had continued to see things in the widest context. He had never sneered at being chief of police in a small town, but he had never thought of it as a position of real importance and power. But now his whole perspective had a new angle. Though Friendship might never know it he had suddenly, this morning, become the most important person in town, the cornerstone.

People were coming out of the houses, going into their two- and three-car garages to drive to church. Some of them stopped to look up at the wracked sky, but none of them appeared really worried. America on a Sunday morning, he thought: does the rest of the world look as smug and secure as we do on this day?

He turned into the Farquhar driveway, parked behind Jack Atcheson's car. The church-goers drove past, some of them slowing as they saw the two police cars outside the big house. Faces showed at the windows of the cars and it struck him that suddenly they no longer looked smug and secure. It was as if the house they were staring at was a symbol that had begun to crumble.

## II

Willis Vanderhorn had not enjoyed the conversation with the President. The two men had never been compatible; their running on the same ticket four years ago had been a marriage of convenience dictated by the shotguns of the National Committee. The same shotguns had insisted that this year's ticket should be the same, but the National Committee and the President knew that in four years' time Vanderhorn intended to be his own man, to run for first place on the ticket. He had never stated that intention; he had lived by his grandfather's dictum that you never told today's men what you meant to do tomorrow. But other men had stated his ambition, without his permission but also without his denial.

"Your security guys have found out you're not at home," said the President. "Kerby, from the Secret Service, has been on to me in a panic. I've told them I know where you are and not to worry, but you know what they're like. They're such conscientious bastards."

"I'm delighted to hear it," said Vanderhorn. "I thought that trait was supposed to have died out in Washington."

"Don't sound so goddam chipper."

"I'm a long way from feeling chipper, John."

"Sorry. I didn't mean that. How long are you going to stay down there? You're due in New York tomorrow at the UN. I hope you haven't forgotten that?"

"I haven't forgotten." He never forgot anything. His mind was crammed to bursting with even the forgettable, like a Civil Service file. It was something he had tried to cure himself of, but his famous self-discipline, in this instance, had not worked. "I'll be coming back to Washington tonight."

"How is she, Willis? Any worse?"

"It's hard to tell. I've just come down from her bedroom. She was asleep and I thought—I hoped—she mightn't wake up. She's in dreadful pain, John." He felt the pain himself: of memories that he knew he would never forget. "But then she woke up and recognized me. I can't leave her, John, not while—Do you understand?"

"Don't jeopardize everything. I don't want to sound cruel, Willis, but she is going to die anyway."

"We're all going to do that," he said. "Don't worry. I'll keep our priorities straight." He emphasized the word *our* just a little but he doubted if it had carried all the way to Washington. The President was not a man with a sensitive ear, a good thing in a politician but not in a President. "I'll be back tonight, whatever happens."

"What about Kerby?" Kerby was Chief of the Secret Service. "Does he know about Rose?"

"I think so. The regular agents on my detail know about her, so they've probably told him. But they'll keep their mouths shut."

"Kerby is likely to guess where you are. Does he know Rose went home a month ago?"

"No. For all he knows, we just broke up and she went off to Europe. I don't discuss my private life with the Secret Service, John."

"Okay, okay." The President sounded testy. "Just remember I've got a stake in you, Willis. Neither of us is entitled to a private life."

"All right." Vanderhorn decided to control his own temper; anything to end the conversation. "Look, Kerby and his men knew nothing of Rose's illness. They know I haven't seen her for a month. So for all they know, she could be in Europe. She went there every spring for a few weeks. It used to be one of my presents to her. Her Easter egg, if you like."

There would be no more presents; and all at once, for

90

the first time, he felt the value of them. The value in the heart: the money that a gift cost had never meant anything to him. He couldn't remember when he had last looked at the price of an article or a service or a trip; everything had always been done for him by his secretary, even the buying of the gifts for Rose. And now it was too late for all that to be changed.

"Tell Kerby I'll be back in Washington tonight. Tell him his conscience is clear and you'll give him a Presidential pardon if by some remote chance anything happens to me."

"I won't, you know. I don't believe in Presidential pardons, not after—"

"I was joking, John. Though Christ knows, I don't feel like it."

When he had hung up he sat on in the study where he had taken the call. It had been the Senator's study and more than just vestiges of the old man still remained. The shelves seemed to hold only books published before the Senator's death. The authors belonged to another era: Lippmann, Krock, Nevins, William Allen White. Even the novels wouldn't be seen in paperback reprints nowadays: *Kitty Foyle, State Fair, The Biscuit Eater.* Vanderhorn suddenly felt an affinity with the dead man: so many of these books had been the reading of his own youth.

He stood up and took down a title that had caught his eye: *Missouri Men.* He opened it, hoping there might be a piece on the Senator in it, but there was none. Then a photo fell out into his hand: a young girl and a young man standing hand in hand in a garden. He recognized Rose at once; it was a few moments before he realized that the laughing, carefree youth beside her was her brother Gilbert. They both looked so happy that it hurt him; everything had been so *right* for them in that long ago summer. The garden, he saw now, must have been

91

the one outside; but it was so much larger then, the house well behind them in the background. He turned the photo over and saw the date on the back in a good firm hand: August 1945. The year he had met Carolyn.

There was a knock on the door and Adele Farquhar pushed it open. She saw him holding the photo and at once he had a feeling of guilt, as if he had opened a locked family album.

"May I have that photograph, Mr Vanderhorn? I didn't know it was in the book." She took it from him and looked at it without expression. Or so he thought till he noticed the rigid control of her mouth. But when she looked up at him and spoke there was no quivering of her lips. "That was such a long time ago. One's children seem like strangers in these days."

He thought of his own children, two boys and a girl, already strangers to him, allies of their mother: "They looked very happy."

"They were good times, Mr Vanderhorn. Their father was still alive. Our whole circumstances were, well, much better than now."

"Rose occasionally told me how things were back here when she was young."

"Did she tell you much?"

"No. I never pressed it—she could be very reticent at times. She never mentioned her brother, for instance. Though they looked very happy together in that picture."

"They were. We were all happy, very much so. Gilbert would tell you about it."

"I don't think so. Your son and I don't seem to have any rapport. I saw him a while ago, going out across the back lawn and into the woods. He seems to be avoiding me."

"He often goes for walks." He hadn't expected her to sound defensive. But she was defending her children,

92

something he had given up doing long ago. "Rose used to like to walk, too."

"She still did, up till a few months ago when—" He gestured lamely, as if Rose's illness should not be mentioned between them. "That was why I bought her the house on Chesapeake Bay. She went walking every day she was there. I wouldn't allow her to walk in New York."

"Why not?"

"I was afraid of her being mugged."

"I'm surprised she took any notice of you. She was a headstrong girl."

He smiled, glad of the relief of it. "Not with me. We got on remarkably well."

"So long as you got your own way? Oh, don't excuse yourself, Mr Vanderhorn. I'm not a Women's Libber. I've always been content for it to be a man's world. Perhaps Rose was just waiting for the right man to come along to prove she was more like me than I thought. Where did she live in New York?"

"I bought her a house on East 61st Street, a small brownstone. She preferred that to living in an apartment. That way we had no doorkeeper or elevator man spying on us."

"You appear to have treated her well. Materially, that is."

"I wanted to divorce my wife and marry Rose fifteen years ago. My wife wouldn't hear of it."

"Is she a Catholic?"

"No." He was going to say her religion was to be a bitch, but he knew that would be a mistake. Adele Farquhar might be on Carolyn's side: you never knew what drew women together in an alliance.

"I thought divorce was easily obtained these days."

"Not by Vanderhorns. I am as restricted by my family as Catholics are by the Vatican. Our faith is the family name, if you like. My mother and brothers defend it with all the fervour of the Curia."

"Did your family know of your association with Rose?"

He nodded. "I wasn't ashamed of Rose, Mrs Farquhar. She and my mother met several times and got on well together. My mother never blamed Rose for the break-up of my marriage. But no Vanderhorn has ever been divorced. We are a little like the British royal family. Or so my mother likes to think."

"The one admirable thing, Mr Vanderhorn, is that you respect your mother's wishes. Or was that just an excuse? I know how politically ambitious you are."

He decided to be as honest with her as he had been with Rose; like Rose, he guessed, she would not be easily deceived. He was beginning to see the daughter in the mother, though Rose was softer and had more sense of humour than her mother. But then he hadn't known Adele Farquhar when she had been young and Adele Vaughan.

"That entered into it. I was selfish and Rose knew it. But she never pressed the point. She used to say that it wasn't necessary for me to make an honest woman of her —she never felt she was *dis*honest. I want you to know this is the truth, Mrs Farquhar. After my wife refused to divorce me, Rose never wanted me to marry her. She said she was not going to let me get a Mexican divorce, anything like that. She was not going to have our relationship dirtied in the interests of respectability, that was what she said. I never fought her on it," he added lamely. "And now, when it's too late, I wish I had."

"As you say, Mr Vanderhorn, it is too late. But thank you for being honest with me. You are not wholly admirable, but I don't think I should like it if my daughter had fallen in love with a man who could not be honest about their affair."

"It was never an affair. It was always more than that, right from the day we met."

94

"I apologize. It was an insult to my daughter—and to you." She looked at the photo again, then turned it inwards against her breast. "What would you like for luncheon? Normally we have our big meal on Sundays at midday, but I'm afraid I don't feel like it today. But Wilma Mae will prepare whatever you wish."

He noticed she had used the word *luncheon,* just as his mother did. The two old women had much in common, perhaps because each belonged to another era. Or perhaps because they had protection: his mother that of her wealth and position, Adele Farquhar that of her isolation here in this backwater.

"Just something light. Rose told me once that Wilma Mae made something called Rum Tum Tiddy that she and the Senator liked. I believe he had got the recipe for it in Boston or somewhere."

Adele Farquhar smiled: she, too, looked relieved, as if a smile were some sort of analgesic. "Tomato soup and melted cheese, with a beaten egg and some seasoning. My husband, who had a Southern gentleman's prejudices, said it was the only thing that ever came out of New England that he liked. You shall have it, Mr Vanderhorn. Even if only for sentiment's sake."

The front-door bell rang: a little shrilly, it seemed to Vanderhorn. But perhaps he was becoming edgy. He had not slept at all last night and yesterday had been a busy day, even though a Saturday. Lunch with Feeney, the labour boss (who certainly wouldn't have called it *luncheon*); an afternoon meeting with the President and his primaries campaign organizers; dinner at the French embassy. His well-publicized energy had suddenly drained out of him; but he knew he was more exhausted by emotion and grief than by the political and diplomatic round. He wondered how strong or weak (shattered?) he would be by the time he got on the plane this evening for Washington.

Wilma Mae tapped on the study door. "Chief Mc-Kechnie here to see you, Miz Farquhar. He's in the drawing-room."

"Again?" But Adele Farquhar addressed the question to Vanderhorn, not to her housekeeper. And he felt pleased at the question, rhetorical though it might only be. She had accepted him into her house, even if only for the day. "What can he want?"

McKechnie wanted Gilbert Farquhar. "I have some more questions to put to him, Mrs Farquhar."

"My son is not here, Mr McKechnie."

The police chief frowned. "Where is he then?"

Vanderhorn had followed his hostess into the drawing-room, feeling certain now that she wanted his support. He said, "I saw Mr Farquhar going out across the back lawn about twenty minutes ago. He was heading into the woods, going for a walk, I presume."

McKechnie glanced out the window at the police car that had been parked in the driveway for the past hour, but he made no comment. He spun his cap in his hands and looked back at Adele Farquhar. "Then I'd like to talk to Wilma Mae."

"May I ask why, Mr McKechnie?"

"You may ask, Mrs Farquhar, but I'm afraid I don't have to tell you."

"There is no need for you to be offensive, Mr Mc-Kechnie."

The exchange was as polite as an exchange of visiting cards. Adele Farquhar, Vanderhorn had already noted, set the tone in her own house.

"That wasn't my intention." For the first time Vanderhorn saw the weariness in the police chief. What sort of day had he had yesterday and last night? What calls of duty? "I am investigating what might be a murder, the murder of your daughter-in-law. That doesn't make this a social call."

96

Vanderhorn waited on the old woman's reaction. He was sure that she had all his own mother's stock of refrigerated anatomy: the cold shoulder, the chill stare. He knew how his mother would have treated this policeman; public servants in her eyes were just that, *servants*. But Adele Farquhar had more tact than that. Or perhaps more respect for this man who was just trying to do his job.

"Shall I bring Wilma Mae in here or do you wish to talk to her in the kitchen?"

"The kitchen will do," said McKechnie. "I feel more at home there."

"You under-rate yourself, Mr McKechnie. I think you would feel at home anywhere."

### III

"I never goes out anywhere at night," said Wilma Mae. "Where the dark catches me, I stays."

"So you were here in the house all night last night?"

"Yessir, chief. Why I wanna go out, anyways? I mean, with Miss Rose sick like she is, nobody knowing when she gonna go to the Lord."

"Who *did* go out last night? I mean beside Mrs Molly? What about Mr Gilbert?"

Wilma Mae was a good-looking woman with a dignity that was partly inherited, partly absorbed: she was a daughter of this house if not of the family. She had once had a husband, a quiet sober man who had worked for the Farquhars as chauffeur and gardener, but he had died ten years ago. She was in her late fifties now, McKechnie guessed, but he couldn't be sure. He had never been expert at reading black faces, their age or their thoughts, and he knew even now that he would leave this kitchen with questions unanswered, questions useless to ask. Wilma Mae knew *her* duty: to the family that was as much hers as if she had been born of it.

She sat at the big table in the middle of the big old-fashioned kitchen and gazed at him with all the confidence of a Farquhar. "What Mr Gil done last night is his business. I dunno he went out or not and I ain't asked him."

McKechnie had already cursed himself for not having questioned Farquhar as soon as Jack Atcheson had told him of seeing the Cadillac going out last night towards the Blamey place. He should have come back to the house at once, but weariness and ten years of easy-going routine had dulled him; the further questioning of Farquhar could wait till later, till *now*. He determined that for the rest of today he would put nothing off. He had done his best to accommodate this family, spare them, if you liked to call it that, and they weren't reciprocating. He'd put out an APB on Gil Farquhar at once and to hell with the consequences. Then he remembered the other man in the house and caution settled on him like snow.

"What about Mrs Molly? Was she upset at all yesterday?"

"She upset like we all is. You be like that, chief, somebody you love dying in your house."

Jesus, he thought, she knows how to raise ghosts. But her face was expressionless and he knew there was no malice in her. "Of course. But Mrs Molly had other things on her mind, too." He took a risk: after all, she was one of the family, she wouldn't go broadcasting any scandal. "She was pregnant, Wilma Mae."

Her face was a dark stone mask.

"Did you know that?" he said, surprised.

Slowly, the words dragged out of her, she said, "She told me. Like she done tell me lotsa things. She had nobody to talk to, she say. She used—confide?—me."

"What else did she confide in you, Wilma Mae?"

Her eyes were deep closets of thought; she had secrets locked away in her that pained her to the point of tears.

But she didn't weep in front of him: that in itself would be a disclosure. "She dead, chief. I respects the dead."

Sure, Molly Farquhar was dead; and he was beginning to realize that he had never known her when she was alive. She had been a bright, sometimes witty woman, gregarious as a sparrow; but it seemed perhaps that no one, he least of all, had ever really guessed at the Molly Farquhar behind the vital, good-humoured image she had presented to the town. Only the three other people in this house had seen behind it; and, he guessed, Clint Blamey. He wondered if Blamey had been confided in as this black housekeeper had been.

"Wilma Mae, Mrs Molly was *shot*. Someone killed her. Don't you want to help me find out who that might be?"

"I ain't one for revenge, chief. Miz Molly wasn't, neither. Leastways I never thought that before."

"Before what?"

Nothing showed in her face or eyes, but he knew she had made a slip. Then she said, "Before she die."

He sat back in the old Windsor-style kitchen chair. This big work room, he guessed, was Wilma Mae's pride and joy: that part of the house which was hers and hers alone. Copper-bottomed pots and pans gleamed like a signature, her mark impressed on them through the vigour of her hands. The table and the work-benches were wood, scrubbed to a pale gold; the wall tiles behind the benches were the sort he remembered from public washrooms. Except that these were decorated by a pale blue symbol: it took him a few moments to recognize that it was a decorative initial, the letter F. The cupboards were of the same pale gold timber; McKechnie imagined he could see the tiny scoring of the scrub-brush in the wood. The only modern note in the kitchen was the double-oven electric stove, but even that had been fitted into the old stone fireplace, as if somehow to disguise it. This was

Wilma Mae's retreat, where she felt safe from the night and whatever other terrors there were beyond the walls of the house. *Where the dark catches me, I stays.*

Then she jumped in her chair and he did the same. There was the loud crack of the rifle shot and, part of the same frightening sound, the crash of glass. McKechnie thrust back his chair, lost his balance and grabbed at the table to keep himself on his feet. By the time he got to the window over the sink, whoever had fired the shot had gone. There was no one on the back lawn; the woods fifty yards back looked empty. He spun round, ran out of the kitchen into the hallway as Adele Farquhar came out of the drawing-room.

"Where's the Vice-President?"

"Upstairs with my daughter—" She stopped, put a hand to her throat.

Then Vanderhorn said from the top of the stairs, "I'm all right. You had better go up to Rose, Mrs Farquhar."

They passed on the stairs, the old woman moving with almost youthful speed, all her dignity forgotten as she hurried to comfort her daughter. Vanderhorn came down to McKechnie.

"Did you see him?"

"No, sir. Stay here. I'll be back in a minute."

He went quickly out through the kitchen again to the back porch. Jack Atcheson was standing in the middle of the lawn looking up at the house, an angry bewildered look on his long face. "Jesus Christ, who the hell—?"

"You been down to the timber?" Atcheson shook his head. "Come on then!"

But whoever had been in the woods had gone. They saw crushed wet leaves where he had stood behind an oak and a trail led off down the slope through the trees. A narrow back road ran along the bottom of the slope and McKechnie guessed that the gunman, if he had had a car down there, was already heading for one of the other back roads that ran out into the countryside.

"Get moving, Jack! Take your car down to the bottom road, see if there are any tyre tracks. Get on to Lucy, tell her to call the other cars into this area." As they ran back up through the woods and across the lawn he said, "What about the houses on either side? Anyone home there? They might've seen something."

"All at church." Atcheson was panting; he wasn't accustomed to running. "You staying here?"

"I'll be here. If there's nothing down there on the bottom road, come back."

Atcheson went on round the house and McKechnie went back inside, careful to wipe his feet on the porch mat before stepping into Wilma Mae's kitchen. She was standing at the sink, staring out through the window.

"Did you see anything, Wilma Mae? Just before the shot?"

"I was looking at you, chief." She gestured at the chairs beside the table; he realized she had her back to the window. "Anybody seen anything, oughta been you. Who they trying to shoot? They trying to frighten Miss Rose to her death?"

He had no answer to either question. He just hoped that whoever had fired the shot had not been trying to shoot the Vice-President of the United States. He went on into the hallway, found it deserted; then saw Vanderhorn through the open doors of the drawing-room. He went in, sure of his authority now but suddenly, sickeningly, aware of his responsibility.

"Were you standing by the windows upstairs, sir?" Vanderhorn nodded. "Did you see anything, I mean anyone?"

"I had my back to the windows. I don't think whoever it was was trying to kill *me*, chief."

101

"I can't rule out that possibility." He felt uncertain, frustrated. He knew he was a better cop than he must appear to be just now, but he was getting no breaks at all. The gunman, even hiding among the trees in the woods, must have been visible to anyone standing or sitting near the windows in the back of the house. Yet he down in the kitchen had seen nothing and neither had Vanderhorn upstairs in the bedroom. "You must have got threats at some time, sir?"

"All the time, I'm told. I never see them, the Secret Service agents intercept them. It's part of the wages of the position I hold. But nobody knows I'm here."

"Would Miss Rose have seen anything? Does her bed face the window?"

"It does. But she'd have seen nothing. She is lying on her back. She is *dying*, chief."

McKechnie nodded, gestured weakly. "I'm sorry. I'll need to go up there later. To look for the bullet."

"I don't know what Mrs Farquhar will say to that, but I'm saying no. She must be allowed to die without any further disturbance. I'm adamant about that, chief."

McKechnie didn't argue. The bullet wasn't going to move from whatever it was embedded in, the ceiling or one of the walls of the bedroom. "How did she react when the shot smashed the window?"

"I thought it had killed her: The shock, I mean. Then I realized she was concerned for me, that I might have been hit." He relaxed, seemed to forget their respective roles, spoke as man to man. "She is dying and her only concern was for me. Do we deserve as much as that?"

"No, sir. My wife died saving me from a bullet and I've never felt I deserved it."

Vanderhorn said nothing for a moment, looking at the policeman with a new interest. "You don't come from around here, do you?"

"No, sir. New York."

"I'd like to know more about you, chief. But I don't think there will be time, not if I'm to go back to Washington this evening."

"I'd like you to go sooner, sir. Just in case that guy with the gun tries again."

Vanderhorn shook his head. "I'm staying. Did you run away when your wife was dying?"

"She died instantly. And the situation was different. I was not the Vice-President of the United States."

"I am still not leaving here till this evening. Unless Miss Farquhar dies before then. I just don't believe that shot was intended for me."

"It might have been." McKechnie wondered at the question in his mind. Had he become infected by the atmosphere of the house, the secrets hinted at by the evasive answers of Wilma Mae? "What is the feeling between you and Gilbert Farquhar?"

Vanderhorn took his time about answering. "None on my part. I had never met the man till this morning."

"What's his feeling towards you?"

Again the answer wasn't immediately forthcoming. "He doesn't like me. Both he and his mother think I didn't treat Miss Farquhar fairly."

"I've already gathered that, sir."

Vanderhorn raised his eyebrows slightly. "You don't appear to miss much. But I think you're building more on your evidence than it will bear. Do you really think Farquhar would try to shoot me in his own house?"

"I've had more experience with murder or attempted murder than you would have had, sir. In New York, anyway. It's usually only cold-blooded hit men, contract guys, who choose where they are going to knock someone off. Most murders are committed on the spur of the moment."

"I'm not going to even *think* that Farquhar fired that shot at me."

"You're making my job more difficult, sir."

103

"I know you are only trying to do that job. But you are a stubborn man, chief. In Washington I don't think I'd be as patient with you as I am out here."

"In Washington, sir, you wouldn't be my responsibility." Then McKechnie gestured again. "I apologize. I don't want to argue with you. Just do me a favour, please. Stay away from the windows. There are my men. Excuse me."

Sirens moaned out in the street and McKechnie, through the drawing-room windows, saw the red lights spinning in the grey day like blood blenders. He went out of the house, turning his face away from the onslaught of wind that suddenly blew up the street. There was no rain, but water drops fell on him as the wind whipped the maples above him. The other three police cars and his own blocked the driveway; it looked like the scene of a major accident. He couldn't remember ever having all the cars together, not since the Kansas City Southern freight train had hit a refrigerated truck at the Bell Street crossing. He sometimes wondered why disaster always had to be a production *after* it happened. But he knew it wouldn't be politic to tell his men to switch off their lights.

"Nothing, chief," Jack Atcheson reported. "There wasn't even any car tracks down there on the bottom road. He was either on foot or he left his car somewhere else."

"You think it was someone out there in the woods shooting at birds or something and he got off line?" Bud Grierson asked. Then he shook his head, answering himself. "Nope, it's outa season. Anyone around here, he'd know better'n to come so close to town."

The policemen had all got out of their cars and stood in a tight dark group beside McKechnie's car, pushed together by the wind. The radios continued to crackle, as if Lucy Chapley back at headquarters was tuned in, not wanting to miss anything that might be said. The newcomers stared up at the big house, the younger men, the farm boys, really looking at it for the first time. They had cruised on this beat every alternate week for several years, ever since they had come on to the force, but they had never had any occasion to get out of their cars and look closely at the houses they were supposed to be protecting. Not up here on Forest View, anyway. When they did look at the houses it was only to envy the owners, to dream of some day owning something like the newer ones in the $70–80,000 bracket. On $525 a month that was some dream. None of them would have aspired to something as old and old-fashioned as the Farquhar house.

"We went back out to the Blamey place, Bud and me," said Roley Trubauer. "No sign of Molly Farquhar's car."

"Any signs of Clint Blamey?" McKechnie said.

"Nothing, chief. You think he might of been the guy who took the shot out back there?"

"He could've been."

Some spectators had begun to congregate at the bottom of the drive, faces pinched with puzzlement. Some kids, sparrows ready to feed on the grain of excitement, came up the driveway, but one of the younger officers shooed them away. Then McKechnie saw the tall stooping figure come down the street and push through the group at the gates.

"It could've been anyone," said McKechnie.

Gilbert Farquhar lifted his head and pulled up as he saw the line of police cars. He was dressed in the old tweed hat, pulled low down on his head, and the dark raincoat; he looked like an old bird, a dark crane or heron in a swamp of doubt. He frowned, then his face clouded with a mixture of worry and anger.

"What's going on? Why all this commotion, chief? What's happened?"

"Let's go inside, Mr Farquhar." McKechnie then turned

to Atcheson and the other policemen. "Take another look around, fellers. I still want to talk to Clint Blamey."

"You want me to come back here?" Atcheson said.

"I'll let you know, Jack. All of you better keep an eye on that sky, too. You see another twister coming, that takes priority."

The men got back into their cars and drove off, waving the spectators away as they did so. McKechnie and Farquhar stood side by side in the driveway, neither of them saying a word till they were alone. Then Farquhar said, "You owe me an explanation, chief. You're supposed to be keeping people *away* from this house, not drawing attention to it."

"Did you hear a gun shot about ten, fifteeen minutes ago?"

Farquhar frowned again, looked quickly up at the house. "My sister—? Good God—"

"Your sister is okay. Did you hear the shot?"

Farquhar, still staring at the house, nodded almost absently. "Yes, I heard it."

"You didn't take any notice of it?"

Farquhar slowly turned his head, his face expressionless now. The wind flung some raindrops from the trees into his face, but he didn't appear to notice them. "What are you getting at?"

"Someone tried to kill Mr Vanderhorn. He was upstairs in your sister's bedroom and someone tried to shoot him through the window. If you heard a shot down in this direction, why didn't it worry you?"

"I thought it was a car backfiring. Or somebody out shooting in the woods. I don't know, I just didn't take any notice of it."

"Your wife was murdered last night, Mr Farquhar. Shot. I'd have thought you'd be pretty jumpy if you heard another shot so close to your house."

It abruptly began to rain again, gun-metal sheets of it

slashing up the street. Farquhar swung round and ran up the steps to the front porch. McKechnie, taken by surprise, took a moment to follow him. Only when he was up on the porch did he realize he had actually been *chasing* Farquhar, not trying to get in out of the rain. He had thought the other man was trying to escape from him.

"Goddam you, McKechnie! Come inside—I've got to phone someone. I've got a witness who'll tell you where I was when we heard the shot!"

He went in the front door, leaving it open behind him. McKechnie followed him, closing the door. Farquhar went to the phone on a hallway table, flipped through a leather-covered phone book with feverish hands. He found a number, started to dial it, fumbled and started again. He was trembling with anger, glaring at McKechnie as he waited for the number to answer.

Then: "Miss Barron? This is Gilbert Farquhar. Could you come down here to our house, please? It's urgent!"

# *Chapter Four*

The tornado front lifted around mid-morning. South of Friendship the sky seemed to lighten, though it continued to rain. People began to hope that the storms had worn themselves out, that maybe there would be no more twisters today. The clouds flattened out, the giant mountains of cumulus turning into a grey desert out of which the paradoxical rain fell steadily. The rolling squall clouds disappeared and the thunder fell silent. But the Severe Storms Forecast Center in Kansas City did not withdraw any of its warnings: it only reduced them from Tornado Warning to Tornado Watch. Their radar screens, the satellite photographs and reports from airline pilots told them that in the upper galleries of the sky the turmoil was still there. The cold air, coming down from the north, bouncing sideways off the Rocky Mountains and spreading east, had risen but had not given up the battle against the moisture-saturated warm air pushing at increasing speed up from the Gulf of Mexico. The cold air blanket, like an army regathering, began to thicken, became heavier. High in the atmosphere, at 65,000 feet, the Jet Stream, sweeping slightly to the south of east, added its contribution to the battle, like a Great Power fuelling up a local war. It pulled pressure out of the path of the warm air front, increasing the speed of the colliding masses. The flat rain-clouds low down over Texas, Oklahoma, Kansas and Missouri were only a smoke-screen hiding the awesome fury building in the upper heavens.

The tornadoes that had already touched down had killed twelve people, injured scores of others and disrupted the lives of hundreds more. They also disrupted the plans of Lew Black, who was white, and Jumpy Cowman, a black. They were the two men whose mug shots were on the clipboards of every cruising policeman in a dozen counties in that corner where Missouri, Kansas and Oklahoma met. They had held up the bank in Columbus, Kansas, on Friday and everything had been going well until the elderly cop had walked into the bank and tried to be a hero. Jumpy, who was well nick-named, had shot him at once and they had had to flee with less than half the money they had hoped to get. They had headed south and they had holed up Friday night and all day Saturday in a deserted shack near Lake Spavinaw over the Oklahoma border. Lew Black, who had once had his own heroes, had remarked that Mickey Mantle had come from around here; but Jumpy, whose heroes were black and more recent, had not been impressed. Early Sunday morning they had set out again, aiming south-west down through Oklahoma to Texas.

They ran into the storms just after they had started out. They drove on through the rain, under the towering thunderheads and the ambush fire of the lightning, until they ran into the police roadblock just north of Wetumka. They pulled up just in time as they came over a crest; the rain cleared and half a mile down the road they saw the flashing red lights. They were not to know that the police cars were not waiting for them but were there to turn back motorists trying to drive through the devastated area on the outskirts of Wetumka.

Black and Cowman turned west, but eight miles along

the side road they saw the red lights blinking at them again through the dark-grey day. They pulled up and held a conference, a low level meeting of low level intellects. It did not occur to them to ask why police cars, if intent on intercepting two cop killers, should advertise their presence by flashing their lights as a warning.

"Cops," said Black. "Looks like they're on to us."

"What the hell we going to do, man?"

Black, as steadily as breathing, let out a stream of obscenity that, alone, would have had him arrested by Chief McKechnie. Finally, the straight unqualified sentence sounding almost prim, he said, "You ever been to Chicago?"

"Jesus, man, when you think I got up there? Let's go, man."

They turned the car round and headed north-east, following the line of the storms straight through to Friendship.

## I

"I saw Mr Farquhar passing my house and I went out to speak to him," said Lee and looked pointedly at McKechnie. "To offer him sympathy on his wife's death."

"Did you hear the shot, too?"

"Yes. I wasn't sure whether it was a car backfiring or a gun going off. A lot of people around here have guns. Too many," she added, sounding for a moment like one of her own editorials.

She could not keep from glancing at the man standing with Adele Farquhar at the doorway of the drawing-room. They had come in only moments after she, ushered in by Gil Farquhar and McKechnie, had entered the room. They had pulled up, obviously surprised to find her in the house. They had not attempted to retreat, though she had seen the quick enquiring look Adele Farquhar had given the stranger. They had remained silent and there had been no attempt at an introduction.

Then McKechnie, apparently satisfied with her answers to his questions about Gil Farquhar, spoke to the man. "I'm sorry about this, sir. I didn't bring Miss Barron in here."

"It looks as if the damage is done. I think the young lady recognizes me."

"I do, Mr Vice-President," said Lee, though till the man had spoken she had not been sure. She had never seen Willis Vanderhorn in the flesh and she knew only too well how different some people could be from their newspaper pictures and their television appearances. "But I wasn't sure that I wasn't dreaming. I'm Lee Barron, owner and editor of the local newspaper."

"That's bad," said Vanderhorn. "Who brought you here?"

"I did," said Farquhar. "It had nothing to do with you being here. I was just trying to prove to our busybody police chief that I wasn't the one who took a shot at you upstairs."

McKechnie had noticed that Adele Farquhar did not appear to have the poise and control that she had shown only a couple of hours earlier. She looked much older, less certain of her small world. She spoke now but it seemed to him that she had less authority in her voice and even the voice itself was just a little ragged at the edges.

"I don't think Mr McKechnie really believes that, do you?"

"Not now," said McKechnie.

"But you believed it up till I brought Miss Barron down here?" Farquhar still wore his raincoat and hat, as if he had no intention of staying in the house; his trembling hands fumbled for his pockets like white rats scuttling for their holes. "You really thought that, didn't you?"

"No," said McKechnie and tried to sound convincing;

111

he realized he wanted to preserve the atmosphere of this house as much as the old woman who owned it. "But I have to check out everything. I'm still trying to find out how your wife died. Don't forget that."

"What is that supposed to mean?"

"It means exactly what Mr McKechnie said." Adele Farquhar had regained some of her composure; she put it on like an actress changing gowns between acts. "I think we have had enough of this. Go up to Rose, Gilbert. I think one of us should stay with her all the time now."

"I'll go back up," said Vanderhorn.

Farquhar had hesitated, as if about to ignore his mother; but as soon as Vanderhorn turned towards the door he said, "Stay where you are. I'll go."

He brushed by his mother and Vanderhorn and disappeared, leaving an edgy vacancy behind him. Those remaining in the room looked at the space where he had been rather than at each other; embarrassment itched at them like an eczema. Adele Farquhar was the first to recover.

"Have you explained to Miss Barron why the Vice-President is here?"

"I haven't had time," said McKechnie. "Perhaps the Vice-President himself would like to do that."

Vanderhorn gave him a quick look, appreciating his shrewdness: he wasn't going to go right out on the end of the limb for the Vice-President. "I'll have to ask you to forget you are a newspaperwoman, Miss Barron. I am here for a very personal reason."

"I can't promise anything, Mr Vice-President. I have a job to do, just as you have."

For Christ's sake, McKechnie told her silently, stop being so goddam professional, just for today. He saw Vanderhorn glance at him again and recognized the unspoken question: *What have we got here?*

"I am not here as part of my job, Miss Barron. I was

a close friend of Miss Farquhar and I came out here because her family called me to tell me she was dying. I—and I'm sure Mrs Farquhar and her son—would like her to die in decent obscurity, not splashed across the pages of your newspaper just because I am here."

McKechnie saw the slight stiffening in Lee, an assertion of the bones rather than any actual movement of her body. You're going about it the wrong way, he wanted to tell Vanderhorn. She doesn't see her newspaper as a scandal sheet: it's her bible.

"Mr Vice-President—" Lee sounded as if she was about to begin a speech. Or an editorial, an open letter to politicians who did not pay proper respect to the freedom of the press.

"Honey," said McKechnie gently; and saw Vanderhorn's eyebrows go up at the endearment. "Miss Barron and I are engaged to be married, sir. I wonder if she and I could have a minute or two alone, Mrs Farquhar?"

"Of course. I'm sure we can trust Mr McKechnie to handle the situation, Mr Vanderhorn. As I said earlier, he is a man of discretion."

Vanderhorn looked at Lee and McKechnie, then nodded. "I know that. I'm in your hands, chief."

"We'll be in the back parlour. Come, Mr Vanderhorn." She went out of the room ahead of him, all her poise and authority recovered, Chief Executive in her own house again. McKechnie thought he caught a wry smile from the Vice-President, but he wasn't sure.

"A man of discretion," said Lee. "You have quite a reputation in high places, haven't you?"

"Forget the sarcasm. Be reasonable—"

"All right, I'll be reasonable. You try and be the same. Good God, don't you see what we've got here? This is the biggest story I've ever had—the biggest the paper's ever had! What do you expect me to do? Just turn my back on it?"

"Yes."

"*Yes?* Jim, how can I? I'm no admirer of that man or what he stands for. What do I owe him?"

"Respect for his position," he said, trying not to sound pompous and priggish; at the same time asking himself why he should be so defensive about stating such a principle. "And for the Farquhars."

"God, you know how to stick the needle in! I don't mean about him being the Vice-President—if he were the President, maybe I'd admit you had a point. But Vice-President—" She shook her head.

"What about the Farquhars?"

"That's what I mean about the needle. I respect *them*. And with what's happened—I mean Molly being *murdered*. And Rose dying—" She looked at him, suddenly frowning. "My God, I've been dim, haven't I? She's his mistress, isn't she?"

"Was. Like you said, she's dying. Doc Stenhouse said she'll be dead *some time today*. Do you have any respect for the dead?"

"All right, stop needling!" She was wearing a bright red raincoat that was at odds with the brown gloom of the room; the sky had darkened outside and all the highlights had gone from the polished furniture. She thrust her hands into her pockets, just as Farquhar had done but with more force, as someone might beat his fists against a wall in frustration. "How long do I have to sit on the story?"

"Forever. He goes back to Washington tonight, whatever happens. After that it will be Mrs Farquhar who will have to bear the brunt of the scandal. In this town, anyway."

"Are you bending the law in any way?"

"Not yet. I'm not going to, not as far as he's concerned. He's not tied up with Molly's murder."

114

She shook her head, dizzy with imagination. "God, what a story that would be!" Then she took her hands out of her pockets, spread them in resignation, sighed. "All right. But I'm doing it for Adele Farquhar, not for him."

He kissed her on the cheek. "I know why I love you. Because occasionally you can be reasonable."

"Balls," she said, because she knew it would annoy him; and might have said something even stronger in other circumstances and in another house.

But he refused to be annoyed: he had won his point. They went out to the back parlour, a bright green-and-white room where Adele Farquhar and Vanderhorn waited with dark apprehension. Vanderhorn, forgetting McKechnie's advice, had been standing at the trembling french doors staring out at the clouds beginning to assemble again in great moving ranges. The wind had increased and new blossoms and dead leaves flew across the lawn like a mixture of white birds and their brown shadows. Beyond the lawn, in the woods, the trees bent their tops under the onslaught of the wind.

Adele Farquhar sat in a rocker, but the chair was still. She, too, was staring out of the french doors but saw nothing. Nothing, that is, but the memories that were now creeping back on her like a sweet illness that she thought she had conquered.

McKechnie and Lee came into the room and at once McKechnie said, "It's okay, Mr Vanderhorn. Miss Barron understands the situation."

"All of it?"

"All of it."

Vanderhorn bowed his head to Lee. "Thank you, Miss Barron. Mrs Farquhar has explained to me what your politics are, that your newspaper is very much against our Administration. So I appreciate it even more, your going along with us."

Lee nodded to him, but spoke to the old woman. "I'd like you to know I'm doing it out of respect for you, Mrs Farquhar."

"Thank you, Lee. Perhaps you would care for some coffee?"

McKechnie could see that Lee was tempted. He did not know how often she had been in this house; not many times, he guessed. But she was magnetized by the situation that prevailed here; even if she had not been a newspaperwoman, he knew she would have found it difficult to resist the invitation to stay. But somehow she did resist it.

"I've intruded enough. But I'll come again—tomorrow perhaps? There will have to be a story—leaving out the Vice-President, of course. But the story on Molly's death—"

Adele Farquhar nodded, knowing she could only ask so much. "All right. Tomorrow then. Shall we say ten o'clock?"

McKechnie once again had to admire her. Her whole life was being demolished, just like Clint Blamey's house, and she was making an appointment, as she might with her attorney, with someone who, by the very nature of her profession, might complete the demolition.

"We'll see ourselves out," he said. "I'll keep checking back, Mr Vanderhorn, just in case. And please stay away from those windows."

Vanderhorn only then seemed to become aware of the french doors behind him. He moved aside, not fearfully but in deference to McKechnie's concern for him. "Mrs Farquhar, may I invite Chief McKechnie to come back and have lunch with me?"

If Adele Farquhar was surprised she hid it well. "Of course. Twelve-thirty, Mr McKechnie. Be punctual, please."

"He always is," said Lee. "He drives me up the wall."

"It is when they don't turn up at all that one is driven up the wall, Lee." But none of the other three in the room believed that any man had failed to turn up for a date with Adele Farquhar.

McKechnie took Lee's arm and led her out into the hallway. They had reached the front door when Gilbert Farquhar spoke from the top of the stairs.

"Stay out of this house till tomorrow, McKechnie. We don't want to see you here again today, you understand?"

McKechnie looked up at the tall thin figure silhouetted against the leadlight window at the head of the stairs. He had taken off his hat and raincoat and looked more long-legged and ungainly than ever. Again McKechnie had a bird image of him: his long arms stuck out and down from his shoulders like the bones of long featherless wings.

"I can't promise that. While he's here in the house I'm responsible for the safety of the Vice-President."

"Damn him! Let him look after himself!"

McKechnie wondered if the conversation could be heard out in the back parlour. Perhaps the noise of the wind obliterated it; or perhaps the two people in the back room wanted none of this further confrontation. McKechnie felt Lee stiff and curious beside him: and frustrated, too, witnessing drama she would not be able to use.

"Mr Farquhar," he said to the awkward, angry figure at the top of the stairs, "where were you going last night at midnight? Your car was seen heading out towards Clint Blamey's place. Was your wife with you?"

"I never left the house last night."

"Then who brought your car back here?"

"That's for you to find out, McKechnie. I never knew it had been taken out."

He turned quickly and disappeared from against the light of the window, like a bird suddenly swinging sideways in flight.

When they got outside the house McKechnie said, "I'll drive you home. This rain's too heavy."

They ran down the driveway and scrambled into his car. Lee took off her rain hat and shook out her hair. Rain glistened on her cheeks like tears; but McKechnie had the odd, irrelevant thought that she only wept when happy. Sometimes after they had made love or, when she had really broken down, the night he had asked her to marry him. But there were no tears now and she was far from happy.

"God damn it! I could have that story on Page One of every paper in the country! Why are you doing this to me?"

"That's a stupid question. *I'm* not doing it to you. You can go ahead and publish it if you want to. I can't stop you."

"But you let me *know*! You were doing better when you kept me in the dark. But to let me *know* and then tell me I can't write it—"

"Wrong. It was Gil Farquhar who let you know, not me. You'd still be in the dark if I had my way." He picked up the microphone, switched on. "PD-Two, this is PD-One. You there, Jack?"

"With you, chief. I'm down on Hickory."

"Get back up here on Forest View, Jack. Sit here in the drive like you were before and keep everyone away." He could see faces at windows in several houses across the street, but the rain and wind was keeping everyone indoors.

"Right with you. Two minutes."

Then Lucy Chapley, always there on the outskirts of every call, chimed in. "Are you coming back to headquarters, PD-One?"

"No, Lucy, not yet. I'll call by the fire station, then I'm heading out to the Blamey farm."

He hung the microphone back on its hook and Lee said, "Can I ride out with you?"

"You know I don't like civilians riding around in police cars."

"I'm not a civilian. I'm your sometimes-loving fiancée and a newspaperwoman to boot."

"Which is what I'd like to do. Boot you where it'd hurt. I'll drive you home."

"I'll get my own car and follow you out to Clint Blamey's."

He swore under his breath and she smiled.

"I think that was a four-letter word."

He didn't reply, just started up the car and drove out into the roadway as he saw Jack Atcheson coming down the street, red light whirling on the roof of his car. He pulled up sharply, got out and ran across to Atcheson as the latter pulled his car into the driveway.

"Jack, for Christ's sake switch off that goddam light!"

Atcheson, eyes slitted against the rain as it beat in against his face, frowned in surprise. "Okay, Jim. I just forgot it, was all."

"Sorry, Jack. I think I've got shit on the liver this morning."

"Sure have. Especially when you come right out and say it."

McKechnie grinned, feeling the rain running off the back of his cap down into his collar. "A coupla hours' sleep and I'll be my pure-mouthed self again."

"Why don't you go home, grab some sleep? We can call you, something happens."

"Maybe later. Don't forget, Jack. Nobody goes in or out."

"You tell that to them inside? Gil Farquhar, f'rinstance?"

"He won't be moving. I think he knows that shot was meant for him. He's not going to risk coming out of that house again. Just stay here till I relieve you, Jack. Every ten minutes go for a stroll around the house, check the back down near those woods."

"You think Clint Blamey'll come back for another try?"

"You think it was Clint?"

"Who else? He killed Molly Farquhar and now he's after her husband. Christ knows why, but there ain't no other way looking at it, is there?"

"I guess not." But McKechnie had begun to learn there were a hundred ways of looking at anything. Rain blew into his eyes, refracting the day. The house in front of him oozed away, like a sand castle under the rising tide. He ran a hand over his face, wiping away rain, weariness and imagination. "Just keep your eyes peeled, Jack."

He went back to his own car, got in beside Lee, took off his cap and shook the water from it. Lee took a handkerchief from her pocket, reached across and wiped the back of his neck. Then she brought her hand round, put the back of it against his lips. He kissed it and she seemed satisfied.

He drove down the curve of Forest View into the business section across the square and into McKinney, the main street leading out of town. He pulled up outside the fire station, ran through the rain, which seemed to have become heavier, and into the station house. Half a dozen men sat in a glass-walled room to one side playing cards, but Al Boatswain, the fire chief, was sitting just inside the front doors, gazing out at the weather.

"Looks like you're kinda busy, Jim." Boatswain was a short, overweight man who, no matter the season, always wore a thick sweater knitted for him by his wife; he complained of the cold and his crew only half-joked that he had only become a fireman to keep warm. "I heard about Molly Farquhar. Shot, eh? Out at Clint Blamey's too. Who'd of believed it?"

"You hear the twister warnings, too?" McKechnie tried to keep the irritation out of his voice; gossip was already running through the town, flooding it like the rain in the gutters. "You got all your fellers on call?"

Boatswain gestured towards the card players. "I got my four regulars there and two part-timers. I got four others standing by, case another twister comes through here. Ain't no cause to worry about us, Jim. Chilly, ain't it?"

McKechnie shivered obligingly. "Don't start any fires to get warm."

"That's an old 'un, I been hearing it every day from my boys, ten, twenty years. Who you got in your car with you?"

"Lee Barron."

"You giving the press transport these days? Or just going for a Sunday joy ride?"

"Some day, Al, I'm going to arrest you as a pyro-maniac."

"Never started a fire in my life."

"No, but you enjoy them. You enjoy gossiping, too."

Boatswain was unoffended. "What else is there for you to do while you're waiting for a fire to start somewhere? You sit here at the station door long enough, you see plenty to gossip about. We got, what, twenty-four, twenty-five churches in this town and I reckon there's more adultery, or anyway the thought of it, than you could shake a stick at."

"Driving Lee Barron around isn't adultery, Al."

"Didn't say it was. My, you're touchy this morning. But what you reckon Molly Farquhar and Clint Blamey was up to? But I'd never of guessed it. Never saw them together, not sitting here at the station door. I saw Clint a while ago—"

121

"Where?"

"Driving through town here. Maybe a half-hour ago, maybe a little more."

"Heading which way?"

"He came down the same way you come. If we get hit by a twister, Jim, you gonna run things?"

"You and me both, Al." McKechnie knew how jealously proud Boatswain was of his position; in his eyes all firemen should be answerable to no one but their own chief. "Anything happens, you'll be the first I talk to. You catch a sight of Clint again, call Lucy Chapley at headquarters, will you?"

Driving out of town towards Route 86 McKechnie got on the radio again. "This is PD-One. Clint Blamey is still in the area somewhere or was half an hour ago. Keep watching for him."

He switched off and Lee said, "You had quite a conversation with Al Boatswain."

"He was comparing the number of churches with the amount of adultery goes on here. How much gossip do you get from your stringers?"

The *News*, like all small town newspapers, ran social columns from part-time correspondents in half a dozen surrounding communities . . . *Mrs Charlene Boswell is entertaining her mother, Mrs Jessie Rock, who says she is looking forward to returning to Chicago . . . Landon Swartz is in Vista County Hospital as a medical patient, having gone there to see his wife Ethel . . . Opal and Pearl Taber, twin daughters of Mr and Mrs Charles Taber, celebrated their 21st birthday Saturday with a twin barbecue . . .*

"More than I can print. Last year I interviewed the Reverend Pressley just before he retired and left town. He said he had only just found out what was going on here in Friendship and he just wished he was Father Indelli hearing confessions up at the Catholic church instead of running the Second Baptist, so he could have confirmed what he could only guess at. He said, and I quote, I sometimes think the churches are just asylums for the morally insane, unquote."

"Pressley said that? He must've been drunk."

"Just drunk on the thought of escaping to California, he said. Out there, he said, you expected moral insanity. But not here in Friendship."

"I don't think the town's nearly as bad as all that. But I'm surprised you didn't print what he said."

"He told me he'd sue me if I did."

"So you do bend the freedom of the press when it suits you?"

But she didn't take the bait, just turned her head and looked out at the pouring rain. Then suddenly the downpour ceased and it was almost a shock to drive out into the clear light ahead. But the sky hadn't cleared; the clouds were still low and down to the south McKechnie could see the long dark rolls, spread horizontally, that he knew were called arcus clouds. They could be frightening to anyone seeing them for the first time, but he knew they contained no danger in themselves. He looked beyond them but could see no thunderheads or the tell-tale funnel of a developing tornado.

A power company truck was just pulling away as the police car drove up to the Blamey farm. The driver leaned out of his cabin. "We just shut off all the power into there, chief. It's safe now for you to walk around."

"You seen anyone around here? How long you been here?"

"Half an hour, mebbe a little more. Nope, ain't seen a soul, 'cept some sightseers pulled up out here on the road. Sure made a mess, didn't it? Anyone hurt?"

The power men came from over in Vista: there was no need to tell them everything. "Not by the twister, no. Nobody was home."

123

He turned in and drove up behind the avenue of trees, following the tracks he had made earlier. The cows, heavy with milk, had come closer to the house and stood in a tight herd by the gate that led to the flattened milking barn. Out in the field beyond them the dead cows lay like dark tan rocks, their udders showing white like huge fungi. In the orchard fields the apple and peach trees still standing raised their jagged, splintered arms to the sky, mute imploring questioners of the devastation.

"The cows will need to be milked," said Lee. They got out of the car, stood in the middle of the yard. "Why did you come out here, anyway? Did you expect Clint Blamey to be here?"

"No."

"If Clint shot Molly and he knows what happened to his farm, why would he want to hang around here? Unless he's crazy and wants to kill Gil Farquhar, too."

"Yeah."

"My, we're very communicative all of a sudden, aren't we?" Then, as if aware of the silence about them but for the bellow of a cow, she shrugged and nodded. "All right, I'm chattering. But I'm—*confused*."

"You think I'm not? For the first time since I came down here, I'm beginning to wish I was back in New York. At least back there, there'd be someone above me I could pass the buck to. Who's this?"

A pick-up truck came up from the road, pulled into the yard. A man got out, slipped back the hood of the yellow slicker he wore and McKechnie recognized Jeb Arahill.

"I come up to see what I could do about Clint's cows." He was a lanky lean man, a hundred seasons or more beaten into his face as the marks of his trade. He raised cows and fruit, on a larger scale than Blamey, on a farm about a mile and a half down the road. "Dang it, that twister sure made a mess. I heard about it on the radio,

124

but I couldn't get up here afore this. I been bringing in my own herd for milking."

"Did the twister hit your place?"

"Nope, I saw it coming up from this way, but it lifted afore it got to them trees down yonder." He waved to a windbreak of trees half a mile away on the edge of the Blamey farm. "I tried to phone Clint, but they wasn't no answer. Then he called me 'bout an hour ago, asked me to come up and take care of his herd for him."

"Did he say where he was calling from?"

Arahill shook his head. "He hung up afore I could ask him that. He sounded kinda upset, jittery-like, not like himself a-tall. But I'm happy to oblige him. He's a good neighbour, Clint, always has been." He looked at the herd of cows. "They can wait another hour or so. I'll get my boys up here and we'll take 'em down over the bottom field there to my place. Looks like I'm gonna be helping Clint out for quite a while. Gonna take him a coupla weeks, mebbe more, afore he gets his plant working again. Sure had his share of bad luck these past coupla years. He's all right, is he, chief? I mean, he wasn't hurt or nothing when the twister hit?"

"No, he's okay, Jeb."

"A real nice feller. Well, I better be getting back, bring my boys up. Guess I'll read all about it in your paper, eh, Miss Barron?"

"Some of it," said Lee.

Arahill drove away and McKechnie moved across to the wrecked house. He walked round till he came to the spot where he, Trubauer and Zeke Norval had pulled away the wreckage to extricate Molly Farquhar's body. He tossed some timbers aside, crouched down and went in under the flattened roof. He was sitting on his haunches, head hunched down, in what had been the front bedroom, when Lee clambered over the wreckage, knelt down and peered in at him.

125

"What are you looking for?"

"A gun. Molly was shot by a .38, a hand gun. Clint, or whoever it was, used a rifle to take that shot at the Farquhar windows."

"He could have the hand gun with him."

McKechnie nodded, bumped his head on a beam of the roof. He was squatting beside a double bed, with an iron-and-brass frame, that helped support the roof from collapsing further. Molly Farquhar's body had been lying beside the bed; he looked down and saw that one of his boots was right in the middle of a dark stain on the carpet. He lay down, twisting his body, and looked under the bed. There was nothing there, no sign of the gun.

It began to rain again, drumming on the iron roof right above his head; Lee bent herself double and crawled in beside him. The wind sprang up again and the house creaked and whispered; the roof shifted as if about to take off. Lee cowered down and McKechnie put a protective arm across her shoulders.

"Go back to the car. I won't be a minute."

"You come, too. I don't want you getting hurt under all this."

The rain became heavier, beating on the roof only an inch above their heads. McKechnie felt as if his skull had turned into an iron vessel and he was being deafened by the sound ringing through it. The wind swept in, fierce and strong as an invisible surf, and the roof lifted, then fell back with a crash. McKechnie pushed Lee down beneath him. The wave of wind hit again and once more the roof lifted; this time it slipped back and away from the bed and McKechnie and Lee were left exposed to the rain. He stood up quickly, his arm around her, ready to push her ahead of him out into the clear. Then he saw the gun, a pearl-handled .38 Smith and Wesson, lying in the middle of the exposed bed.

He let go of Lee and grabbed the gun by its barrel.

Then, as abruptly as it had begun, the rain and the wind stopped. The arcus cloud rolled on over them, like a long horizontal funnel of tumbleweed, and the sky lightened, though the higher clouds still moved swiftly in an agony of shifting darkening patterns. Still holding the gun by its barrel, he took Lee's arm and moved to help her out over the wreckage. Then the phone range right at his feet.

"Jesus!"

He stumbled with shock, almost losing his balance. Lee fell against him and he had to brace himself against the frame of the bed to hold them both upright. The phone continued to ring, an everyday sound that was now as bizarre as musical chimes from outer space. Lee found the phone, down behind the smashed bedside table beneath the crushed wall. She pulled it out, stopped the ringing, and handed it to McKechnie.

"Hello?" said a woman's voice. "Mrs. Farquhar?"

"Just a moment." McKechnie put his hand over the mouthpiece, gave the phone to Lee. "You're Molly Farquhar. Answer it."

Lee, puzzled but not arguing, took the phone. "Who's this?"

"This is Ozarks Airlines at Joplin, ma'am. You booked two seats out of here on our noon flight today for Kansas City. I'm sorry, but all flights for today have been cancelled because of weather conditions. Weather permitting, we'll be flying again tomorrow. Shall I hold the seats for you?"

Lee looked at McKechnie, who was standing close to her, his ear against the phone. He took it from her. "This is Chief of Police Jim McKechnie, down here in Friendship. When did Mrs Farquhar book those aeroplane tickets?"

"Police? How do I know you're that? What's going on down there?"

McKechnie stood amongst the wreckage, the phone to

127

his ear. Down on the road four cars pulled up, farmers and their families on their way back from church. If their eyesight was good 'enough and they could distinguish what he was doing here, he could imagine how ridiculous he must look.

"Look, we've had a twister down here—I'm standing in the middle of a wrecked house taking this call. Now I can go back to headquarters, have you call me there, but you can save me and yourself a lot of time and trouble if you just tell me when Mrs Farquhar booked those seats and where she was heading."

"Why don't you ask Mrs Farquhar? She's there, isn't she?"

"Mrs Farquhar is dead. That was—my despatcher. All I want—"

"All right, chief. You just kinda put me off-balance, that was all. Just a minute, I'll check." McKechnie waited, staring down at the cars on the road, willing them not to turn in and come on up to the house. Then: "The booking was made at 5.20 p.m. yesterday and the tickets were to be picked up half an hour before flight time this morning, to be paid for in cash. Mr and Mrs Farquhar were flying to Kansas City to connect with a Continental flight for Los Angeles, California."

"Did she give this number for your return call?"

"Yes. There is a note here saying she would be at that number after 8 a.m. this morning."

"Do you usually call up all your customers to tell them when a flight has been cancelled?"

"No. But Mrs Farquhar has been a regular passenger on our flights and it was a courtesy service to her."

"How regular? And where did she go?"

"I'll have to check that, sir. Can I call you back?"

"Not here. Call me at headquarters in half an hour. That's 999–1234. You better cancel the reservations."

"I guessed as much. I'll call you, chief."

128

McKechnie hung up, put the phone down on the bed. Then he took Lee by the arm and helped her over the wreckage into the mud of the yard. He saw a car begin to move out on the road, turning in at the gates, and he ran across to his own car, started up the siren and stood back, waving to the occupants of the car to stay where they were. The car pulled up, stood still a few minutes, then it backed into the road, swung round and disappeared in the direction in which it had been heading. The other cars moved off, following it, and in a moment the road was deserted.

"Goddam ghouls!"

"Not necessarily," said Lee. "They could have been offering some help. It's natural with farmers and that's who they'd be. That car coming in the gate was Clair Bristow's—he's a devout church-goer who believes in Christian help. I know, I've seen him at work. You better try and relax, darling. You're going to give yourself a nervous breakdown, trying to keep this whole thing to yourself."

He drew a deep breath, calming himself. "Okay. But the last thing I want right now is questions, and they'd have been full of them. I've got enough questions of my own."

"So have I. For instance, where were Molly and Gil going on Ozarks Airlines?"

"Kansas City, then Los Angeles. But I'll bet it wasn't Gil. It was Clint Blamey going with her. But something stopped them. Why didn't they go up to a motel in Joplin, stay there last night? If two people are going to run away, they don't hang around where the wife's husband can find them. Unless he *did* find them." He examined the gun, which he still held by its barrel. "There are only two bullets left in this. Where did the others go? One went into Molly, but where did the others go?"

He glanced down towards the road where a car had

slowed down. For a moment he thought it was going to turn in at the gates, then suddenly it accelerated and went on up the road at a speed that should have got its driver a ticket.

Lee was looking curiously at the gun. "It's a fancy one. Men around here usually don't have pearl-handled guns, not unless they're collectors. Clint wasn't a collector, was he?"

"Not that I know of," he said. "Did you ever run any pieces in your social columns on Molly? That girl at the airline said she was a regular passenger of theirs."

Lee shook her head. "We never ran an item on the Farquhars unless they were at some big event. They're not the sort of people who call you up to tell you they're going to visit their mother or whoever in Oshkosh. Molly could have gone out of town regularly on short visits and nobody need have known."

Driving back to town Lee said, "Take me to the office first. There's something I want to check."

"What's on your mind?"

"I'll let you know if I find it in the morgue." She smiled, but it was a weary smile; as if she were relieving him of some of his exhaustion. "An unfortunate choice of words in the circumstances. The files."

When they reached the *News* plant McKechnie went into Lee's office with her. He sat there on the leather couch against one wall, relaxing with his eyes closed, while she went out to another office. He wanted to stretch out and go to sleep, but resisted the temptation. Sunday morning there was only one staff member on duty, a junior girl there to answer the phone, take the kicks from people whose newspaper hadn't been delivered and to keep an eye on the wire service teletype. He could hear Lee and the girl talking, but here in the editor's office there was only quiet, the wind and the rain shut out beyond

130

the brick walls and the double-glazed windows. The winters were never really cold in this part of the country, but Lee liked her comfort. The office showed that. Without looking too expensive, it had more the air of the office of the editor of a woman's monthly magazine than that of someone responsible for getting out a newspaper six days a week and a Sunday edition. There was wall-to-wall carpet, neat bookshelves, the leather couch and two leather chairs in an elegant Scandinavian design, a large modern teak desk on which yesterday's flowers stood in a stainless steel vase. It was a contrast to the Barron home up on Forest View and he knew which he preferred. He never felt comfortable here, as if there were a side to Lee that he preferred not to know.

She came back with a file of clippings. "I've got a good memory for inconsequential things. Look at this story. It was written by my father."

The story, headed by a photo of Senator Robert Farquhar, ran only to four inches of a single column. It said that the Sheriffs Association of Missouri had presented a pair of pearl-handled Smith and Wesson pistols to Senator Farquhar on the occasion of the 25th anniversary of his being a member of the US Senate. Also at the presentation dinner had been Mrs Farquhar, daughter Rose and Dr Russell Stenhouse.

"Doc Stenhouse, eh? But where was Gil?"

"I don't know. When I came home to take over from Dad I spent a couple of weeks going through the files on all the prominent people around here. Just for background, that was all—I'd been away from here for almost five years. I didn't think that particular item was important at the time. But it is now, isn't it?"

He handed back the clippings. "Are you going to use it in your story on Molly?"

Lee went round and sat down behind her desk. The

131

mere action seemed to him to change their status. If asked, he would deny that he was a male chauvinist; but would admit to himself that his claim had never really been tested. Not, that is, until Lee had come home and taken over the town newspaper. Then, for the first time, he had had to deal with a woman who, in her own way, had as much power to influence as he had. Maybe more.

He was listening to an editor now, not the girl he was going to marry: "Since I dug out that information myself, you can't say it's classified. I'm entitled to use it."

"I haven't said anything yet. I'm just asking."

"I'll use it if you come up with proof that the gun outside in your car is the one that shot Molly."

"You'll look pretty foolish if the Senator's guns are still together as a pair. Mrs Farquhar could have them somewhere up in their house. Have you thought of that?"

"I'll check that first." She reached for the phone, but he stood up, reached across and held her wrist.

"Not till after I've done it. That's a police order."

"On what grounds?"

"The obstruction of justice. Abusing an officer. Wilful harassment of citizens. I'll dream up something and throw you in the can for the rest of the day."

"You wouldn't dare!"

"Try me."

"You *are* a son-of-a-bitch, you know that?"

"I'm beginning to believe it. It beats having a conscience." He let go her wrist, stood back. "I promise you, if one of those guns is missing I'll let you know. And if the bullet that killed Molly matches those in the gun outside in the car, I'll let you know that too. Fair enough?"

She was studying him carefully. "You've got something else on your mind."

He nodded. "If you print those facts and I arrest Gil, for instance, for Molly's murder, any smart lawyer is going to claim that your story will have already prejudiced

132

any jury in advance against his client. The judges down around here are conservative—they don't like trial by newspaper editors. They might agree with the lawyer."

She sat back in her chair, drawing composure about her like a shawl. But it was camouflage, too: to hide her anger and frustration. For she was far from feeling composed. She was no romantic, the young journalist dreaming of the story of a lifetime that would win her a Pulitzer, give her national headlines, an offer to go to work on the *New York Times* or the *Washington Post*. She knew she was indeed sitting on one of the stories of the year; she wondered what her father and grandfather would have done with it. Her father, a simple decent man, would probably have stayed with the story but in the end weighed local consequences against national interest and held off writing it till publication was unavoidable. Her grandfather, a muckraker and proud of the title, would have printed the story even before he had had all the facts and let the lightning strike where it might. Her mother, who had never liked the responsibility of owning a newspaper, would have asked why any part of the story had to be printed at all. But *something* had to be printed. The people of Friendship might tut-tut at an unsuspected secret of the town being exposed to the nation at large; small towns valued their secrets just as families did. But they would relish having been told the secret, having had it exposed to *them*. And if they learned of it from somewhere other than the town newspaper, and they undoubtedly would in time, they would want to know why it had not been published. A newspaper had no duty to protect the sins of the respectable or even the powerful; it also had no duty to cultivate the voyeurism of the public. She was confused by the number of elements in what had happened and was happening to the Farquhar family.

At last she said, "I think you're trying to protect the

living as much as pay your respects to the dead. I think the Vice-President being up there at the Farquhar place has put poor Molly into second or third place."

"You're wrong," he said, but not with enough emphasis even to convince himself. He looked at his watch. "I haven't got time to go back to headquarters to pick up that call from Joplin. Can I call the airline from here?"

He got the girl at Ozarks Airlines. "Oh, chief, I was just about to call you. Mrs Farquhar flew out of here on an average of once a month. She's been doing that for at least a year. If she was flying with us longer than that, I'd have to check with head office."

"No, that's okay. Where did she fly to? Was she alone?"

"Always to St Louis. And always on her own. Today's booking was the first double she made."

McKechnie hung up and Lee said, "What's the matter?"

"I'm beginning to wonder if the real Molly Farquhar ever stood up in this town."

## III

"I have a great many faults," said Vice-President Vanderhorn, unconsciously confirming the opinion of a great many of his fellow countrymen. "My idea of a good conversationalist is someone who is prepared to listen to me. Not necessarily agree with me, but *listen*. Miss Rose was a good listener." He paused, then said, "Miss Rose. I never called her that before today. Do you like this Rum Tum Tiddy?"

"It's all right," said McKechnie unenthusiastically. "I was hoping Mrs Farquhar would have had lunch with us. I like to listen to her. Her voice, I mean."

"You never heard Miss Rose, did you? No, you couldn't have. It was like her mother's, not as trained but as

134

pleasant to listen to. Not now, though." He bent his head towards his food.

"What time are you planning to leave this evening, sir? I'll have to get you over to Springfield."

Vanderhorn pushed his empty plate away from him. "What time does it get dark out here?"

"This time of year, about six, maybe a little later." McKechnie glanced out the window. "It could be earlier this evening."

"Do you think we could have a tornado through here?"

"Your guess is as good as mine, sir. I've been here ten years and there's been one in the county, maybe two or three, every year. None of them serious and we've never had one hit the town. Frankly, I wish you were back in Washington."

"Don't think I haven't given thought to your concern for me. And to the President's concern for me, too. He spoke to me this morning. If it's any consolation to you, he feels the same as you, that I shouldn't be here." He sat looking out the window of the small back room where they were having lunch, where he had had breakfast with Adele Farquhar. All the blossom had been stripped from the dogwood and redbud by the wind and rain and the trees had a wintry look again. "I apologize to both of you, but I just can't leave. Not till the last moment, anyway."

"I think I understand. As a man, I mean. Maybe not as chief of police, though."

"What is it like at your level of responsibility?" Vanderhorn changed the subject slightly, trying to keep his mind off the thought that Rose could be dead in a matter of hours. He could feel grief taking hold of him like a paralysis, a heaviness creeping through him that made him suddenly afraid that he might break down in front of this stranger; a man he liked but still a stranger. He

135

tried to transfer his attention to the policeman, away from himself. "I don't mean to sound patronizing."

"Everything's comparative, I guess. It depends on your capacity to stand up to it."

"Have you read anything about the Vanderhorns?"

"A couple of books. One was by a British writer, I've forgotten his name."

"That was a fair one, fair to us, I mean. The British have always thought more of us than our own people have. Possibly because my grandfather was English and the English always admire one of their own who makes good over here. Sort of compensation for having lost the colonies. Nowadays it's only their actors and pop stars, but they still remember people like my grandfather."

"Vanderhorn? I thought that would have been a Dutch name."

"It was originally. The family crossed to England from the Netherlands in the late eighteenth century. They were cotton merchants then, but they weren't very successful. There were three brothers, but two of them died childless. My grandfather was the third generation born in England and by then the family had forgotten they were Dutch. Grandfather came to America when he was eighteen years old and by the time he was thirty he had made his first million."

McKechnie grinned, beginning to understand that the Vice-President just wanted to talk. "My grandfather was an Irish immigrant. I don't think they'd have got on too well. I remember when I was a kid, he used to tell me that rich men were the curse of the world. He'd never met a rich man. Neither had I till I met you, sir. There are some wealthy ones around here, but no one who's rich."

"What's the difference?" said Vanderhorn, who knew it well.

McKechnie pondered the question for a few moments.

136

"I guess a wealthy man can go bankrupt, but a rich man can't. But I wouldn't know."

"It's as good a definition as any I've heard. But there are a lot of wealthy men who'll never go bankrupt, no matter what happens to their ventures. They're the devious ones, the curse of the world, as your grandfather said."

"He said the *rich* were the curse. I don't think he knew the difference between the two. He never earned more than twenty-five bucks a week in his whole life."

"What do you earn, chief?"

"Nine hundred and fifty a month. I could go bankrupt without any effort."

Vanderhorn shook his head, looked out the window again. He had long ago given up being ashamed of or embarrassed by the family riches, realizing the futility of it. It was a fact of life, of his own immediate life and of that of the nation. The money came from an empire that rivalled those of the Mellons, the Rockefellers, the DuPonts, the Pews; it had begun in railroads but the family had got out of those right after World War Two and now the holdings were in oil, chemicals, automotive parts, banking, farming and a dozen other interests. The Vanderhorn Foundation gave away millions each year but seemed to make little impact on the family wealth; to have given away the family empire would have meant an assault on the nation's economy. For better or worse, the Vanderhorn money was part of the fabric of this country of which he was Vice-President: a heart-beat, as the saying went, away from the Presidency itself. In his deepest heart he felt the circumstances were wrong: not evil but wrong. But even had he been a poor man he would have been just as politicially ambitious, would have worked just as hard to rise to the top. Or so he told himself.

"Are you happy?" he asked.

"I think so."

"I'm not going to say that's the important thing."

"I'm glad you didn't. Happiness can be added to. I'd be just as happy as chief of police on twenty thousand a year. Or thirty. Well, no, maybe I wouldn't. That would mean being chief in a bigger place than this and maybe I wouldn't be so happy then."

"Are you afraid of too much responsibility?"

"I never really thought about it. Until today," he added.

"I've never been afraid of responsibility," said Vanderhorn without conceit. "But that was because I was brought up to it."

"Your father never liked it."

Vanderhorn looked at him shrewdly. "You read that book pretty thoroughly. No, he didn't. That was why my grandfather made me his protégé. I'm just sorry he didn't live long enough to see me as Vice-President. It would have pleased him. When he was building his first railroad, his arch-enemy was E. H. Harriman. I think he would have jumped off the top of his headquarters in San Francisco if Harriman's son had ever made it to the Presidency of the United States. And Averell Harriman was just as ambitious as I was."

"Were you always ambitious?"

"Yes," Vanderhorn confessed without hesitation. He could not remember when he had trusted a stranger so quickly as he did this man. But then he had never been in these circumstances before: it was a day for truths, not politics. He remembered something Rose had once said to him: *In my presence do me a favour, always be honest.* He was in her presence now, the presence where she had grown up and become the woman she had. "Some of the rich have to prove themselves. Most don't, but I did."

Wilma Mae came in and cleared away the dishes. "You didn't like the Rum Tum Tiddy, chief?"

138

"The what? Oh sure. I just wasn't hungry, Wilma Mae."

"I liked it fine," said Vanderhorn. "I'd like to take the recipe back to Washington with me, if I may."

"You surely can, Mr Vice-President. Miss Rose'd admire know you done that. It her favourite, long time ago. What you like follow? I got peach upside cake or some pecan cookies."

Vanderhorn and McKechnie agreed upon pecan cookies and coffee and Wilma Mae looked disappointed. Then McKechnie said, "When we've finished, Wilma Mae, will you tell Mrs Farquhar and Mr Gil I'd like to see them in the front room?"

"I don't tell Miz Farquhar nothing."

"I'm sorry. Will you *ask* her and Mr Gil if they'd see me in the front room?"

"You still worrying them?"

"Only because I have to, Wilma Mae. Not because I want to."

But that didn't satisfy her. She went out of the room, rattling the dishes like the sound of her nerves, and Vanderhorn said, "She will protect them as if they were her own. Rose used to tell me about her."

McKechnie remarked that it was Rose now, not Miss Rose. "I hope I can protect you too, sir. It'll be bad enough for you if it ever gets out about you and Miss Rose. It'll be ten times worse if your name is linked to this murder."

"I'll do my best to survive that," said Vanderhorn quietly. "What I want you to remember is that Rose is the one to be protected. No matter what the outcome of Molly Farquhar's murder."

"That mightn't be easy."

"I'm relying on you."

"You're putting a lot on me, sir. If you don't mind me saying so."

Vanderhorn gazed steadily at the younger man across

the table, all at once marvelling at their relationship. The feeling was probably only temporary, but he felt as confident of this quiet, open policeman as he did of men he had known for years. He had always been careful of trust ("one thing a rich man can't afford," his grandfather had told him) and he could not remember ever having trusted anyone so quickly before. Except Rose.

"I know. And I don't like doing it. I wish I could help you—" He *could* help, but that would only involve Rose more. And he was still getting over the shock of what he had learned since he had arrived here in this house.

Then Wilma Mae came back with the cookies and coffee and the lunch finished in small talk between the two men. Fifteen minutes later McKechnie was in the drawing-room waiting for Adele Farquhar and her son. In one hand he held the pearl-handled gun, now wrapped in a plastic bag.

The Farquhars came in, Adele composed but haughty, Gilbert belligerent. "I thought we had done with you for the day—"

McKechnie held up his empty hand as if stopping traffic. "Hold it, Mr Farquhar. I'm trying to give you and your mother as much privacy as I can, but things keep cropping up."

"What's cropped up now?" Farquhar was in no mood for appeasement; all semblance of the courteous man he had once been had gone. "Why the hell can't it wait till tomorrow?"

McKechnie looked at Adele Farquhar. "Do you understand that I'm not enjoying coming back here today?"

"I do, Mr McKechnie."

But she remained standing, made no attempt to offer McKechnie a chair. Manners went just so far: you did not have to make the enemy comfortable. She was politer than but just as strongly opposed to him as her son. He wondered what had happpened, what she had learned in the hour or so since he had last been here.

"Please go on," she said.

He decided to keep his trump card for a few more moments, put the hand holding the gun behind his back. "I understand your wife used to leave town about once a month, go to St Louis. Do you know why she went there?"

"No," said Farquhar flatly. "My wife did lots of things she never explained to me."

McKechnie looked at Adele Farquhar. "Did she ever explain her trips to you?"

"No," she said just as flatly.

McKechnie recognized he was not going to get anywhere with that line of questioning. He changed tack: "You have only two cars in the family? The Cadillac and your wife's Buick?"

"That's all," said Farquhar. "Everyone knows that."

McKechnie nodded. "I thought Wilma Mae might have a car. Even in a town this size, a chief of police doesn't check on every car bought and sold."

"My wife drove Wilma Mae downtown when there was shopping to be done. The rest of the time she hardly moves away from the house."

"Can she drive?"

Farquhar looked at his mother, then back at McKechnie. "I guess so. Yes. But it would be years since she drove."

"You and your wife always drove your mother around?"

"You know that is so, Mr McKechnie," said Adele Farquhar. "We have often passed each other when I have been with my son or my daughter-in-law. What is the purpose of all this? Surely this sort of questioning could have waited till tomorrow?"

"I guess so." Then McKechnie took the gun from behind his back, took it out of the plastic bag and held it by the barrel. "Do either of you recognize this?"

There was no expression on either face. Then Adele

141

Farquhar said, "It is one of a pair that belonged to my husband."

"Where is the other?"

"In the study. Come."

The two men followed her, the police chief pausing to let the son go ahead of him. In the study the old woman went to a glass-fronted cupboard set at an angle in one corner, opened it and took out a felt-lined case with insets for two guns. In one inset there was a pearl-handled .38 Smith and Wesson; the other inset was empty. A small silver plaque told who had presented the guns.

"Did you know this gun was missing?" McKechnie held up the gun in his hand.

Before his mother could reply Gilbert Farquhar said, "I knew it was missing. I discovered it had gone about an hour ago."

"Did someone tell you or did you discover that yourself?"

"Nobody told me. I came in here and saw it was gone."

"Were you looking for it? You must come into this room every day. Do you always look to see if the guns are still there?"

"No-o. I don't know why I looked there this morning, I just did. Maybe it was because of that shot Clint Blamey took at the house."

"Were you going to use the gun? For protection?"

"I don't know. Maybe."

"Do you have ammunition for it? This one still had two bullets in it when I found it."

"Where *did* you find it?"

"Out at Clint Blamey's. It was on the bed, only a couple of feet from where we found your wife's body. What about the ammunition?"

"There's a box of it in the desk." He opened a drawer, took out a carton, handed it to McKechnie. "It should be

142

full. None of it has ever been used. My father brought it home with him years ago."

McKechnie opened the box. "Some of it's been used. Not a full chamber load, maybe three or four bullets. It's pretty old stuff, it's a wonder it fired. I'll take this with me." He put the box in the plastic bag with the gun. "Did you know the gun was missing, Mrs Farquhar?"

There was a flicker of surprise on her face, as if she had expected no more questions to be directed at her. Then: "Yes. My son told me it was gone from the case."

"That was the first you knew of it?"

"What are you implying, Mr McKechnie?"

"I'm not implying anything, Mrs Farquhar." He wondered how formal his questioning would be of anyone else in town on a matter of murder. But he sensed that the best way to meet this old woman was on her own terms. She had been accustomed to them too long for her ever to change. "I am trying to find out who killed your daughter-in-law, possibly with this gun. You and your son seem to want to forget that that is the only reason I'm here at all."

Adele Farquhar was once again assailed by her years: her face seemed to age even as McKechnie looked at her. She glanced behind her, took an uncertain step backwards and sat down in one of the chair, straightening herself; there was a regal air about her, but it was as spurious as her strength. It seemed to McKechnie, in a moment of insight, that she was losing the will to go on living.

"I am sorry I admitted you to my house, Mr McKechnie."

"I'd have had to come anyway. I wouldn't have enjoyed taking out a warrant to get in to see you."

"You keep using the word *enjoy*. Is that how you look at your work—as enjoyment?"

"Not today, anyway," said McKechnie wryly. "I'll try

and think of another way of saying it. In the meantime you are beating about the bush. When did you first learn the gun was missing?"

She was not accustomed to being told she was beating about the bush: her cold indignation made her look suddenly stronger. But she was too intelligent to be tiresome about McKechnie's seeming lack of respect for her. She looked at her son, then back at the policeman. "I found the gun had gone when I came in here last night. The cupboard door was open."

"What time was that?"

"Some time after eleven-thirty, I'm not sure exactly. I don't wear a watch. Time hasn't meant anything for years," she added almost irrelevantly. But it was the confession of a secret and she abruptly looked annoyed, as if she had committed some social gaffe in exposing herself to the stranger in her house.

"Who do you think took it? Your daughter-in-law?"

She hesitated, then nodded. "No one else would have taken it. I heard her go out just before I came downstairs."

"Why would she have taken it?"

"Who knows?" But Gilbert Farquhar sounded as if he didn't care. "Maybe she was frightened of that son-of-a-bitch Blamey."

"Watch your language." But his mother spoke automatically, as if the atmosphere of the house was as it had always been.

Farquhar looked at his mother with impatience, on the point of rebelling after fifty years. "What else do you expect me to call him? The son-of-a-bitch killed Molly!" He had been standing behind the desk and suddenly he, too, sat down as if all his strength had run out of him. "Jesus God! Why don't you bring him in, McKechnie, and get all this over and done with!"

"We'll get him," said McKechnie quietly. "Just one more question, Mrs Farquhar. You say your son always drives you wherever you want to go. But can you drive yourself?"

The famous voice had no projection at all; McKechnie had to lean forward to hear it. "Yes. I took my son's car out to Mr Blamey's farm last night."

"What time was that?"

"Again I don't know exactly. Some time between eleven-thirty and midnight, I suppose."

"How long were you out at the Blamey place?"

"Perhaps half an hour, a little more. Then I came straight back."

"Did you talk to your daughter-in-law and Clint Blamey?"

"Mr Blamey didn't say a word all the time I was there. I made no impression at all on Molly, I mean about her coming back here. She told me she was finished with— with this family."

"Did she say why?"

"I understood why. But that, Mr McKechnie, is the family's concern."

"Maybe," said McKechnie, but did not press the point; he was beginning to recognize how far he could go at one time. "Did your son know you had gone out there?"

"No," said Farquhar. As with his mother, all resistance seemed to have run out of him. One hand crawled aimlessly across the desk in front of him, like a sightless crab. "But I guessed it when you told me this morning that my car had been seen going out that way last night. Then when I found the gun gone—"

"You thought your mother had killed your wife?" McKechnie's own voice was still quiet: he could have been a member of the family discussing a terminal illness.

Farquhar looked at his mother, painfully seeking forgiveness. "For a moment, yes. I'll never forgive myself—"

"We all jump to conclusions." But there was no note of forgiveness in her voice. That's what has changed her,

145

McKechnie thought: that her son could think her capable of murder. But he found that his own sudden suspicion of her wouldn't go away.

"Did you know your wife was going away with Blamey? She had booked two aeroplane tickets to Los Angeles. They were going out on the noon flight from Joplin."

Farquhar shook his head. "I didn't know that. But when you told me there was over 2000 dollars in her handbag—well, I guessed she must have been thinking of going away."

"She couldn't have been afraid of him, not if she was going to run away with him. She took that gun for another reason. Maybe she was afraid you would come after her. Would she have tried to kill you?"

Farquhar looked at his mother. The two of them exchanged a silent confidence that locked McKechnie out completely. Then Farquhar said, "She might have."

"Miz Molly'd never kill nobody," said Wilma Mae from the doorway. "Was me took the gun."

# Chapter Five

Down in the Gulf of Mexico the day, like Saturday and Friday before it, had become hot and humid. The winter had been unusually mild even for a region accustomed to mild winters and the waters of the Gulf were warmer than their average temperature of seventy-five degrees. Moisture from the sea was pushing heat upwards and the Gulf air mass began to stream north again at an even faster rate than earlier. The reinforcements were arriving for another battle of the elements.

Thunderstorms built up over northern Louisiana and northern Texas. They moved on, rolling through the skies like tank battalions; they were weightless but the ground seemed to flatten out beneath them. Lightning blazed and stabbed, shattering trees, killing cattle, setting fire to a barn and burning a man and his son to death. Wetumka, Oklahoma, still reeling from the tornado that had hit the hamlet just north of it, suddenly was pounded again, this time by lightning, thunder and hailstones the size of small grapefruit. One woman was killed, her head split open, and a dozen were injured, some seriously with concussion. The windshields of over 200 cars were smashed as if some lunatic pedestrian had gone among them with a baseball bat.

Several local storm spotters throughout eastern Oklahoma reported that another, possibly even more severe, front was on its way. Reports were already coming in from other sources. The satellite SMS–1, marking time 22,000 miles above the lower Mid West, was beaming pictures that suggested the planet was dissolving into the inferno of gas from which it had been born. Aeroplanes, like terrified birds, fled from the area, leaving the sky to the elements.

Lew Black and Jumpy Cowman, listening to their static-riddled car radio, knew they had done the right thing in turning back and running away from the storms.

"Man, we could of gotten our asses blown off by them storms. They got twisters up in Chicago?"

"How do I know? Jesus, Jumpy, you ask some dumb questions. Where are we now?"

"We still on 86. I seen a sign back there, something about Friendship. What sorta friendship they mean? Dames, that sorta thing? Or milk and fucking cookies?"

"You dummy. That's a town, Friendship. We're heading in the right direction, anyways. Kee-rist, looka that!"

Black slowed the car on the long stretch of road, peered through the dull grey light at the flattened farmhouse up beyond the splintered trees. Then suddenly he slammed his foot down on the gas pedal, jerking Cowman's head back.

"There's a police car up there! You want some of that sorta friendship?"

# I

McKechnie took Wilma Mae back to headquarters to question her further. Adele Farquhar had invited him to question Wilma Mae at the house; then, when he had refused, had tried to insist. "You must talk to her here, Mr

McKechnie. She will answer your questions just as well here as down at your office—"

"I don't think so. She'll be afraid all the time that you will overhear her."

"Are you suggesting my son and I will be eavesdropping?"

"I'm suggesting that Wilma Mae will be afraid of the *house* eavesdropping on her."

He wondered if that sounded too fanciful, then saw that the old woman understood what he was getting at. She was still a woman of the theatre, even though she had long left it, and she understood the meaning and influence of atmosphere. But he was surprised at himself for thinking of her now as old: the thought had not occurred to him when he had first come here this morning.

"Wilma Mae is entitled to have our lawyer with her. We'll have to get him over from Springfield."

"I don't want no lawyer man, Mr Gil. I confused as it is."

"That's why you need him." Farquhar was gentle and solicitous towards her; McKechnie saw a side of him that he hadn't even suspected. "He'll be there to help you, not confuse you."

She shook her head stubbornly. "No. We got enough outsiders worrying us now."

"That's true." Adele Farquhar didn't look at McKechnie, but he knew that he and Vanderhorn were the unwelcome intruders. "But you mustn't get yourself into trouble because of us."

"I is *us*!" Wilma Mae's vehemence seemed to surrprise the Farquhars as much as it did McKechnie. "Holy Lord, Miz Farquhar, you think I don't belong with you?"

Adele Farquhar moved to her, took her arms and looked into the dark face that was no longer a closed mask, that was about to break apart. "Wilma Mae, you

149

know we'd never think that. I'm sorry. We'll do as you ask—no lawyer."

"I'll have to put it to her again when we get down to headquarters," said McKechnie. "That's the law, that she must have the chance to talk to her lawyer."

"Whatever you say, Mr McKechnie. But you are not to intimidate her, you understand?"

Hauteur didn't come easily to McKechnie, but he tried for a little of it himself. "I don't run my department that way, Mrs Farquhar."

But she didn't apologize. All her respect and admiration for him as a man of discretion seemed to have been put away, like something taken out of a drawer by mistake. He was one of the elements threatening her house: the wind and the rain rattled the windows, providing a sound-track. She looked out the window as if she might be associating him with the storm, then back at him. But she still said nothing, letting him know by her silence that they were foes. He felt a sudden disappointment that had nothing to do with his role as police chief.

"Maybe I'd better come down with you," said Farquhar.

"It'd be better if you didn't." McKechnie did his best to sound patient, to tell Adele Farquhar, if not her son, that he was not entirely unsympathetic to their situation.

But if she caught the hinted gesture, she showed no sign of it. Her son said, "I don't practise, but I do have a law degree. That should satisfy the law about having an attorney present—"

"I don't think so. You're involved in this, Mr Farquhar."

"You mean I'm still under some sort of suspicion?"

"If you want to put it that way." McKechnie gave up trying to sound patient; neither of the Farquhars was in the mood for gestures. "I'll bring Wilma Mae back as soon as I've talked to her."

"Then he isn't going to arrest you," Adele Farquhar said

to the black woman; the beautiful voice succeeded in sounding both comforting to Wilma Mae and sarcastic to McKechnie. "Just tell him the truth."

Jack Atcheson was sitting in his car when McKechnie and Wilma Mae came out of the house. He had gone away for lunch when McKechnie had arrived and had asked no questions as to why the police chief should be having lunch with the Farquhars. He asked no questions now as McKechnie put Wilma Mae into his own car, but McKechnie knew he must be strangling himself with restraint.

"I'm wasting my time here, Jim. I could be out looking for Clint—"

"Just a while longer, Jack."

Driving through the intermittent rain back to headquarters, McKechnie said, "When I start asking you the questions, Wilma Mae, tell me the truth, like Mrs Farquhar said. All of it, not just part of it."

She sat with her head leaning wearily back against the wire grille that separated the front seat from the rear. She moved her head, feeling the grille and rolling her eyes backwards. "That where you put the bad 'uns, chief?"

"Just the violent ones. You're not one of those."

"I ain't done a violent thing my whole life. I feel like it sometimes. But I never done it."

"Did you feel like it last night?"

But, her head still resting against the grille, she closed her eyes and said nothing. He glanced sideways at her, wondering if she was being shrewd, determined now to have a lawyer present while she was being questioned. Then he saw that there was no antagonism to him at all in her. If she refused to answer it was not because of her insistence on her rights. Her silence was that of resignation: she had no will or energy left to fight him. And he knew from experience that that sort of attitude was more difficult to break down than belligerent defiance.

151

He turned on the radio, keeping the volume low. A sports announcer, voice as doom-laden as if disaster had already struck, was broadcasting that the Kansas City Royals–New York Yankees game had been called off because of the weather. Then the message came in over the announcer's voice: "A Tornado Watch is in effect—"

McKechnie switched off. He knew the warning was in effect for his area; the sky alone told him that. But as he drove down past the smaller homes beneath the bluff of Forest View he saw some of the more cautious residents at last coming out of their houses, taking things down into their cellar shelters. Some were carrying blankets, boxes of food, mattresses; a man and his wife were struggling with a large television set, evidently their most prized possession. But the cautious ones were the exception; most of the houses, blandly expressionless, still were an outward sign of the complacency inside them. The majority of the townsfolk, or anyway the men, were more concerned at the cancellation of the ball game and were looking for alternative entertainment on their television sets. If the kids were out of the house, McKechnie guessed, Mom and Pop might go to bed where Pop would find some consolation entertainment for having been deprived of the ball game. He wanted to switch on the horn, yell at them to get down into their cellars. But, once again, he told himself, no one was going to listen to his bones.

He took Wilma Mae into his office, sat her down, gave her coffee. He put the gun and box of ammunition in a drawer in his desk, then went out to Lucy Chapley. "Anything in from anyone?"

"Negative. The cars are still out looking for Clint Blamey, but no sign of him yet. What's wrong with Wilma Mae, chief?"

"Nothing. I just have a few questions to put to her."

"Everything all right up at their house?" He just looked at her and she suddenly was flustered. "I mean—"

152

"Someone's already dead and someone else up there is dying. You think everything should be all right?"

Then a call came in over her radio and he left her to it, angry at her yet angry at himself, too. He was long accustomed to Lucy's busybody approach; sometimes he had taken advantage of it when it provided a short cut to needed information. He was just taking out his frustration on her because she was so readily available.

He went back into his office and closed the door. Wilma Mae sat with the coffee untouched in front of her on his desk, exactly where he had placed it. She neither turned her head nor glanced at him when he came in, but waited till he had gone round and sat down at his desk in front of her. Then, he felt, he appeared in her gaze like a suddenly developed photograph. She stared at him, waiting for him to begin.

"Why did you take the gun?"

"I was scared for Miz Farquhar."

"Which Mrs Farquhar?"

"They only one Miz Farquhar, far's I concerned. I don't mean Miz Molly."

"Okay, why were you scared for Mrs Farquhar?"

She frowned as if puzzled that he should ask. "She going out at midnight on her own, only me with her. I told you this morning, I don't trusts the dark."

"Was that the only reason—you didn't trust the dark? Come on, Wilma Mae. You were scared of more than that. Why did you go with her anyway? Did she ask you to?"

"Course she did. I mean, after I offered. I hear her go downstairs and I follow her——"

"Where were you? Isn't your bedroom off the kitchen?"

"Yeah. But I was upstairs, sitting the end of the hall near Miss Rose's bedroom. Just in case I hear her call."

"Where was Mr Gil?"

"He in the bedroom with Miss Rose. But he asleep in

153

his chair. I peeked in, seen him like that. Then Miz Farquhar go downstairs and I go after her. She told me go back upstairs, go to bed, anything, but I just stand there with her and in the end she ask me to go with her. She glad to have me, I think. She go out to get the car outa the garage and I go'n get the gun."

"Did she know you had it?"

"Not then."

"What do you mean—not then?"

She stared at him a while and he waited, trying to read behind the deep opaque eyes and failing utterly. Then she shook her head. "I done tell you enough, chief."

He kept a calm face, showing no expression: tried his own version of a stone mask, "I can lock you up, Wilma Mae, till you decide to tell me all you know."

Again she stared at him, then she nodded slowly. "I knows that, chief. It don't worry me none, being locked up. 'Cept I wanna be home when Miss Rose goes to the Lord. You gonna stop me being there then, chief?"

He let out a deep breath, half-sigh, half-hiss. "If I let you go home till—till Miss Rose dies, will you promise to tell me the truth tomorrow?"

"I done tell you the truth."

"Not all of it." Unlike a loaf of bread, half the truth was not much better than none.

"Mrs Molly was going away with Mr Blamey. Do you know if she took much with her, clothes, things like that?"

She took her time about replying. "I look in her room this morning. She took two bags, mebbe three. All her good clothes, they gone."

"Did she ever confide in you about why she went up to St Louis every month?"

"No." There was no hesitation this time. "That her business she keep to herself."

He stood up and at the same time she got slowly out

154

of her chair. He hadn't thought of her as being old but now all at once he realized she was not much younger than Adele Farquhar. And like her mistress she had suddenly been hit by her years. There was a stiffness to her movements that he hadn't noticed before, there was grey in her face as well as in her hair.

"Thank you, chief. You an understanding man."

An understanding man and a discreet one: he had never received so many citations in one day. I'm protecting that family as much as you are, he thought. And damn it, she knew it. Their reasons were different, but they had the same commitment.

There was a knock on the office door, then it opened and Roley Trubauer said, "Bud and I've just had dinner, chief. We're going out again now."

"Hold it, Roley. Maybe you can drive Mrs Roberry home."

"I can walk," said Wilma Mae, gathering her coat and her strength about her. "I ain't had a breath of air today."

"There's plenty of it out there," Trubauer grinned. "Hang on to your hat."

Wilma Mae nodded, unsmiling, and went out past Trubauer and Bud Grierson as they stood aside. There was something of Adele Farquhar's dignity about her exit. She was right: *I is us*, thought McKechnie.

Trubauer and Grierson lingered in the doorway, waiting to be informed, curiosity making them look incongruously gauche. McKechnie sat down, put his feet up on his desk, let his bones fall where they might. But he wasn't relaxed, not at his core.

"Old Mrs Farquhar and Wilma Mae paid a visit out to Clint Blamey's last night. They went there looking for Molly."

Trubauer whistled softly and Grierson looked dourly surprised. "They tell you why they went? I mean, had Clint abducted her or something?"

"Clint's not that kind, you know that."

"I dunno," said Trubauer. "He took that pot shot at the house this morning and I didn't think he was that kind, either."

"No, Molly went out to his place on her own. They were going to go away together, but something went wrong." He opened the drawer in his desk, took out the gun and the box of ammunition. "I haven't had the bullets checked yet, but it's odds-on that's the gun killed Molly. I'll send them up to Joplin tomorrow, have their ballistics guys look at them."

"Clint's?" said Grierson. "I wouldn't of expected him to have a fancy gun like that."

"It belonged to Senator Farquhar, one of a pair. Wilma Mae took it out with her last night."

"You mean she shot Molly? Shot Molly?"

"If she did it was an accident. But I don't think she fired the gun or even intended to. She was just scared of the dark, that was all. She took it for protection."

"That what she told you?"

"Yes."

Grierson's expression said that if that satisfied the chief, it was okay by him; but he, personally, wouldn't have been satisfied. McKechnie had never heard Grierson use the word *nigger*, but he was old enough to have used it in other times. And, McKechnie was sure, he still *thought* it. There had never been any racial strife in Friendship in McKechnie's time, not even during the civil rights tension of the Sixties, but there were still some in the town who thought of blacks as second-class citizens who should be no better than that, who wouldn't want to take a black's word without the corroboration of at least two whites to back him up. McKechnie had no concrete evidence to support his opinion but he believed that Grierson was one of those.

"Who took the gun off'n her then?" said Trubauer. "To shoot Molly, I mean."

"That's something I'm still working on." McKechnie sounded on the defensive even to himself. "That's why we need Clint in here soon's you can get a hand on him."

"Ain't caught a scent of him, not since he got away from me this morning. Dunno where he's got that automobile of his hid, 'less he's to hell'n gone, over the state line and still going. Still going."

"Where's Molly's car?"

"It could be in one of the lakes or ponds," said Grierson. "If they were gonna run away together like you say, maybe they ditched it like that. But we know where she is and if we pick Clint up, it ain't gonna be important about the car, is it?"

For the first time McKechnie had the feeling that Grierson was trying to tell him how to do his job. Or was he becoming too sensitive? "You better start looking for him again, then."

"You gonna be here?"

McKechnie put his feet down, sat up. Either his ear was becoming too acute or out of tune: even that simple question by Grierson sounded critical. "I'm going to move around town, find out more about Molly. The more I get into this, the more I realize we don't know much about her. Unless you guys know something?"

"Me?" said Roley Trubauer. "Never passed more'n the time of day with her. I used to admire her ass, but I never knew nothing about her. Nothing."

"What about you, Bud?"

Grierson shook his head. "Don't think I even looked at her ass. Why don't you ask Lucy? She knows everything worth knowing in this town."

"She didn't know about Clint and Milly." He would come back to Lucy Chapley only if all else failed. He wanted facts, not gossip.

"Molly Farquhar had her own account," said George Milburn. "So has Gil. They've always had separate accounts, long as I can remember."

McKechnie had called Milburn, the president of the bigger of the town's two banks, asked if the Farquhars banked with him, then suggested that Milburn should meet him down at the First Citizens'. The banker, puzzled but curious, had been waiting for McKechnie when the latter arrived.

The police chief had been delayed by a demand by Lucy Chapley that he glance through her morning's reports; then he had walked across the square to the bank. It stood on a corner, the most modern building in town, all granite and glass in accordance with what seemed to be the theme of modern banks: no secrets from anyone, come and see who's inside asking for a loan. McKechnie would have liked more privacy, but even the president's desk was out in the open, the biggest island in an archipelago of desks. McKechnie, glancing out through the huge glass wall that fronted the bank, was glad that the weather seemed to have kept most of the citizens at home.

"Molly took out 2200 dollars Friday," said Milburn, running a well-manicured finger down an account statement.

"Did she often take out amounts as large as that?"

Milburn shook his head and his fine silvery-blond hair seemed to dance like a nimbus. He was middle-aged, a short square man with a face that seemed oddly out of joint, as if there was some quarrel between the flesh and the bone. One cheek seemed higher than the other and the nose somehow didn't seem to be at right angles to the brows. It was not an ugly face, but it was disconcerting. He had a soft voice, unobtrusive good manners and was always impeccably groomed, even on a wet Sunday afternoon. He was one of the leaders of the First Baptist, the town's biggest church, and he had twice been mayor. He was also, like McKechnie, a man of discretion.

"I take it, Jim, that all your questions are going to be necessary?"

"I wouldn't have troubled you, George, if they weren't." Was he going to meet the same obstruction here in the bank as up at the Farquhar house?

Milburn somehow managed a nod and a shaking of his head at the same time. "I understand. I'm still getting over the shock of what you told me—that she was shot. It was a shock when we learned at church this morning that she was dead—and *where*. But we all thought it was because of the twister. I tried to have a few words with Clint Blamey—"

"With Clint? *Where?*"

"At church. He came in late, but left early. He sat in a back pew—"

It was McKechnie's turn to shake his head. While he and the other policemen had been looking for Blamey after the shot at the Farquhar house, Blamey had come down to the church.

"What's the matter, Jim?"

"I'm kicking myself. I've been looking for Clint all morning—I just never thought to look for him at church."

"You're not a religious man, are you? Clint *is*—you forget to give him credit for that."

McKechnie accepted the criticism; then went back to his original line of questioning. "Did Molly often draw out large amounts?"

Milburn ran his finger down the statement again. "No. Usually her withdrawals were average, fifty, sixty a week. Except—wait a moment—about every four weeks she'd take out a couple of hundred."

That would tie in with the trips to St Louis. "Her husband told me she had a private income. Did that arrive regularly and how much was it?"

Milburn examined the statement again. "Every quarter she got a cheque for 1500 dollars. It doesn't say here where from, but I could look it up."

"Later." McKechnie looked down across the lesser desks and the wide expanse of terrazzo floor and through the glass wall into the square. The Confederate soldier, the grey iron of him glistening in the rain as if he were being spruced up for a new war, stared imploringly across the street at him. You're not the only one who's exposed, McKechnie silently told him. "What sort of woman was she, George?"

The soft accent hardened, turned a little cold. "You can't expect me to denigrate her, if that's what you're looking for. There'll be enough gossip about her as it is, her being found where she was."

"I'm not looking for gossip. I could have got that without coming across here." Thinking of Lucy Chapley ready with another report.

"Well—" Milburn, too, looked out at the square, pursing his lips; he was not usually asked for character references of the dead. "She was a kind woman and a wonderful worker. For the churches, the Red Cross, everything. She never seemed to be able to do enough to fill in her time. That was why—" he paused, then decided he was offering an opinion, not baseless gossip— "that was why I always thought she was unhappy. But it never occurred to me that she might walk out on Gil. She was very strict, I mean about the morality, the sanctity of marriage. She didn't judge other people harshly, those whose marriages failed, but I don't think anyone would have suspected her of—You're sure she was having an affair with Clint Blamey?"

"I don't have it in writing, but I'm sure enough. You

160

said you always thought she was unhappy. What do you mean by always? Ever since you first met her?"

Milburn nodded, the silver-blond hair lifting on his head again. It was the finest, lightest hair McKechnie could remember seeing on a man, like a baby's that had turned grey early. "Right from the first day. I don't say this conceitedly, but I think I can read people, it's part of my job."

"It's part of mine, too. I don't reckon I score better than fifty-fifty."

"Obviously I was wrong about Molly. Or partly wrong, I mean about her and Clint. I was wrong about him, too, I guess. I'd never have suspected him of being a philanderer."

Milburn had some old-fashioned terms: McKechnie wondered whether that was because he was a conservative banker or a pillar of his church. "Did Clint bank here? Do you know if he drew any money on Friday, too?"

"I can tell you that without having to go to the files. No, he had no money, no large amount, to draw. Clint had a bad year last year. That big hailstorm last summer ruined all his fruit crop and you remember his wife had been ill for a long time before she died around about the same time. He'd had a lot of medical expenses. No, if Clint had wanted to draw any large amount, they'd have sent him to me. With what's happened to his farm this morning, I don't know what he'll do. He must be feeling pretty desperate."

He's desperate all right, one way or another. "This is just between you and me—" Milburn looked offended, as if McKechnie should not even have hinted that he, a bank president, didn't know how to keep a secret. "Molly and Clint were planning to run off together. They had aeroplane tickets for Los Angeles."

Milburn pursed his lips again, dropped the statement on his desk and steepled his fingers. McKechnie was having trouble separating the banker from the church deacon.

But maybe he shouldn't be trying to do that: there was no reason why the man's morals should not be the same whatever hat he wore. McKechnie, the occasional Catholic, the full-time police chief, had become too accustomed to compromise.

"This is just between you and me—" The rebuke was gentle but unmistakable. "Clint owed the bank close to $80,000. That's not a lot of money to some people, but it is in this part of the country. He was not the sort of man who would go off leaving a debt like that behind him. It just wasn't in his nature."

McKechnie sat slumped in his chair, wondering how *he* would feel about being $80,000 in hock. He looked around the bank, at the empty desks, the empty counters; the place was inhabited only by himself, Milburn and whatever money and valuables there were in the vault. The aura of money had never affected him, probably because he had never been exposed to it; he had tried to conjure up an atmosphere of money about Vanderhorn while talking to him, but had not succeeded. Even debt had never had much effect on him, mainly because he and Paddy had tried to live within their income; they had had simple tastes and, if anything, his tastes had become simpler still since she had died and he had moved to Friendship. But he understood the sometimes unbearable weight of debt: in New York and even here he had been called to suicides who had chosen death instead. But Clint Blamey was not a man, he was sure, who would have chosen to kill himself and Molly because of his debt to the bank. And he had not killed himself, so why had he killed Molly? If he had . . .

"I think that's all, George." He stood up, feeling himself moving as stiffly as he had seen Wilma Mae do. Out in the square a grey car was circling, seeking the way out of town; it had out-of-state plates, ones that he couldn't distinguish because of the dirt on them, and he wondered who would be travelling on a day like this. He suddenly wished he was with the travellers, heading anywhere out of town. "Thanks for your help, even though you've confused me."

"How's Rose Farquhar? Things must be dreadfully sad up there. A state of shock, too."

"I'm trying to make it as easy for them as I can."

"That can't be easy for you. I mean, in the circumstances." He began to escort McKechnie towards the front door of the bank. "There was one thing about that situation—"

"What situation?" The grey car had disappeared, the travellers finding a way out of town. Which was more than he could do.

"About Rose Farquhar coming home. No, I better not—"

"George—" McKechnie stood in the open doorway, the wind already tugging at him. "You owe it to me to give me all the facts you can—"

"This wasn't a fact—that's why I'm hesitating. It was just—interpretation, if you want to give it a name. And perhaps I misinterpreted what he said."

"What who said?"

"Gil Farquhar. He came in here about a month ago to make a substantial withdrawal. I went across to speak to him, just pass the time of day, and he said he was going to Maryland to bring his sister Rose home. That was the first time I've ever heard him mention her name. He said she was very ill and they were bringing her home for good."

"Go on," said McKechnie, who had been told nothing new yet.

"I asked him if his wife was going with him to Maryland. He seemed very upset, otherwise I don't think he would have said what he did. You know he's not normally a very communicative man."

"What did he say?" You're not being very communicative yourself, George.

"He said Molly wouldn't go with him at any price."

"Did he say anything else?"

"Nothing. He seemed to realize what he'd told me and he left very abruptly. He's been in the bank a couple of times since, but it has seemed to me he's been avoiding me. Perhaps I *am* misinterpreting—"

"Maybe, George. But you said yourself you're good at reading people."

He left Milburn and walked back across the square. It was deserted except for four cars parked outside Bazeley's drugstore next door to the picture theatre. A small group of teenagers, who would normally have been out driving in the cars, stood under the marquee of the theatre staring glumly out at the miserable day. Above their heads the marquee sign said that, by popular demand, *Jaws* had been brought back. Just the movie for weather like this, McKechnie thought.

He crossed the road. Soggy scraps of paper inched along the gutters like oil-logged birds. Rainwater dripped like tears from the Confederate soldier's iron eyelids: had it been raining at Appomattox? McKechnie wondered. But couldn't remember the weather of history.

He went into headquarters, noting that no police cars were in the parking lot. That meant they were still looking for Clint Blamey, the possible murderer who would never leave a bank debt unpaid, whose natural hiding place had been a church.

"Any messages?"

Lucy Chapley had gone home for a two-hour break and would be back to finish off with a final two-hour tour of duty. She had been replaced by another part-time despatcher, Dorothy Kidmann.

"Dr Stenhouse called. He said it wasn't important, but you might like to call him back." Dorothy was a pretty girl

164

with a beehive hair-do and short, bottle-shaped legs that she tried to hide with longer-than-fashionable skirts. She continually reminded McKechnie of someone out of a 1950s high school movie. But she was efficient and not a busybody. "Thre's nothing else except they're repeating the Tornado Warning."

He went into his office and called Stenhouse, who answered the phone himself. "Chief? I've just come back from another visit to the Farquhars. What the hell's going on there? They tell me someone tried to shoot our friend through the bedroom window."

"Doc, can I come up and see you?"

"So long as you don't stay too long." Stenhouse never wasted time on politeness. "I'm pooped. I was going to have a nap."

"Just close your eyes when you want me to go, doc."

"If I fall asleep it won't matter a damn to me whether you go or stay."

McKechnie drove up again to Forest View. He'd been up here more times today than he had in the past month. As he drove along between the elms that lined the street he saw faces at several windows and wondered whether they were waiting for him or the tornado to appear. He turned into the gravel driveway of Stenhouse's home, a long, low ranch-house built of fieldstone and timber. It had been the first place up when the Farquhar estate had been cut up into lots and sold and it had weathered into its setting, looked less conspicuous than some of its neighbours. There was no rain falling as he got out of his car and the air seemed a trifle warmer, even humid.

Stenhouse opened the door to him, looked out at the weather. "Goddam rain! I was supposed to go over to Little Rock this weekend, play golf. I like to try out other courses when I can."

"You couldn't have deserted Rose Farquhar anyway, could you?"

"No, I guess not."

He led McKechnie into a room that was a combined study and office. The doctor's surgery was in the medical centre next to the hospital and he was notorious for his temper if anyone came to his house expecting to be treated. All emergency cases were expected to go to the hospital and he would go down there to attend to them. The study-office, McKechnie guessed, was where Stenhouse just added up his accounts.

"My wife's gone out to the country club, damn fool. Says she wants to make sure everything's been cleaned up after last night's wing-ding. Always damn well housekeeping. Well, what's on your mind?"

The room was cosy and warm. McKechnie sat down in one of the two deep armchairs, wondering if he might follow the doctor's example, when the time came, and fall asleep. He had cast a quick eye around the room when he came in, saw the rows of books, the sporting prints, the photos of Stenhouse with various golfing partners. It was the sort of room he hoped he might have himself some day, when he had moved into Lee's house.

"Doc, tell me something about Molly Farquhar. Where did she come from, what was she like when she married Gil?"

Stenhouse took a pipe from a rack, filled it, lit it and sat down in the other armchair. He was dressed as if he still hoped to get in some golf: a turtleneck sweater, corduroy trousers and something McKechnie couldn't remember seeing before, blue-white-and-red argyle socks worn with a pair of leather slippers. Stenhouse saw where McKechnie's eyes were hooked and he held up a leg like a woman admiring her ankle.

"Genuine argyles. I got them in Scotland when I was over there last summer, playing at Gleneagles, Troon, places like that. My wife and I go separate ways for our vacation—she can't stand me playing golf all the time. I'm going to Japan this year. My wife wants me to bring back a happy-coat. You know, one of those things makes you look like a samurai on his day off. Or a male masseur in a brothel." He yawned, took a puff on his pipe. "What makes you think I know anything about Molly?"

"You treated Gil, so you must have gone to the house occasionally. You'd have seen her out at the country club—"

Stenhouse nodded, puffed on his pipe again. "Well, she came originally from Jefferson City—her old man was the Senator's ward boss up there. A very respectable ward boss, not like some of the Democrats we've had. Pendergast, men like that. Harry Paterson never had any money and as far as I know Molly never had any, either. Not of her own."

"Fifteen hundred dollars a quarter. Even cops earn more than that."

"Glad to hear it." But Stenhouse made it sound as if he was only glad because it meant cops could pay their medical bills. He ran his thumbnail along his moustache, squinting through the smoke of his pipe while he tried to remember more about Molly Farquhar. "She looked a bit like Rose, you know, when she was younger. A plainer version—well, no, not plain. A less beautiful version of Rose. Then she dyed her hair and I guess a lot of people forgot about the resemblance."

"Did anyone remark on it at the time?"

"I suppose so. My wife did, but she remarks upon *everything*." His pipe went out and he relit it. "Well, at first Molly seemed happy enough with Gil—or so it seemed to those of us who came in contact with her. As I said this morning, she was never my patient. But that was only for a while, her being happy. It wasn't long before we began to notice things were a bit strained between them. Nothing you could put your finger on, but it was there. Gil came to see me about two years after they were married, said things weren't too good and asked me to look at him, take some tests. That was when I found out he was impotent."

"What about Molly?"

"It was just after that she started being the eager beaver she's been ever since. Anyone started a committee, she had to be on it. Down at the hospital she was more god-dam nuisance, being a do-gooder . . . I shouldn't talk about her like that. She had her problems and she was working them off in the only way she knew how. Gil was no goddam help to her."

"How was that?"

"Well, she wanted to travel, for one thing. Sometimes, out at the club, she'd let her hair down to my wife. She was never a real drinker, but she might have one or two and then her tongue would start to rattle. She said every year they'd get a card from Europe from Rose, the only time all year they'd hear from her except at Christmas when Rose would call her mother. She said those cards used to drive her up the wall with jealousy. Or maybe she said envy, I don't know. Anyhow, she used to ask Gil to take her on a trip, but he'd never move out of Missouri. Damned near never moved out of Friendship."

"Molly used to give herself little trips. To St Louis, about once a month."

"Where'd you find that out?" Stenhouse's pipe had gone out and he lit it once again.

"Something I dug up. What about Rose?"

"What about her?"

"Tell me something about her. I've left her out of all my calculations about Molly's death, but she seems to be cropping up now."

"She had nothing to do with Molly's death, get that idea out of your head." Stenhouse sounded testy, made a loud sucking noise on his pipe. "Are all you cops such suspicious bastards?"

"It's the first thing they ask you as a rookie, have you got a suspicious nature. I almost failed, but I had enough."

Stenhouse allowed himself a grin: it looked like the side-effect of a stroke. "You and I should get together more, chief. Well, about Rose. It was a long while ago that anyone here in town knew her. I've got to confess I had my eye on her and I wasn't the only feller in town felt like that about her. That was before I married the wife. There was no country club in those days, but there used to be dances at various places and Rose was always there. She was the best-looking gal at any of them, best-dressed too, as I remember it. She had a wonderful gaiety about her that was sort of infectious. She made everyone feel *good*, even the other girls. I don't think any of them were ever jealous of her."

"Did she go with any particular feller?"

"She tended to play the field. I don't mean by that she was promiscuous. She liked a good time, but she wasn't —I hate the term—an easy lay. Gil looked after her pretty well, he was very protective. Most of the fellers who had their sights on Rose thought he was a pain in the ass. But in a way I suppose you couldn't blame him. Moral standards were different back then, the late Forties, the early Fifties. Jesus, on the calendar it seems like only yesterday, but it was another age." He shook his head, took his pipe out of his mouth and looked at the glowing bowl of it: which went out, even as he looked at it. "Brothers cared about their sisters' reputation, there was still a bit of Andy Hardy in them, I guess. I've heard one of my grandsons up in Kansas City, told to take care of his sister, ask what the hell for, she was on the Pill. I offered to cut his balls out, finish the Stenhouse line there and then, but his mother, my daughter-in-law, said that's the way of the world now. You're lucky you have no kids, chief."

"Yes." Paddy had been four months pregnant when she died.

"Well—" Stenhouse considered the way of the world in the second half of the twentieth century; then relit his pipe and blew out angry puffs of smoke. McKechnie, a non-smoker, was beginning to feel choked by the heavy air. "Rose wasn't a girl who'd have used the Pill if it had been available then. She believed in sin in those days and the wages of it."

"How do you know? Were you one of her fellers?"

"What makes you ask that?"

"Something I dug up."

"You're much smarter than I thought." Stenhouse decided to let his pipe go out. He sighed, then looked directly at McKechnie. "I might as well tell you. We were unofficially engaged for a week. We went away together, over a July Fourth weekend. But she called it all off when we came back. It hurt me like hell at the time and I couldn't understand it. The weekend had been, well, satisfactory. More than satisfactory, I thought. But something happened when she came home and that was the end of it."

"She never told you why?"

"Oh, she told me she'd decided we couldn't be compatible. Maybe she was right. But she hadn't talked about compatibility while we were over at Lexington, Kentucky. We went there because she was nuts about horses in those days. If she'd wanted to look at a skunk stud farm, I'd have taken her. But all that was long ago," he said and tapped the ash of his pipe into a big stone bowl. "And if ever you mention any of it outside this room I'll cut *your* balls out."

"No chance, doc. Both ways." McKechnie stood up; he knew when a man had given more of himself than he had intended. "I wish I could have met her just once. You make her sound pretty attractive."

170

"She was more than that." Stenhouse stood up, sober and sad; the bottoms of his trousers slid down to hide the gaiety of his socks. "She was the most beautiful, charming girl I ever met. I could cry to see her now."

"You mentioned she was always gay. Was she like that after she broke it off with you?"

Stenhouse looked back at years he had tried to forget, down a corridor of memory where he had tried to close all the doors. "I've really forgotten. I went away for six months, took a temporary job over in St Louis, and when I came back she had gone. Then I met my wife and I put Rose out of my mind. Or tried to. I would think about her once in a while, but after a while you find those sort of things don't hurt any more. There is no such thing as one true love, not unless your true love stays alive and stays with you."

McKechnie nodded: he loved Lee as much as he had loved Paddy. "You're not the sour son-of-a-bitch you try to paint yourself."

"I am about certain things. I still hate kids and cats and whining old women like Mrs Ness. But I'm still capable of a tear for a girl I used to know named Rose Farquhar."

McKechnie noticed he had not mentioned his wife. "I think our friend the Vice-President is capable of a tear for her, too."

"I've always had respect for him. And not because he's rich and a Republican. Now I feel sorry for him."

"So do I. For a poor Democrat to say that about a rich Republican is something. Thanks, doc. Have your nap."

"I'm wide awake now. When this is all over, come up again and spoil another Sunday afternoon for me."

"I'll look forward to it."

As they reached the front door it opened and Gwen Stenhouse came in, pulling a scarf from her head. She had never been a pretty woman, but there was a healthy

171

heartiness to her that made her attractive. "Hello, chief! Something wrong?"

"Nothing," said her husband. "Did you polish up the clubhouse?"

"Naturally. You'd be the first to complain if we left it like a pigsty. Well, see you, chief. Got things to do!"

She disappeared towards the back of the house and her husband scowled. "Always goddam housekeeping. When she gets to Hell, which is where I hope she goes, she'll have them polishing the goddam grates before she's there five minutes. Is Lee Barron a housekeeper? No? Then don't let her change."

## III

Willis Vanderhorn had gone through every room on the ground floor of the house, walking restlessly back and forth like a politician caged by his election promises. All his life he had been active, impatient of boundaries whether they were stone walls or mental concepts; his only frontiers had been those of a code of behavior, the sole influence his father had had on him. Several times in his youth he had broken away from the protective screen put up by his kidnap-conscious parents and grandfather and gone wandering incognito; the experience had excited and, to a degree, educated him, but he had always been glad, like a prodigal prince, to return to the palace. He had never been one of the rich unhappy at being rich; he had no more worries than the rest of men and a good deal fewer than most. He had been perfectly happy to be a rich man's son and, eventually, a rich man himself.

There had been restrictions on him once he had assumed the Vice-Presidency. The Secret Service agents had been a running barbed-wire compound that had at times driven him almost to distraction; but he had accepted the need for them and twice, during violent demon-

172

strations abroad, had been glad of them. Once, during a so-called goodwill tour of South America, he had spent twenty-four hours cooped up in an embassy while a crowd, showing badwill, had threatened to stone him if he appeared. Those had been part of the wages of the job and he had accepted them. He had become bad-tempered sometimes and taken out his frustration on those appointed to protect him, but he had never attempted to stop them doing their job. Not till he had stolen away from them early this morning.

Now he was confined to this house by devotion to the dying woman in the room upstairs and to be bad-tempered about it would be to deny that devotion. He had spent an hour with her, sitting beside her bed and watching her die by the minute. We all die by the minute, he had told himself; but that had been no consolation, watching Rose who had so few minutes left. He had become bad-tempered then, angry at God for prolonging her pain. He was not a religious man, never had been, but he had always believed in God and His mercy. But there was no mercy in letting a woman die on a rack that was not of her own making.

He had been shocked when he had been taken up this morning to see Rose. She had been wan and thin when she had left the house on Chesapeake Bay a month ago, but she had still been beautiful and all her charm and humour, though the latter may have been drier, had still been there. As they had said goodbye in the bedroom where they had spent so many happy nights, she had said, "Forgive me if I don't vote for you in November, darling."

"Voting isn't compulsory in this country, thank God."

"That's always been one of the good things—that nothing between us was ever compulsory. I'll confess it now—in all the time we've been together I've never voted Republican. Daddy would have enjoyed that."

But the talk about voting had been only a brittle screen

173

and both of them had known it. She had leaned against him, a beautiful complement of bones and huge dark eyes, and whispered, "All I wanted was for it to have gone on forever."

They had both wept, holding on to each other, closer than they had ever been in their love-making. When he had gone downstairs and he had gone out to his car to drive back to Washington, it had been like giving up forever a part of himself. A cliché, he had told himself, but the wound was real and would never heal. He had driven away and then her brother Gilbert, whom she had insisted he must not meet, had come to the house and brought her home to Friendship.

When he had seen her this morning he had wept again, had found it hard to believe that he had known and loved the skeleton lying in the big four-poster bed. The lovely head and face, now just a skull, had turned away from him; the once-beautiful eyes, already dark with death, had wept and the tears, catching the light, had seemed more alive than the yellow transparent cheeks on which they ran. He wondered if he had been cruel to her in coming to see her die; but it would have been crueller to himself to have stayed away. And the living, in death, are always the selfish ones.

When he had come downstairs twenty minutes ago he had phoned the President. It was the first time he had ever had to dial his own call to the White House. He dialed direct, having to look up the Washington, DC, area code; it amused him that he didn't know it, though Washington had been his home town for the past four years. He knew the White House number, 456–1414, and he got through to the switchboard in the Executive Office Building. He gave his code name and was put through to the Presidential aide on duty. The aide wanted to know where he was calling from, but he had shut the aide off and told him to connect him to the President at once.

When he got on to the President he asked him to secure his end of the line, though the Farquhar end was open. If anyone bothered to listen in they would hear only half the conversation and he was careful of what he said.

He had called not to report anything but because he knew the irascible man in the White House would be wondering why his Vice-President, absent without leave, should not call in even if only to say he was still alive. The President had always been polite to Rose on the few occasions when he had met her, but she had never been invited to the White House and he had never mentioned her in his conversations with Vanderhorn. He was not a prude, but he had never learned to trust the voters' more permissive attitudes and, by omission rather than suggestion, he had let it be known that Vanderhorn and Rose Farquhar's romance was to be clandestine, the more clandestine the better. The President had his own boundaries, those of the voters' prejudices.

Vanderhorn walked back through the house, familiar with it now and beginning to understand why Rose loved it so. She had been born in it and been both happy and unhappy here, she had told him; and with no real home of her own, none that he had been able to provide her with, she had chosen to come back here to die. Perhaps it was the size of the house he had been born in and the houses and apartments in which he had lived: somehow this seemed to him more like a *home*. There was a dimension about it that one could feel, a warmth from and identity with the family that had occupied it for over a hundred years. No interior decorator had been allowed to put his mark on this house; it spoke for itself and the Farquhars. There were pictures, ornaments, furniture that had belonged to several generations of Farquhars before those who had built and lived in the house. He had noticed several pieces that reminded him of Delaware River Valley furniture he had seen in a museum the Vanderhorn Foundation had funded; his family bought early American furniture for a museum but the Farquhars lived with theirs. It struck him that he, the Vice-President of the United States, was less American than this family who were now at the end of their line.

He went into the drawing-room, stood back from the windows but looked out through the curtains. The police car was still there in the driveway; he was glad of its presence. Several cars had attempted to pull in off the street, townspeople coming to pay their respects or to see what they could do for the Farquhars, but the policeman on duty had got out of his car, gone to speak to the visitors and they had driven away. The phone had rung half a dozen times and Adele or Gilbert Farquhar had answered it. They had been polite but short and the word must have got around town that the Farquhars just wanted to be left alone today. There had been no more calls for the past two hours.

He saw Wilma Mae come up the driveway, walking past the policeman in his car without looking at him. She went round the side of the house and he went out to meet her as she came in the kitchen door. She paused, looking at him with respect and the expectation that he was about to ask her to do something for him, which he knew she would do willingly. She was an old-fashioned Negress, he thought, one who still used the word *coloured* instead of black and didn't resent him because he was white or the symbol of white supremacy. She was no Aunt Jemima, he was sure; she was just secure in the Farquhar world, small as it was. More secure perhaps than any of the others in it.

"Did Chief McKechnie give you a bad time, Wilma Mae?"

She took off her hat and coat, looked around as if wondering what to do with them. He was not to know that she prized the neatness of her kitchen, that a wet coat and

176

hat should not be left hanging over the back of a chair; but he was the Vice-President of the United States and she could not leave him and go into her bedroom to hang up the coat and hat. So she stood holding them, giving the impression that she did not belong here and would go as soon as he dismissed her.

"No, sir. He ask me some questions, I give him some answers. He ain't a bad man."

"He's only doing his job. I think he's a very good man —at least at his job."

"I dunno, sir. This family, we never had no trouble with the police before."

He hesitated, feeling he was about to embark on his own grilling of her: "Did he ask you any questions about Miss Rose?"

She shook her head slowly. "Miss Rose don't belong in this business, he know that."

He felt an immense relief, but hid it. There were no more questions to be asked and he was glad of it, for his own sake as well as hers. "We must keep it that way, Wilma Mae."

She gazed steadily at him, the difference in their status for the moment forgotten. She *knows,* he thought. "She gonna go to the Lord in peace, Mr Vanderhorn. She never done no wrong and she deserve that."

"Indeed she does," he said.

There was nothing more to say. He had the reputation of being the rich man with the common touch, a consummate politician; but it was a reputation built by his own public relations men. He was at ease with his own servants, but there had never been any real cause before this to talk confidentially with someone else's servants. It was sufficient to know that he and Wilma Mae had reached an understanding without having to state it.

As he walked back through the hallway Gilbert Farquhar came down the stairs. The two men paused, looking at each other with suspicion. I'm on his territory, Vanderhorn thought. But he could not allow the other man sovereignty, not while Rose was still alive.

"The police chief wasn't too tough with Wilma Mae."

Farquhar nodded, as if he had not been prepared for Vanderhorn speaking to him. He came on down the stairs and went into the drawing-room. Vanderhorn hesitated, then followed him. The Sunday edition of the *News* lay on a chair, tossed there carelessly by Vanderhorn when he had finished glancing through it.

Farquhar picked it up, frowned and shook the pages together. "I like my paper neat."

"My grandfather was like that. He had an English butler who actually ran a warm iron over the papers before he took them in to my grandfather."

"That's ridiculous."

"We all thought so. But none of us ever told my grandfather. He didn't care for other people's opinions about his behavior."

"Do you?" Farquhar folded the newspaper neatly, put it down on a side table. He hadn't glanced at even a headline, as if the world's news was trival and unimportant today.

"In certain regards. Just as you do."

"How do you know what I feel?" There was agitation in him but he tried to hide it; but his bony knuckles cracked as he put one hand into the other. "Did Rose ever talk to you about me?"

He wondered if he should tell the truth and say no. It was difficult to know whether Farquhar would be reassured or hurt. He hedged: "Not specifically. She would sometimes talk about the family, but you were all lumped together."

"Lumped together?" Vanderhorn knew he had used the wrong phrase; but Farquhar seemed more puzzled

178

than insulted. "That does not sound like her. She used to be very specific. About people, I mean."

Rose had been specific about the people she had met in Washington, often bitingly so. *The President doesn't trust women; our emotions are too honest for him to understand.* She had been equally candid about members of the Cabinet and the Majority and Minority leaders in the House and the Senate; but always only to him and never to anyone else. She had a quick microscopic eye for character analysis, pinning people against a wall like specimens without their ever realizing it; several times he had relied upon her judgement and found it correct. But she had always been vague about her family and it had not taken him long to realize that she was deliberately so. He had never pressed her, not really wanting to know the Farquhars he had never met. He had known almost from the start of their romance that they would never be able to come out in the open, that the Farquhars here in Friendship would never be his in-laws.

"Perhaps it was my fault," he said placatingly: he didn't want any more encounters with Farquhar. "I never pressed her to talk about any of you. To be honest, I never thought we'd meet."

Farquhar pondered this a moment, then nodded. He seemed less antagonistic, as if he knew it was pointless, as if he was beginning to appreciate that Vanderhorn didn't care how he felt towards him. "I suppose if she hadn't fallen ill . . . Would you have stayed together? I mean as you both got older?"

"That was the way she wanted it. The way I wanted it, too."

"Would you have married her—eventually? I mean if your wife, um, died?"

"Yes."

Farquhar nodded to himself: it was impossible to tell

179

whether the answer satisfied him or not. But he did say, "That would have pleased my mother."

"What would have pleased me?" Adele Farquhar came into the room, *sweeping* in: she had regained some of her style and poise.

"The Vice-President was saying that eventually he and Rose would have married. If his wife died."

"Yes, that would have pleased me, Mr Vanderhorn." She picked up the newspaper, opened it, glanced at the front headlines, then dropped it carelessly on the side table. She, too, cared nothing for the rest of the world today. "I've just been listening to the radio. The storms further south are getting worse. Do you think it would be safer for you to leave now?"

"I am not concerned for my safety. I am concerned for Rose. I shall have to leave before it gets dark, but until then . . ."

She looked out the window, drawing the curtain aside to scan the darkening sky. Vanderhorn moved to one side, so that the policeman, now out of his car and walking up and down the driveway to stretch his legs, would not see him. "A tornado is all we need . . . Rose is awake. She would like to see you."

"How is she?"

"I think you should say goodbye to her now. Not in so many words—you know what I mean. Then I think I shall call Russell Stenhouse and ask him to give her an extra-strong sedative—"

"No!" Farquhar had picked up the newspaper, was re-folding it. But now suddenly he crumpled it in his hands.

"It's for the best. She has suffered enough. Don't you agree, Mr Vanderhorn?"

"I don't know. I can't—"

Then through the net curtains he saw the policeman suddenly run up the driveway, reach into his car and grab the microphone. He said something excitedly, then he wrenched open the car door and quickly slid in.

"Something's happening!" Vanderhorn said.

The police car backed out of the driveway, the red light starting to flash on its roof, then it went down the street at speed, its siren beginning to wail.

# Chapter Six

The President had been less than satisfied with his conversation with the Vice-President on the phone. It was his wife who at lunch had mentioned the weather in the Mid West.

"I heard it on the radio. They have already had seven or eight tornadoes and they say the weather is getting worse." The First Lady came from Nebraska and knew the threat of tornadoes. "I hope Willis is keeping an eye out. He probably isn't. He'll be more worried about Rose Farquhar than the weather."

"I wish he'd come back here. He says her condition is hopeless."

"If ever I'm in a hopeless condition, will you desert me?"

"You'll live a damn sight longer than I will."

"Who told you that—Dr. Gallup? You usually accept his diagnosis on everything, don't you?"

"Sometimes I think you're not really the girl I married. You're an impostor planted by the *Washington Post*."

"But I love you. Don't tell the *Post*."

When Vanderhorn had called, the first question the President had asked him had been about the weather. "John, you've never asked me about the weather all the time I've known you."

"Don't bullshit me, Willis. You know what it's like down there. Have you had a twister or anything?"

He had noticed the slight pause before Vanderhorn had replied. "A small one outside of town. No real damage."

"Willis, I think you should get back to your plane and get back here while you're still all in one piece."

"Is that an order, Commander-in-Chief?"

"Ah, come on. What would you say if I said yes, it is an order?"

"I'm afraid, John, I'd ignore it. I've already told you, I'll be on my way by dark. But not before."

"Well, if you get caught in any sort of bad weather don't try to fly out of there. Catch a bus, take a cab, any damn thing. Jesus, Willis, you're more damn trouble—"

"Than I'm worth? Go on, John, say it."

"I'm beginning to think you're trying to bring me on a heart attack, so you can step into my shoes."

"Never into your shoes." The President's one sartorial vanity was his hand-made Italian shoes that, Rose had once said, made him look like the only backwoods gigolo she had ever met or was likely to meet. "My feet are too big and clumsy. Relax, John. I'm feeling pretty depressed, but I'm a long way from feeling suicidal. If the weather gets really bad, I'll find a safe way out of here. There's a very competent police chief in this town who is very concerned for my safety."

"Jesus Christ, the chief of police knows you're there? That means the whole goddam town! I *come* from a small town, I know what they're like—"

"This police chief is not a small town boy. He comes from New York."

"Christ Almighty, that's worse! No New Yorker can keep his mouth shut if he can make a buck by opening it."

"Mr. President, you have no faith in America—"

"Okay, cut the corn." The President swallowed, tried for a calmer voice. "Come back now, Willis. That's no order, just a request. Come back before you get you and Rose spread across every newspaper and television screen in the country."

"I'll leave here before dark, John, I promise. Now watch your ear—I'm about to hang up on the President of the United States, may God forgive me."

"You're a son-of-a-bitch, Wil—"

Almost a thousand miles to the west and slightly south, Lew Black and Jumpy Cowman were having their first argument. "What the hell you doing, Lew, driving right inna the goddam town? You crazy, man!"

"You think I did it on purpose? Shut up, Jumpy."

When they had come along Route 86 and seen the flattened farmhouse, Black had slowed the car. Then he had seen the police car and at once speeded up again. A mile down the road he had turned off into a side road with thick timber on either side; he had pulled off on to a track, cut the engine and waited. But they hadn't been followed and they had decided to stay there a while and rest. They had both dozed off and two hours passed before they got going again. Black had pulled out on to the side road and headed in the direction away from Route 86. He had driven down between some farms, come to some warehouses and then suddenly realized he was heading into town. There had been no turn-offs and in a few more minutes they were surrounded by houses. He had kept going and in another minute they were in the town square.

Then he had seen the flag wrapped around the top of the pole; it looked like a giant striped lollipop sucked down to the last mouthful. He saw the blue squad car standing outside police headquarters and all at once the old recklessness came back. He began to circle the square, like a lost traveller looking for the road out of town; he even began to hope that some cop would come out of headquarters and give him directions. It was crazy, he knew, but it made the adrenalin run. He didn't know what adrenalin was but a doctor in the Federal pen in Atlanta had told him he had too much of it.

Beside him Jumpy began to curse, obscenities running out of him like dribbling saliva. He ignored him, driving slowly round the square a second time. They passed two banks, on opposite sides of the square; in one of them, the First Citizens', there appeared to be two men sitting at a desk at the rear but he wasn't sure. He gave a mock salute to the statue of the Confederate soldier: his own great-granddaddy had fought on the Union side. But there was only one war now, between him and *them,* the cops and the sons-of-bitches with money. Like those banks: he was tempted to go completely crazy, to go into that First Citizens' and stick up those two guys, make them open up the vault.

"Lew, you crazy, man! Let's get outa here!"

He completed the second circuit of the square and drove down the street that ran into the north-west corner. The street curved up the side of a bluff, then flattened out into a tree-lined avenue between expensive houses set back in thir own lawns and gardens.

"You look at 'em, Jumpy? All sitting on their fat asses, Middle fat-assed America!"

Jumpy didn't like it when Lew started to talk like that. He was black but he was no black militant; he had no political views at all and he had turned bank robber because he could think of no quicker way to earn big money. He didn't resent people who had loot, whether they were white or black; he dreamed of the day when he could sit on his own fat ass in a street like this, in a house like those they were passing. It was a useless, impossible dream, but even a dummy like himself, and he knew he couldn't match brains with Lew, couldn't stop his skull from some-times filling up with hopes.

Then he saw the police car standing in the driveway of the big house with the copper dome on top. Black saw it

185

at the same time, but stopped himself from slamming his foot down on the gas pedal. They went on down the street, cruising sedately, and the police car, with the cop at its wheel, remained behind them in the driveway.

"Relax, Jumpy. We gonna get outa town without no trouble at all. Here comes the rain again. Nobody's gonna be looking for us in this."

He was wrong. Two miles out of town, driving through heavy rain, they passed a police car. In the driving mirror he saw the brake-lights of the police car suddenly go on, saw the car swing sideways on the greasy road as the driver tried to do a U-turn. Black stepped on the gas and went down the highway, looking for a side road, wondering where the hell they were going to go now.

**I**

McKechnie was sitting at his desk doing rough, childish drawings of .38 Smith and Wessons when the red light went on on his desk. It was the signal that something important was coming in over the communications radio, that the despatcher at the console needed him to give instructions. His first thought was that a twister had struck somewhere and, forgetting the ballpoint pen he held, he closed his fist and thumped it on the desk with such force that the pen snapped in half. Another twister: all he goddam needed!

He went out quickly to the glassed-in section behind the front counter where Dorothy Kidmann was waving a frantic hand to him as she spoke into the microphone.

"Got it, PD-Four. The chief is here—hold it." She looked up at McKechnie as he leaned over her. "Roley and Bud are out on Route 60. They said they recognized the car those bank robbers used over to Columbus. Roley and Bud followed them, but have lost 'em."

McKechnie took over the microphone. "Roley, Bud—where are you now?"

"Out on Nut Ridge Road, chief, just past the sawmill." Bud Grierson's scratchy voice wasn't improved by static. "We lost 'em in the rain, but we reckon they're still somewhere in the area. Ain't that many exit roads leading off'n this 'un. Plenty of back roads, but they all lead back to the main roads."

"Okay, sit there. I'll get all the other cars into the area right away. I'll be out soon's I can make it."

"What about Clint Blamey?" That was Roley Trubauer, who liked to get his priorities right. "We forget him for a while?"

"No, you don't forget him! But you concentrate on those guys till I get out there and we look at the situation. Ten-four." He handed the microphone back to Dorothy. "Get me the other cars quick."

"Everything's happening today, right?" Dorothy was excited; her hair-do wobbled like a hive whose bees had gone berserk. She had been working for the department for only four months and nothing exciting or out-of-the-ordinary had happened while she had been on duty.

The other cars reported in and McKechnie told them to get out to Nut Ridge Road. Jack Atcheson was a little slow in reporting in and sounded out of breath. "You want me to go out there, chief? I thought I hadda stay here at the Farquhar place—"

McKechnie hesitated only a moment. He was sure now that nobody up at the Farquhar house was going to run away, and it really was not the Police Department's job to protect them from unwelcome callers. As for protecting the Vice-President . . . But he didn't have time to debate the pros and cons of that. "Get out to Nut Ridge, Jack. I'll see you there. Move!" He tapped Dorothy encouragingly on the shoulder. "Get two of the volunteer men in

187

here right away, whoever's available. You're holding the fort till they turn up."

Her face shone as if she had just been proposed to. "I can handle it, chief."

He went into Bud Grierson's office which was also the ammunition store. He opened up the safe with his master key and took out a dozen boxes of ammunition for the carbines that would be in each police car, plus a dozen tear-gas bombs. He didn't know whether they were going to have any sort of shootout with the bank robbers, but the *Wanted* fliers had said they were dangerous and he didn't want any of his men caught short of firepower. As he went out of his office on the run he thought what a hell of a Sunday it was turning out to be. Something flashed into his mind, a religious notation on his desk calendar: Low Sunday. Never had a day been better named.

The rain was heavy, coming from the south in great gusting sheets like heavy grey sails billowing in a Roaring Forties wind; the wind itself seemed to be trying to force the car backwards. It took him fifteen minutes to get out to Nut Ridge Road, a trip that normally would have taken him no more than five minutes. But as he arrived at the spot where the other four cars were congregated, the rain abruptly stopped.

The men got out of their cars as he pulled up. He joined them and they all stood in a bunch in the middle of the sealed surface, away from the mud of the shoulders of the road. The wind still blew but it had dropped a little and wasn't uncomfortable. This was wooded country, a mixture of ash and hickory with some flowering dogwood, its blossom protected from the wind by the other trees, showing like frozen smoke back in the timber. The road was long and narrow and just up beyond where the cars were parked it crested before dropping down towards thicker wooded country and a series of small lakes and ponds.

McKechnie knew that if the bank robbers had got in here amongst the timber it might take weeks to flush them out.

"We gonna need a helicopter, chief," said Gerry Hankesen, one of the younger men.

"You'd never get 'em to put a chopper in the air on a day like this. But I'm going to have to call in the sheriff and the Highway Patrol."

"Ah, geez, chief, we need to do that? Those guys come in, they just take over. They think they're the goddam FBI or something."

"There's them, too. The FBI, I'll have to call them."

The area was suddenly looking crowded; but he would have to keep the outsiders out of the Farquhar affair. He sometimes thought the American law enforcement system had too many cooks in the kitchen; in theory they were all supposed to cooperate but sometimes the jealousy and rivalry resembled that of organizations on the other side of the law. He knew he was as much an offender as anyone else. He treasured his authority and independence and wouldn't have welcomed any suggestion that he should be just a cog in a national or even state police force. At least, today, he could keep quiet about the Farquhar affair and not break any rules.

"You and Bud better stay in this area, Roley. Don't go on to any of the trails through the timber. I don't want you getting bogged down and being a sitting duck for those guys if they find you."

"What about us, chief?" said Hankesen.

"You and Andy swing round over the other side of this timber, down through the lakes. Larry—" He looked at the other young farm boy, seeing the nervous excitement in his stamping feet and his constantly moving shoulders. As far as he knew the boy had never yet had to draw his gun in the course of his duty and he hated the thought of his coming up alone against someone of the calibre of Black and Cowman. "You get out on the open road, keep

189

out there so's you can't be jumped. And don't forget, all of you, we're still looking for Clint Blamey."

He kept to himself Milburn's information that Blamey had been at church this morning while they had been out looking for him on the back roads. He was becoming sensitive, already conditioning himself for failure.

"What about me?" said Jack Atcheson.

"You better come back with me."

He saw the disappointment on Atcheson's face; he was afraid of missing something. They had all lived a quiet life for so long and now, when Atcheson had the chance of being a real cop for a change, of experiencing some of the excitement that a New York cop like McKechnie must have seen, he was being told to accompany the chief back to headquarters. Over the years the local men had coaxed stories of New York out of McKechnie and even though he had tried to underplay the excitement or import-ance of anything he had done, they had obviously envied him. None of them had ever queried him about the death of Paddy and the shooting of the junkie, but even the rest of his stories had left them with the feeling that a small town cop missed a lot. The French Connection was never likely to reach Friendship.

"I want you to run things from there, Jack," McKechnie said soothingly as he and Atcheson walked back to their cars. "There's only Dorothy and a couple of the volunteer guys there now. I can't leave any of them in charge. Any-how, Jack, you're too old to get your ass shot off."

"Bud's older'n I am."

"Bud's got Roley to look after him."

"You gonna tell him that?"

McKechnie grinned. "You think I want my own ass shot off by him?"

Atcheson, mollified, got into his car. "What about the Farquhars?"

"I'll drop in there, tell 'em to stay put. If the sheriff and

190

the Highway guys are down at headquarters before I get back, put them in the picture. I'll be there before the FBI arrives."

He contacted Dorothy, told her to inform the other law agencies what was happening and to ask them to come to headquarters. "I have a call to make at the Farquhar place. And honey—" He would never have called Lucy Chapley *honey*; he was glad she was off-duty right now. "Not a word to the sheriff, the Highway guys or the FBI about what happened to Molly Farquhar. That one is still our show, okay?"

"Ten-four, chief." For a moment she sounded like Lucy. Then he forgave her: this must be the biggest day of her life.

He drove back to town, slowing for a moment when he came out on the crest of an open ridge. He looked down towards the south. The clouds were still surging up from there. Over to the west he could see the pouches of mammatus clouds, like inverted toadstools; they looked threatening, but he knew they were harmless. But then all clouds were harmless until you saw the funnel beginning to form at their base. And clouds, on a day like this, took only moments to change shape. He turned on the radio, got the local station playing music as a fill-in for the cancelled ball game up in Kansas City. For a change it wasn't country-and-western: it was symphony music, soft and suggestive of a peaceful spring day. It was a pity that its counterpoint, coming in at the end of it, was the Tornado Watch.

The streets were still deserted as he drove through them and up to Forest View. The citizens might not be ready to go down into the storm cellars, but at least they had the sense to stay at home and close to shelter. He just hoped that if a twister struck there would be enough warning for everyone to hunker down in a safe hole. He made a mental note to remind the Farquhars to do just that. He didn't want the Vice-President of the United States picked up

191

and deposited outside the city limits like some unwanted welfare bum. If you could liken a Vanderhorn to a welfare bum . . .

Wilma Mae opened the door to him, ushered him in without a word as if accepting now that he had right of entry whenever he wanted it. At least for today.

Adele Farquhar came out into the hall from the study. "What is it now, Mr McKechnie?"

He had worn out his welcome with her. "I'd like to see the Vice-President. Something's come up."

"Something to do with my daughter-in-law?"

"No, ma'am. Something separate from that."

"Have you made any progress?"

"A little." But he didn't know if she would appreciate what he had learned. "Mr Vanderhorn, please, ma'am? I'm in a hurry."

She stared at him, but he couldn't read her expression. He did not know whether she was offended at being told to hurry or whether she wanted to question him further on what progress had been made. But she was not a selfish woman; she appreciated that other people had their jobs to do. She nodded, left him standing in the hall, making no attempt to be polite this time, and went upstairs. In a moment Vanderhorn came down to the hall.

"I thought you better know, sir—the roads out of town are going to be over-run pretty soon with the sheriff's men, the Highway Patrol and the FBI." He explained about the sighting of the two bank robbers.

"I'm not going, chief—"

"You will be later, sir, if you still plan to go back to Washington tonight. I have to get you over to Springfield somehow and it may be that I won't be the one to drive you—I may be needed here. If you leave now you can go with Mr Farquhar—" It was a risk, but Farquhar was the only driver he could think of right off. He couldn't turn Vanderhorn over to one of his men and Adele Farquhar

192

and Wilma Mae were not the sort of drivers to be out in weather like today's. "You'll be gone before they put up any roadblocks."

"I'm not going, chief." Vanderhorn was quietly adamant; there was nothing unfriendly about his stubbornness. "First, I'm staying with Miss Rose till the last minute. That may sound pigheaded to you, but I'm afraid that's the way it has to be. I hope you might understand the real reason why I intend staying."

McKechnie nodded reluctantly. They had had to tear him away from Paddy, even though she was dead.

"Secondly, I don't think Mr Farquhar would drive me to the end of the street. He is just as reluctant as I am to leave this house while his sister is still alive. She may die at any time and I don't think either of us would forgive ourselves—." He trailed off, made an odd tentative gesture that was out of character, like a man running out of reserves of strength.

"We'll have to get you out of here eventually, sir. I'll drive you myself, if I possibly can. But that will depend on what happens in the next hour or two. Otherwise—" He suddenly thought of another driver. "Otherwise I may have to ask Miss Barron to drive you over to Springfield. I can tell her the roads where the roadblocks will be set up and she can avoid them."

"I don't want you to get into trouble on my account. I've been thinking—in my situation, a personal one, I really don't have the right to ask any help of you."

"I've thought of that, sir," said McKechnie, trying to make his frankness sound respectful. "I'm doing it for personal reasons."

"I hope I have the opportunity some time to ask you about those. But if you're in a hurry now—"

"If you decide to leave, let me know. Call headquarters—do you have a code name, sir?"

"Yes. Charger."

"Ring headquarters and tell the despatcher that you're Mr Charger and you want to get in touch with me immediately. I'll let the despatcher know I may be expecting a call from you. She'll call me and I'll get back to you."

"You've managed to keep it secret that I'm here?"

"So far. I'll do my best to see it stays that way."

"What about the other business? Rose's sister-in-law? Any progress?"

He was trying to keep the Vice-President out of that business and the less he knew the better. But there was something about Vanderhorn's manner that made him ask, "Do you know something, sir?"

"Eh?" Vanderhorn for a moment was suddenly remote; then he recovered. "No, nothing."

But McKechnie had the feeling the Vice-President was holding something back and he was abruptly angry: the man owed him something. But you couldn't push the Vice-President for information he didn't want to divulge: Congress might, but not a small town police chief.

"We'll be in touch," he said shortly, turned on his heel and left.

He went back to headquarters. He had an urge to go home, take a quick shower, change his clothes, freshen himself up; weariness was starting to cloak him like a thickening layer of dirt, clogging his brain cells. He rented a small house on the south side of town, but he never really thought of it as home. It was no more than a place where he kept his few possessions, slept and showered. He made his own bed with a neatness that impressed the woman who came in twice a week to do his cleaning and laundry; he mowed his own lawn and trimmed the few shrubs in the garden and raked up the leaves of the scrubby elm in the back yard. He occasionally cooked for himself, but most times he ate out. After years in it he would move out of the house without regret or a worthwhile memory of it. All at once and unaccountably, for

194

envy had never been one of his failings, he felt envious and resentful of Vanderhorn, the man who never had to lift a finger to help himself. Who wasn't going to lift a finger to help *him* in the Molly Farquhar business.

Lee and the *News* photographer, Billy Greb, were waiting in the outer room when he got to headquarters. He looked at her, but spoke to Dorothy first. "Anything new?"

"Nothing chief. The sheriff and the Highway Patrol are inside. The FBI won't be here for at least an hour. Their Joplin agent is in bed with the 'flu."

"I didn't think they went down with common things like that." But it meant he would have one less organization to deal with: he restrained himself from saying *good*. He turned to Lee and Billy Greb. "What brings you in?"

"We heard about the bank robbers," Lee said. "Billy was out looking for pictures of the storm and saw Gerry Hankesen. He called me on the citizens' band."

McKechnie was against the citizens' radio band. The air was becoming too cluttered, already some of the bands were too close for comfort. Pretty soon the armchair generals in Ogallala, Nebraska, and Murphy, North Carolina, and points north, south, east and west would be chiming in on the Pentagon's band. The Tower of Babel had been granted an FCC licence . . . "Sometimes I think there is too much freedom of the press. Why don't you stay out of this till we've got it all cleaned up?"

"That's pretty Fascistic, isn't it, chief?" Billy Greb was young and enthusiastic and had the longest hair of any man in town. He had even begun to grow a beard but it had been wispy and blotchy in colour and he had given up the attempt.

"What's wrong with that?"

"Holy Pete, I never thought—"

"He's pulling your leg, Billy," said Lee. "We want the full story, Jim—that's what our readers expect. The public gets the press it wants."

195

"Or vice versa. Okay, hang around. I'll give you a few facts when we've decided what we're going to do."

"If it's a big enough story it could fill all of tomorrow's front page and keep everything else off it." Lee's face said no more than a blank sheet of paper; McKechnie cynically wondered when she had last looked so innocent. "I'm sure you'll be on our side, chief."

"I'm sure I will," said McKechnie, almost going cross-eyed trying to look equally innocent.

The real innocent, Billy Greb, twisted his face in puzzlement, but McKechnie left Lee to handle him. He went into his office, which was crowded with Jack Atcheson, the Vista County sheriff and two of his deputies and four Highway Patrol officers. The conference lasted only ten minutes, everyone eager to be out on the road and have Black and Cowman in custody before the FBI arrived and started telling them how to run things.

## II

Lew Black battled with the wheel, fighting it as the car slid and skidded from side to side of the narrow muddy track. Twice the car scraped a tree, but Black managed to keep it going. It was raining hard, but the overhanging branches, leafless though they were, broke up the downpour. The wipers flipped back and forth across the windshield, but they only marginally improved the view; the track and the trees ran off the glass like a film dissolve that didn't know when to stop. Two deer skittered across in front of the car, their wet backs much darker than their bellies, their thin legs looking much too fragile to carry them through the mud. They disappeared into the trees and Jumpy Cowman, a city boy from Miami, Florida, where deer were less indigenous than retired Mafiosi, let out a hoot.

"You see 'em, Lew! Goddam deer—how about that! We must be out in the middle of nowhere!"

Black had also been born in a city, St. Louis, but he had been educated on prison farms and become familiar with wildlife. both inside and outside the wire. " 'Cause you see deer don't mean there ain't no cops around. We gotta find somewhere where we can unload this heap."

The car suddenly stopped going forward, the rear wheels spinning wildly in thick mud. *This was where they were gonna have to leave the heap.* Then the wheels took and the car shot forward and he was wrestling with the wheel again. Then the rain suddenly stopped, the windshield within the arc of the wipers cleared and up ahead he saw the small clearing and beyond it, through a thin screen of trees, the gun-metal skin of a small lake. He drove into the clearing and only then did he see, off to one side, the small cabin and, behind it, the barn.

Cowman was first out of the car, tottering on his thin legs and having to grab at the car door to stay on his feet. It was four hours since they had last got out of the car. Black opened his door, got out carefully and stretched his arms and arched his back. For the first time he began to wonder if the heist had been worthwhile. There was only just over $4000 in the canvas bags in the trunk of the car and it seemed to him that he and Jumpy had been running for a year. He was tired and stiff and hungry and, all at once, pessimistic.

Cowman went on awkward legs, like a man on stilts, across to the cabin. He was only twenty, a tall thin stick of a boy whom Black sometimes regretted having picked as his partner for a bank heist. But he had needed someone quickly and Jumpy had been available, walking out of the pen with him that same day in Atlanta. They had looked at banks in small towns as they had worked their way west across Mississippi, Arkansas, Oklahoma and then up into Kansas. But there had always been something that had stopped them from knocking off any of those banks and he had been about to ditch Jumpy, fed up with his dumbness, when they had come into Columbus, Kansas and there was the bank just waiting to be held up. And everything would have gone all right if the cop hadn't come into the bank, tried to be a hero and frightened Jumpy into pumping two bullets into him. Black had been behind the cop, had had him covered without his knowing it, but before he could open his mouth and tell the cop to drop his gun, Jumpy had started shooting. He would dump Jumpy just as soon as they got out of this part of the country and take the four grand and head for Utah where, he'd heard, there were no coons, nervous or otherwise, and all those Mormon banks were stuffed with money.

"Hey look, Lew!" Cowman had stepped up on to the low veranda and pushed open the door of the cabin. "Someone's been using this place."

Still easing the ache in his back, the white man walked across to the cabin. He was a short muscular man, middle-aged, with a broken nose, scar tissue on both eyebrows and receding curly hair that looked as if it might have been worn back by too many bulldozing gloves. He had fought preliminaries in more cities and towns than he could remember, but he had given the fight game away over ten years ago when he had finally realized that welterweights, even good ones, no longer made fortunes. Not unless they were Mex, spicks or coons and they, being what they were, always settled for less.

He walked past Cowman into the cabin and saw at once that this wasn't a place that had been closed up for the winter and was still waiting for the owner to come here for the spring and summer. There were two thick coffee cups on the table in the room that made up virtually all the cabin; there was a partition in one corner which hid a shower and a toilet. A double bunk was in one corner of the room and two single bunks along two of the walls.

198

There were blankets on the double bunk, rumpled and thrown back as if someone had been sleeping under them. In the far corner stood a portable gas stove and beside it was a bank of shelves on which were tins of food and coffee.

It was the sort of cabin he sometimes wished for, somewhere to get away from the shit of the city. He envied the guy who could afford this sort of retreat, and then the envy made him curse the absent owner. He felt like burning the joint down.

On the table was a red leather key-case. He picked it up, bounced it up and down in his broken-knuckled hand, then on an impulse went out of the cabin, his aching back forgotten, and crossed to the barn.

"Hey, Lew, where you going—?"

Rough double doors blocked the entrance to the barn, but they were held together only by a rusted bolt. He slid it back, swung open the doors and looked in at the dirty cream Buick with the Missouri plates. He went round the car, got into the front seat and tried one of the keys in the ignition. It fitted. He switched it on and the engine started up, coughed, then died. He tried again and this time the engine caught, then settled down. He had a mechanic's ear for the sound of an engine; this one sounded rough, but it would do. The gas gauge showed almost full; enough to get them up to Kansas City. He switched off the engine, got out and went back to the cabin.

Cowman trotted after him, towering over him, flapping his big awkward hands as if they were birds he was trying to stop from flying away. "What you say, man? They's enough food there keep us for a month, man. Let's—"

"Load it in the car. Quick!"

"Which car? Ah shit, Lew, let's stay here a while—"

"In the Buick! Get the food while I get our things outa the Dodge. Move, for Crissake! Move!"

His weariness and aches had fallen from him just the

199

way they sometimes did in the last rounds of a fight. He had always been a strong finisher; his trouble had been he had been a bad starter and by the time he got to the last rounds he was always so far behind on points only a knock-out could get him a win. And he had had too few of those. But now he suddenly felt he was going to win.

It took them only five minutes to run the Buick out of the barn and fill its trunk with food, blankets, the canvas bags of money and their two cheap suitcases. Then Black ran the grey Dodge into the barn, came out and closed the doors on it.

"Hey man, how about that, eh? Finding them keys!"

"Dumb people just encourage crime, right? You ready? Okay, we're heading north again and we gonna make it this time."

"We going to Chicago, man?"

"You bet." He'd dump Jumpy somewhere north of Kansas City, then he'd head west across Nebraska and down to Utah and those Mormon banks. "You know how that song 'Chicago' goes?"

"You kidding, man? That went out with 'Swannee River'." Jumpy switched on the car radio; the violins of a symphony orchestra made him screw up his face. "Who the hell ever listens to stuff like that?"

"I do," said Black, who had never listened to a symphony in his life; but he was tired of having to put up with this dumb coon. "Leave it on."

"Ah shit, man—"

"Leave it on!"


## III


McKechnie's car was parked by the junction on Nut Ridge Road where the side road came in through the trees. The police car was off to one side, not too con-

200

spicuous to anyone coming up the straight stretch and hidden from anyone coming round the curve. McKechnie had a clear view down the straight stretch and would be able to pull out and block the roadway if he was suspicious of any car coming towards him; if Black and Cowman, or even Clint Blamey, came round the curve he would be in a position to take off after them right away. But he had been here almost half an hour and so far the main road had been as deserted as any back trail in the hill country.

Then the yellow station wagon suddenly appeared, braked sharply and pulled in behind the police car. Sighing resignedly, he got out as Lee got out of the station wagon and came up to him.

"We've done the rounds," she said. "Nothing happening anywhere."

"Thanks for the report. I've been on the air, but you can't trust anything a cop tells you. Especially Fascist cops."

Lee ignored his sarcasm. "Are you just going to sit and wait for those guys to show? Aren't you going to try and flush them out?"

"I can see you're already building up an editorial on police incompetence. Or are we supposed to be complacent? Honey, why don't you get the hell out of here, please?"

"What's happening with our friend back at the Farquhars'?"

"He's minding his own business. Which is an example we should all follow."

"I'm doing my best to keep sweet-tempered, but it's not easy. I'll be doing you a favour if I can spread this bank robbers story across Page One tomorrow and bury Molly's murder inside."

"Who are you kidding? You'll have both stories on the front page. And I know which one the town will read first. And if it leaked out that the Vice-President was in town at the Farquhars', the hold-up guys, even if we have a shoot-out with them, will finish up on the back page in the local social news. You're not about to do the Police Department any favours." He paused, then changed his tone. "But I might have to ask you to do *me* a favour."

She looked suspiciously at him. "What?"

"If I'm still stuck out here, or anywhere for that matter, trying to pick up Black and Cowman, will you drive the Vice-President over to Springfield so he can pick up his plane?"

"You've got to be joking!"

"Why?"

"Well—" Then she turned her head angrily away, looked back at Billy Greb still sitting in the station wagon. She said nothing for a moment, then looked back at Mc-Kechnie. "You really do know how to screw me, don't you?"

"That wasn't what I had in mind."

"I don't mean it that way and you know damn well I don't! I mean—" Still angry, she drummed her fist on the roof of the police car. "I'm already choking on the biggest story I'm ever likely to get and now you want to make it worse by making me part of the story. Smuggling him out of town—dammit, why can't you get one of your men to do it if you can't do it yourself? Or Gil Farquhar?"

"You're the only one I can trust."

She shook her head. "No. I haven't made up my mind yet what I'm going to do about him. I mean, so far we don't know how much is going to come out about Molly's death. If he's involved—"

"He's not." Yet he was sure that Vanderhorn knew something that he himself didn't know. "He didn't arrive here till after she was dead. Stop trying to blow the story up—like you say, it's big enough as it is. Don't start linking him to Molly's death, that's a separate issue." But even as he said it he wondered: nothing in the Farquhar

202

house was what he had first assumed it to be. But his tongue went on defending Vanderhorn: "I thought you'd have a bit of respect for the Vice-Presidency itself, if not for the man and Rose Farquhar—"

"You're not going to convince me that way, so don't try it." She stared down the road past him, not saying anything. She was not wearing a hat and her dark hair blew about her face, increasing her angry look. Then: "I'll think about it. But—"

Then the cream, mud-spattered car came round the bend and went past them, gathering speed as it did so. Lee said, "Isn't that Molly Farquhar's car?"

McKechnie wrenched open the door of his car, fell into the seat and was swinging out on to the blacktop before he had the door shut. He switched on the red light and the siren, grabbed the microphone and called the other cars as he accelerated.

"I have the missing Farquhar Buick in sight, heading north up Nut Ridge. Clint Blamey's in it, plus another guy. Try to head him off before he hits 86."

The Buick was a good quarter-mile ahead of him and he wasn't gaining on it. It disappeared round a curve at the end of the straight stretch and he followed it, having to flick the wheel as the rear end began to slide away from him. The road was slippery, streaked with mud from side roads, and he was constantly having to correct as the car threatened to take over and plunge off into the trees. The Buick was in sight again and he could see that Blamey was having just as much trouble in staying on the road. He had kept the radio open and through a blur of static he could hear the other cars responding; but he was not concerned about them now, he couldn't play police chief and keep the rogue car on the road at the same time. Suddenly, breaking out of the frustration of the whole day, he began to take risks, putting the car through curves and

203

round bends at a speed that slowly began to diminish the distance between him and the Buick.

He was coming up on the car ahead when he saw the passenger lean out, facing back towards him and taking aim with the gun. Then the windshield suddenly had a spreading star in it and he flinched to one side as the bullet hit the grille just behind his head. The car swerved and for fifty yards he was fighting it as the nearside wheels tried to take to the mud at the side of the road. Then he was back on the blacktop and the Buick had pulled ahead again, had gone round a bend out of sight.

Still shaken by the bullet that had come so close to him, he went round the bend at reduced speed and almost ran into the Buick as it finished a U-turn. It went back past him, the black passenger leaning over past the driver to take another shot at him. The bullet this time went through the window of the rear door; then the Buick was gone from sight again back round the bend. The sheriff's car and the Highway Patrol car that had been blocking the road went past with roaring engines as their drivers accelerated in pursuit of the fleeing Buick. There was a screech of tyres and in his driving mirror McKechnie saw both cars narrowly miss the yellow station wagon as it came round the bend in the middle of the road.

He swung his own car round, ignoring the silently yelling face of Lee as it hung out the window of the station wagon. He was not after Clint Blamey, after all; but Black and Cowman, the men in the Buick, might be able to tell him where Blamey was. He suddenly realized he didn't care very much about the bank robbers, that they were only another part of a day that was proving too full.

Four miles down the road he saw the five cars pulled up beside the turn-off, their occupants out and crouched down behind the screen of cars. He recognized two of his own PD cars, plus the sheriff's and the Highway Patrol's; the unmarked fifth one, he guessed, must be the FBI's.

He skidded to a stop, pulling his car into line behind the others, drew his gun and slipped out on the blind side where the other men were crouching.

"They're up there on top of that ridge, Jim." Sheriff Doug Jorgesen was a heavily-built man with a devotion to duty that was in constant conflict with his urge not to upset the citizens who voted him into office. He liked his law-breakers to be out-of-county visitors and honestly straightforward about their crimes. The men up on the ridge were just what he would have ordered. "They got their car up there somehow, but they're not gonna go anywhere. That trail just runs straight into a cliff. This is Special Agent Carradine, the FBI."

"Just a minute." McKechnie looked at Jack Atcheson crouched beside him. "Jack, get down there around the bend. I think Lee Barron and Billy Greb are following me in their station wagon. Keep them back or they might get their heads blown off. Stay there and flag down any other traffic."

"Hell, chief—" Atcheson had come out from head-quarters without asking McKechnie's permission. Like the younger men he didn't want to miss the excitement. But he was a good officer, seeing McKechnie's point about keeping this section of the road clear, and, though he scowled, he went away in a crouching run.

McKechnie looked at Jorgesen. "You got someone up around that bend ahead?"

"One of my cars. Relax, Jim, you're out in my territory, you know that? Town limits finished a coupla miles back. This is Bill Carradine."

"Sorry." McKechnie looked at the blond man in the raincoat. There's no mistaking them, he thought, once you've identified them. They manufacture them, scaled-down government issue of the Six Million Dollar Man. He guessed there had been a lot of other officers like himself who had felt a secret malicious delight when the investigations in Washington had exposed some of the FBI cogs as rusty and less than perfect. "I believe in safety first. For the local citizens, that is."

Carradine nodded and smiled with genuine warmth: this one was human. "I believe in it for myself, too. We want those guys up on the ridge, but I don't think any of us should get shot trying to bring them down. You and the sheriff know this country better than my partner and I do. What do you reckon we should try?"

"Burn 'em out," said Jorgesen. "We got more firepower than they got. Toss some tear-gas up there, then go in with everything we got. You don't care if you get 'em dead, do you?"

"We'd prefer them alive. But we'll take them dead if it means none of your men get hurt. They're dead, anyway. If they don't get the rope over in Kansas, they'll get ninety-nine and a bit. They're never going to get outside again, not after killing a cop."

"I want them alive," said McKechnie quietly.

"With all due respect, chief," said Carradine, "these guys aren't your case. We appreciate your help—"

"I've got a possible murder on my hands," said McKechnie and explained about the shooting of Molly Farquhar and his need to question the missing Clint Blamey. "Those guys are driving Mrs Farquhar's car. I want to know where they got it."

"You kept that one pretty quiet, Jim," said Jorgesen and looked at McKechnie suspiciously.

"Politics," said McKechnie and let it go at that; any sheriff in election year would understand what it meant, even if he didn't know the details. "Let's see if we can talk them out. You got a bullhorn?"

Up on the ridge Lew Black and Jumpy Cowman had left their bogged car, taken the canvas bags and were holed up in a thick stand of hickory. They couldn't see the road, but they knew there were at least three or four police cars down there. Jumpy was nervous and excited, long thin limbs bending and stretching like those of a mechanical doll that was about to run down. Black could feel the adrenalin pumping in him, but he knew he was going to get more than excitement out of this situation. He might be dead in the next five minutes.

Then the amplified voice came up the slope, tattered a little by the wind: "Black! Cowman! This is the FBI! Come down with your hands up!"

"What the hell we going to do?" Jumpy stood straight up, thin and stiff as one of the trees beside him; then abruptly he folded and sat down again. "What we going to do, man?"

"First thing, we gotta find another place." Black looked around him, saw the clump of rocks further along the ridge on the edge of the timber. He stood up, tucking the shotgun under one arm, transferring his pistol to that hand and grabbing two of the canvas bags with his free hand. "Come on!"

They had just reached the outcrop of rocks when the first of the tear-gas canisters landed among the trees only twenty yards from them. The second and third soon followed; then the top of the ridge blossomed with smoke. It lasted only a moment, then the wind whipped it away through the trees and it was gone like last year's flowers. Black, watching it go, began to laugh, felt the adrenalin quickening. Maybe they were going to get out of here after all!

McKechnie, coming up slantwise along the ridge, slipping in the wet clay, saw the smoke coming at him and ducked his head, thrusting his face into the crook of his elbow. He shut his eyes tight and held his breath; he remained crouching like a frightened man waiting to be hit. Then he lifted his head, took a quick look and saw that he was in the clear. He just hoped that the man down on

207

the road firing the gas canisters would realize that they were going to do no good in this wind.

He came up on to the top of the ridge, stood flattened against the rough trunk of a shagbark. So far there had been no shooting and the silence worried him; he could feel himself beginning to sweat and wondered if he was going to be afraid. He'd be a damned fool if he wasn't; fearless heroes rarely finished up winners. Since coming to Friendship he hadn't had to draw his gun more than half a dozen times; but today might be the first time he would have to fire it. He tightened his grip on the Magnum 357 carbine; it comforted him more than the .38 pistol in his holster. But even in New York he had never had to use a carbine.

Then the shooting started, half a dozen or more shots somewhere beyond the timber where he was hidden. He started moving towards it, running from tree to tree, slipping on the wet dead leaves, feeling the hickory nut-husks crunch beneath his boots. The firing stopped, then started again, its sound blurred a little by the wind swishing the bare branches above his head. But no one was shooting in his direction and he kept running, feeling himself beginning to heat up and the sweat starting to run on him. Then the timber started to thin out and he dropped flat behind a fallen tree in the same instant as he saw the two men crouched behind the rocks up ahead.

They were facing away from him, shooting down the slope at the FBI agents and the sheriff's men who were hidden from McKechnie's view. He wondered where his own men were; then saw Roley Trubauer off to his left, down on one knee behind a tree and aiming his carbine. But he took too long: the black one of the two bank robbers suddenly swung round and fired and Trubauer had to duck back behind his tree.

McKechnie settled his carbine on the tree-trunk, took aim. He had the black in his sights: he could kill him and

208

force the other one to surrender. His finger began to squeeze the trigger; then the black turned and looked straight at him. His finger stiffened, wouldn't move, arthritic with fear and disgust: he couldn't kill a man in cold blood again. He shifted his aim as the black brought up his shotgun, fired and the black dropped the shotgun and clutched his arm. It was a good shot, the best McKechnie had ever made: it is not easy to hit a man exactly where you are aiming for.

The white man swung round and McKechnie yelled, "Drop your gun or you're dead!"

Lew Black looked down at the shotgun in his hands. He seemed to take his time, as if debating whether to die now or later; then he threw the gun away from him and stood up, holding his hands above his head. He looked down at the moaning Jumpy Cowman and grinned sourly.

"Wasn't worth it, was it, man?"

## IV

"Where'd you get that Buick?" McKechnie said.

"No questions, pig. I wanna see my lawyer. Fuck off."

"Use that language to me again," said McKechnie, "and I'll shove this gun-butt down your throat."

"Who we got here—Billy Graham?" Lew Black looked at Carradine. "You the FBI joker? I'm your prisoner, right? Tell the pig to get lost."

They were all standing by the line of cars on the road below the ridge. Billy Greb was swooping about, camera bulbs exploding, and Lee was scribbling furiously in her notebook. Cowman, still moaning, was lying on the back seat of the sheriff's car. Black, angrily nervous, like a fighter who had just lost a close points decision, stood with the law officers grouped around him like ring officials.

McKechnie knew he had no authority here. He had captured Black and Cowman, but he was outside the town limits and they were not his prisoners. They would be taken into Vista, held in the county jail until the FBI could move them across the state line into Kansas. There was no knowing, once they were even in Vista, how long it would be before McKechnie could question them for his own purpose.

He looked at Carradine. "You're taking them in for killing the cop over in Columbus, right?"

"Not me," said Black. "It was the coon shot him, not me."

McKechnie ignored him. He looked at Carradine, hoping the latter would read what he was getting at. "The owner of the Buick is dead. I think this guy killed her."

Carradine nodded, face perfectly straight, going along with the play. "It looks like it. He's going to get it anyway for the Columbus job, whether he fired the shot or not that killed the cop. But we can tie him up properly on this Farquhar murder—"

"Hey, hold it! Who you trying to railroad? I dunno nobody named Farquhar—"

"That's her car up there and she's dead," said McKechnie. "You want to tell me where you got it?"

"Look, I tell you we never saw any dame with the car. Look, we found it—I'll tell you where—"

"You want your lawyer?"

"What lawyer? Look, we found the car up by some lake—"

# *Chapter Seven*

The President of the United States had been hoping for a quiet, relaxed Sunday. Last week had been hectic, when he had had to double as both President for the present and Presidential hopeful for next November. He had played host to a visiting Head of State who had come bearing gifts with one hand and a hand-out plea with the other. He had had to replace a Cabinet officer who, thinking he was on a sinking ship in Washington, had gone home to calmer waters where he could run for governor. He had visited four states and preached to the converted that all was not lost next November. Trying to inspire party members whose faith had begun to falter had been harder than trying to recruit converts: the political faithful, like religious believers, took mystic signs for the truth. And the mystic signs of the Gallup and other polls told them that, unless a miracle occurred, their leader would run second in November. Political brethren had less faith in miracles than their religious counterparts.

Tuesday he would be leaving Washington again on the same errand. He had looked forward to regathering his strength and his optimism this weekend. Then Willis Vanderhorn had gone and let him down by scooting off halfway across the country to say goodbye to a woman who, if her name got in the papers, would put paid to Vanderhorn's own chances of being on the ticket with him. He had never really liked Vanderhorn and only politics had made them friends; but when he needed moral support and a boost to his confidence it seemed that the Vice-President was the only one he could rely upon. Vanderhorn owed him nothing, but he was the best of counsellors. He had an unerring instinct for picking the positive aspects from even the worst of predictions and his advice for the coming week would have been invaluable.

The President had conferred with his staffers who were on duty, but fortunately that day the world at large was quiet and no meetings had had to be called. The Secret Service chief, Marvin Kerby, had been on the line to him twice to enquire about the Vice-President; each time he had told him, the second time rather sharply, that the Vice-President was safe and well and would be back in Washington that evening. Kerby had tried to persist in his request that at least he be told where Willis Vanderhorn was—"in the interests of national security, sir"—but the President had cut him off with the curt comment that *he* didn't need any lesson in national security. Maybe Willis Vanderhorn did, but he didn't voice that thought to the Secret Service chief.

He had been accustomed to keeping secrets, or anyway being secretive, when he had been a Congressman and Senator. One also had to keep secrets when one became President; but they were usually secrets shared with other members of the Administration. But now he felt he could take no one other than his wife into his confidence. Fortunately the man closest to him, his White House chief of staff, was in hospital having his gallbladder removed. Chief-of-Staff Steinlauf, who suffered from pedantry as much as gallstones, would have been a pain in the ass in this situation.

Miss Delamaide came into the office. With her was John Olney, the assistant press secretary who always took Sunday duty. He was a short, moustachioed young man who, the President thought, looked as if he would dearly love to press relations with Miss Delamaide but stood no hope against the competition of bachelor ambassadors from oil-rich countries.

"Sir, I've had the *New York Times* on the line. They've been trying to get in contact with the Vice-President about his visit to the UN tomorrow. His own press secretary is already up there in New York, but I haven't been able to raise him. I've tried Mr Vanderhorn's house and his butler said he was spending the day in bed and he wasn't to be disturbed. Is he ill or something?"

The President, politically wise, had learned that the simplest lie was often the best. "He's got some bug. I talked to him first thing this morning and he said he wanted it kept quiet and wanted nobody bothering him. He'll be okay for tomorrow."

"What do I tell the *Times*?"

He had several suggestions to that question: the *New York Times* had never been a fan of his Administration. "Tell them he's working on his speech and doesn't want to be disturbed. It's been done before, John."

The last bit of sarcasm wasn't needed, but he had that sort of tongue and it had handicapped him all his life. He, as much as other people, made him the irascible man he was.

Olney flushed, nodded and left the room. The President looked up at Miss Delamaide, who looked as if she could take the irascibility out of a bear with haemorrhoids. "Are there any newsmen out in the lobby?"

"A few, sir, not many. It's been a very quiet day, hasn't it?"

"Just the way I like it Natalie. Will you get me a line?"

"Do you want me to get the Vice-President for you?"

He gave her a sharp look: had she been listening in on those other calls? Then he recognized what she was doing: she was the sort of secretary who would always be just that much too helpful, who would always have an eye towards making herself indispensable. This girl, he thought, will never have to answer to the voters: she would never need them.

"No, thanks, Natalie. Just get me the line. Oh, could you find out how the weather is out in the Mid West? I heard on the news that they've had some bad storms out there."

"It's got worse. I heard John Olney discussing it with the reporters. You're going out there Tuesday—I hope it's all cleared up by then."

"So do I. Get me the line, please."

## I

"Washington seems perturbed about you," said Adele Farquhar, pouring tea. "I hope you prefer tea rather than coffee in the afternoon?"

"Always," said Vanderhorn, thinking again how well his mother and the woman opposite him would have got on together. "I was brought up on afternoon tea. My mother has the tea and biscuits imported from Fortnum and Mason's in London—she's not very patriotic when it comes to such things. Thank you, no sugar. The President, I'm afraid, always considers the political view before the personal."

"You mean he doesn't like tea—? Oh, I see what you mean. No, I suppose one can hardly blame him. Cake or scones? There's strawberry jam and whipped cream. Wilma Mae always giggles at the thought of a coloured girl from Missouri making a Devonshire tea. I first had it when I was playing on Broadway in one of Freddy

Lonsdale's plays. Leslie Howard played opposite me, a charming man. Is the President a tea and scones man?"

Vanderhorn shook his head, smiling. "Just about now he'd be having his first bourbon and a handful of cashew nuts. I don't think he'd be toasting my good health, either."

He had not really wanted afternoon tea, but felt it would have been ungracious to refuse. He had recognized that Adele Farquhar wanted some diversion, any prop to lean on while the hours crumbled away. As for himself he had begun to feel the pressure of being confined here and he had become impatient to return to Washington. And was deeply ashamed of himself for wishing Rose to hasten her dying.

"You should be thinking of leaving soon, Mr Vanderhorn."

Adele Farquhar sat back in her chair and, above her raised cup and saucer, studied him. They were in the drawing-room, which faced east, and the grey afternoon offered little light through the windows. She had been about to switch on some table lamps when he had asked her not to, pointing out that then he might be able to be seen from the street. So they sat in the brown-and-green gloom of the room, the furniture and drapes dulled with nothing to highlight them. The compensation was that it provided her and him with an intimacy, a dusk in which both knew something was coming to an end for them. She had been studying him all day and she had come to appreciate something of what her daughter had seen in him.

"The weather is getting worse, the radio says. If you don't leave for Springfield in the next hour, you may not get away at all."

He nodded, not arguing. He had not really concerned himself about the weather, despite the warnings by the

215

police chief and the evidence of the turbulent sky beyond the windows. All his life he had been almost totally unconscious of weather, taking it as it came: like Pascal he had his foggy and fine days within him, and he could not remember an occasion when the weather had spoiled anything for him. Some politicians watched it, especially on election days, with the apprehensive eye of a foundering sailor; but he had always had the confidence of a man living in a perpetually cloudless spring. It had helped, of course, that he had held a Senate seat for a state whose Republican sympathies were as predictable as its weather was not. But the President, in their phone talks, had twice brought up the threat of today's storms and he could no longer ignore them.

"You know I don't want to leave, not till Rose . . ." Strange, he thought, how I can't bring myself to say *dies* when I'm speaking of her. "What does the doctor think? I mean, *when*?"

"I don't know. We'll ask him when he comes down. I hope she goes soon." Her voice was quite calm and steady; but the cup rattled ever so slightly against the saucer. "She has suffered enough pain."

"She was always very good at putting up with pain. I remember once when she broke her leg ski-ing at Klosters in Switzerland, the only time we ever went to Europe in the winter. She had to be carried down off the mountain. She was in pain all the way, but she never once broke down."

"She had very beautiful legs. She inherited them from me."

"I know." Then he smiled. "I mean I know about *her* legs. Not yours."

She smiled, too: the room gleamed for a moment with some humour. "I am a vain woman, Mr Vanderhorn. I think most actresses are. Or ex-actresses. But as I remember her, Rose never was. She was a beautiful girl

216

when she was young, but she seemed to be the only one who never gave it a thought."

"She never changed. But I was vain about her—it was always one of my regrets that I could never show her off more widely."

"You are an old-fashioned male chauvinist, Mr Vanderhorn. Women today, I'm told, don't like being paraded around by their men."

"You don't approve of my being proud of Rose?"

"Of course I do. I delighted in being shown off by my husband. If it pleased him, it pleased me. And as I say, I'm vain. Unlike my children. Both of them," she said as Gilbert Farquhar came into the room.

He poured himself some tea but took nothing to eat. He sat down on a chair apart from the two of them and stared out the window, seeing nothing. "Russell Stenhouse says it won't be long now. She's almost gone."

There was silence for a few moments but for the clink of china like brittle bones. Outside the wind had its own noise, but none of them heard it. They were in another dimension of sound: death spoke to them in their own skulls. Then Vanderhorn felt the selfish fear go and the grief began to assert itself. Before she actually left the life they had lived together he tried to remember the high moments. He strained to experience again the pleasure of her as she had been before her illness; the fingertips of memory reached out to touch the flesh that had once been so warm and sensual. His mind's eye struggled to recapture sights they had enjoyed together, that had linked them like a bond: sunrise one winter morning on the Chesapeake, an avalanche one moonlit night in the Swiss Alps, some blind children in Central Park suddenly laughing with delight as the sun came out from behind rain clouds. But memory failed him: the fingertips had no sensation, the mind's eye was almost as blind as those of the children.

He suddenly had the feeling that all point, all focus, was about to die with her.

Then Adele Farquhar said, "It will be a release."

"Who for?" said her son, turning his head awkwardly to look at both of them.

"For all of us," said the mother honestly. She had never avoided the facts of life or death. "I'm sure Rose would say the same if we could ask her."

"I'm surprised you don't try. You never loved her."

"You're wrong, dreadfully wrong. But spare Mr Vanderhorn our family differences."

Farquhar hadn't touched his tea. He put down the cup and saucer and looked at Vanderhorn. "When you leave here we never want to hear from you again."

"If that's the way you want it," said Vanderhorn, looking not at him but at Adele Farquhar.

"It would be best, I suppose," she said, but sounded as if reluctant to agree with her son. *She is buried here,* Vanderhorn thought: *I wonder how much she has missed Broadway and Washington since her husband died?* "It would lessen the chances of people putting your names together."

"There is still the matter of your wife's death," Vanderhorn said to Farquhar. "How much of that will touch Rose?"

"None of it." But Farquhar sounded neither convincing nor convinced.

"Does Rose know she is dead? I mean, did you tell her—?"

"Of course not! How much do you think I want her to suffer?"

*At least we agree upon that about her.* "She knows there was a big row here last night. She heard it and asked me if you had told me what caused it."

"What did you tell her?"

"What could I tell her? You've told me nothing."

218

"Then leave it at that," said Farquhar flatly.

Vanderhorn had felt himself stiffening with anger at the other man's attitude. But now he mentally shrugged: he had enough conflicts on his hands back in Washington without taking this one away with him. "All right, we'll leave it at that."

"It would be best," said Adele Farquhar and he couldn't tell whether she was siding with him or her son.

"I'll be leaving within the hour. If she hasn't died by then—" the word was like a bitter pebble in his mouth— "I'll call from Washington this evening. When you tell me she is dead, that will be the end of it between us."

"It is a pity it has to end this way," said Adele Farquhar, encompassing the relationship of them all.

"I may as well mention something now. There will be the matter of her estate to be attended to. The house in Maryland and the one in New York are in her name. I got her to make a will just before she left to come home. She has left everything to you, Mrs Farquhar. It will come to quite a bit of money."

"What's quite a bit of money?" said Farquhar. "Your standards or ours?"

He refused to answer that, did not even look at the embittered, grief-stricken man. "Shall I have my lawyers attend to it? Perhaps you would rather they did it than have your own lawyer find out—"

"Of course. But she should not have left them to me. They are your houses—"

He shook his head. "They were hers. Everything was hers. What is the matter?"

Adele Farquhar was shaking her head. "Molly was jealous of Rose. One of the reasons was that Rose used to travel abroad, had a house in New York . . . And now I'm going to own a house in New York that Molly could have had. Do your appreciate irony, Mr Vanderhorn?"

"It is one of the elements of politics."

"Did Rose leave anything to Gilbert?"

He hesitated: it gave him no pleasure to wound the man further. "No."

Farquhar closed his eyes for a moment. Then he opened them and looked directly at Vanderhorn. "Did she ever tell you why she left here?"

Again he hesitated. Then: "Yes. But only at the end, since I came down here this morning. I asked her, the last time we spoke—"

Then Dr Stenhouse came into the room. "Ah, tea! Am I too late?"

"I'll have Wilma Mae bring in a fresh pot." Adele Farquhar rang the little silver bell on the tray: again Vanderhorn was reminded of his mother. "How is Rose?"

Stenhouse sat down, stretched his short legs in front of him. The argyle socks were a jarring note in the atmosphere of the room, confetti at a funeral. "She won't wake up again, I'm sure of that. This is when I'm all in favour of euthanasia."

"Don't be brutal, Russell." But Adele Farquhar was composed as she turned to Wilma Mae as the latter came to the door. "Some fresh tea, please, Wilma Mae."

The black woman didn't go away at once, but looked at Stenhouse. "How Miss Rose, doctor?"

Stenhouse shook his head. "Have you said goodbye to her yet?"

"Not yet. I been praying for her."

"Pray for her soul, Wilma Mae. That's all she has left now."

She stared at him, then nodded dumbly and went out to the kitchen. Stenhouse said, "They don't make them like that any more. Will your servants miss you like that when you go?"

It was a moment before Vanderhorn realized it was he who was being addressed. "Probably not. But my mother has one or two who will miss her." He wondered

220

who *would* miss him, now that Rose was almost gone. Not his wife and possibly not his children. "Perhaps things are different in this part of the country? A tradition of the servants belonging to the families."

"Not around here," said Stenhouse and looked at Adele Farquhar for confirmation; but she was isolated in her own thoughts. "Further south and back east, maybe, Alabama, the Carolinas. But not even there now. Democracy is triumphant everywhere, Mr Vanderhorn. The message just hasn't got through to innocents like Wilma Mae."

Adele Farquhar lifted her head, her eyes clearing. "I was thinking about you and Rose, Russell. When you were going out together."

"I thought you had forgotten that. It was all so long ago and for such a short time." Stenhouse glanced at Gilbert Farquhar, but the latter appeared to be ignoring him. Then the doctor looked at Vanderhorn. "Rose ever mention me?"

"No." Vanderhorn was surprised. He looked at Stenhouse with new interest, trying to see him twenty-five, thirty years ago, whenever it had been, looking at a rival from the past. "She was always very reticent about her life here in Friendship."

"Well, I was nothing to boast about. Gil knew me then. I wasn't exactly the Robert Redford of our day, was I?"

"I can't remember what you were like," said Farquhar. "Should I?"

"No." Stenhouse seemed unperturbed by the other's rudeness. "I guess you've had other things to think about."

All at once it occurred to Vanderhorn that they were all talking of Rose, the woman who was about to die. But Molly Farquhar, the woman already dead and in mysterious circumstances, was forgotten or ignored. Had she been forgotten or ignored like this when she had been alive? He began to wonder what sort of woman she had been that she had survived for so long in this sort of atmosphere. Without ever having met her he felt a sudden sympathy for her. Wells of feeling were opening up in him that he had never suspected in himself. Despite his involvement in public life and politics, he had been sheltered by his wealth; he had been protected from strangers as the man in the street could never be. Today, he recognized, might prove a watershed in his life.

Wilma Mae came back with a fresh pot of tea. Adele Farquhar poured and handed the cup to Stenhouse. "Just as it is," he said, declining sugar and milk. "No, nothing to eat. I have no taste today. That's not normal with me. Seeing Rose, I guess. I mean, thinking about her as she was a long time ago . . ."

"You don't have to bring it up," said Farquhar.

"No, I guess not. What's new on Molly's death?" Stenhouse sipped his tea, looked casually at Farquhar. A little tea, a little chat, thought Vanderhorn: Christ, what charades we go through! "Chief McKechnie come up with anything new?"

"We haven't seen him for an hour or two. Thank God."

"He came up to see me." Stenhouse continued to sip his tea. He looked at the Farquhars over the rim of his cup. "Don't worry. I was very circumspect."

Vanderhorn got up, went to a side window of the room and looked out. He had to get out of this house! Rose would understand; she had never wanted him to come down here anyway. The wind had dropped again and the sky to the west and south had darkened. But the clouds had lifted above the southern horizon; a long thin strip of strange green light hung there. It was eerie, the colour of decay. Then the horizon, a line of distant hills, seemed to be bubbling; it lifted unevenly, rising up to blot out the band of light like the upheaval of an earthquake. Then he realized he was seeing another storm coming and even while he watched the light narrowed till it was just a thin line; then it was gone and the sky was once more a boil of clouds and lightning blazed like gunfire. Far away he heard the rumbling threat of thunder.

"I think I should be going," he said abruptly.

"Who will drive you over to Springfield?" Adele Farquhar did not ask him why he had suddenly decided to leave. She knows the score, he thought, she knows I can't stand any more of this.

"Chief McKechnie is arranging that. I'll go up and have a last few moments with Rose. Then I'll call him."

Stenhouse put down his cup and saucer, walked out into the hall with him. "I spoke to Rose this morning after you arrived. I asked her if she had been happy with you and she said yes, very happy. I thought you might like to know that. She said you owed her nothing."

"She was wrong about that—I'll always owe her something. But thank you for telling me. Did you love her—I mean all that long ago?"

"Yes. I'm not an emotional man, but I wept when they called me in a few weeks ago, when I saw how she was."

"I won't be back after I leave here. Can you ensure that nothing touches her after she dies? I mean *nothing.*"

"I'll do my best, that's all I can promise."

Vanderhorn nodded. Then he said, "Why did Rose break it off with you and leave town?"

"It took me years to find out. Just as I gather it has taken you."

The front-door bell rang, tinkling like a sound from the past. The two men stood in the gloomy hallway as Wilma Mae went past to open the door.

"I mustn't be seen," said Vanderhorn and turned to go up the stairs.

"Come in, chief," said Wilma Mae, no welcome in her voice, and closed the door behind McKechnie as he stepped into the hall.

Vanderhorn came back down the stairs. "I was going to call you, chief. I think I should be leaving soon."

"I can't take you over to Springfield, sir," said McKechnie, then turned to Adele Farquhar and her son as they came to the door of the drawing-room. "We've found your wife's car, Mr Farquhar. Two bank robbers we were looking for had stolen it."

Farquhar looked puzzled; but he seemed beyond shock or surprise. "You mean they killed my wife?"

"No. They found it out at a cabin on Gilly's Lake. We've traced the owner of the cabin—it belongs to Clint Blamey's brother-in-law. I'm on my way out there now."

"Do you expect to find Mr Blamey there?" said Adele Farquhar.

There was no passion and very little emotion in the voices of either of the Farquhars, Vanderhorn remarked. Rose's impending death seemed to be all that concerned them at the moment: grief, anger, recrimination for Molly's murder would have to wait.

"I don't know, Mrs Farquhar. I just have to look for him wherever I get a lead. You and your son haven't been as helpful as you might have been, *should* have been, considering whose murder I'm trying to solve. You called me a discreet man this morning. But I'm telling you—my discretion's fast running out. When I find Blamey I'm hoping he'll clear up this whole mess. And I'm going to keep none of what he tells me off the record!"

Vanderhorn was surprised at the police chief's outburst, even though it was controlled. But he recognized the symptoms: the man was exhausted, was being asked to do more than his endurance could bear or his conscience demanded.

Adele Farquhar looked at her son, but neither of them seemed to have an answer for McKechnie. All the old woman could say was, "I'm sorry you feel that way, Mr McKechnie," then she turned and went back down the hallway towards the study. Gilbert Farquhar stood a moment, awkward and irresolute, then he, too, went down the hallway to the study. The three men left in the front hall heard the door close, gently but firmly, shutting them out like the closing of a mind against them and their arguments.

Stenhouse broke the silence that had been left in the hall. "I'll drive you over to Springfield, Mr Vanderhorn."

The Vice-President looked at McKechnie. "That would solve your problem. With all due respect to Miss Barron, I think it might be better if we didn't call on her. She might just be tempted to remember that she is a newspaperwoman."

McKechnie smiled wearily. "I'm having trouble with her that way, sir. I'd appreciate it, doc, if you would take the Vice-President over to Springfield. Only thing that worries me is the weather. If we get hit here, you might be needed."

"We've been waiting all day for it, chief. I'll keep my radio on. If a twister hits, I'll turn straight back. The Vice-President will have to take his chances on that."

"Of course," said Vanderhorn.

"I have to go down to the hospital to look at some patients." Stenhouse looked at his watch. "I'll pick you up in an hour. It'll be dark before I get you over to Springfield, but your plane will be able to take off. Is the weather still clear over that way, chief?"

"The last I heard, yes. We're just on the eastern edge of the storm belt. It's cloudy over in Springfield, but the wind's not as strong as here and they've had no rain all day. There'll be no trouble, your plane taking off, sir."

"Then I'll be waiting for you, doctor."

Stenhouse and McKechnie moved towards the front door together, but Vanderhorn put a hand on the police chief's arm. "I'd like a word with you, chief. We may not see each other again."

Stenhouse looked at the two men, paused, then nodded and went on out the door, closing it behind him. McKechnie said, "It hasn't worked out as I'd hoped, sir, but Doc Stenhouse is reliable. And," he grinned, "discreet."

"I'm sure he is. I want to thank you for your help. Perhaps I can help you."

"How?" McKechnie frowned.

"I mean about Molly Farquhar's murder. I don't know whether I really should be telling you this, but I owe it to you." He glanced down the hallway towards the closed study door, then looked back at McKechnie. "The reason Miss Rose left here twenty-five years ago, why she never came back till a month ago, was that her brother was in love with her. Still is."

McKechnie's frown deepened. "You mean *incest?*"

"It never got to that. But the situation had become unbearable for her. Her mother knew, but couldn't do anything about it."

"Who told you this?"

"Rose did, only today. She was fully conscious for a while and she talked. It was another agony for her, on top of what she was already suffering. I don't know why she told me, except perhaps she felt she had to explain the peculiar atmosphere in the house. I mentioned it to her when I first saw her, said I couldn't understand her brother's antagonism towards me. I shouldn't have done that, but we often say things we regret later. It must have preyed on her mind, because an hour or two later she told me what had happened."

"Did Molly know about it when she married Gil?"

They were speaking in whispers now, both of them facing the hallway and the closed door of the study. They were shadowy figures in the gloom: conspirators, ambushers. Whatever we are, thought Vanderhorn, we are assassinating the Farquhars. And regretted now that he had volunteered the help to the police chief.

226

"Apparently not. When she did learn of it, from then on she was always jealous of Rose. When Gil and his mother brought Rose home, that was the final straw. Molly herself told Rose that last night. She burst into Rose's room in a temper and Gil threw her out. I guess it was just after that that Molly left the house."

"Then Gil could have—?"

"Killed his wife? Perhaps. But somehow I don't think so. Do you?"

"No," said McKechnie after a long pause. "My money's still on Clint Blamey."

"I don't know about this man Blamey. I'll be interested to know if he does turn out to be the murderer."

McKechnie looked at him, man to man. "I don't think you will. When you leave here, you don't want any part of this catching up with you, no matter how indirectly. You'll want to forget as much of it as you can."

"Jim? Jim, you're right. I'd give anything to walk out of this house and forget everything I've heard and seen here, including watching Rose die. But that's selfish and impossible."

"Knowing how Gil feels—he must be as jealous of you as Molly was of Miss Rose—I don't know if I should leave you here with him for the next hour."

"I'll be all right." Vanderhorn had never been lacking in courage: at least physical courage, he told himself. He had been a coward for far too long about his relationship with Rose. "He's completely shattered now. He won't attempt anything."

"I don't know—"

"I'll be all right, Jim. Really. I'll be gone soon and he'll be glad to see me go. He's not going to try to do anything to me in front of his mother. She's my protection." He held out his hand. "Don't worry. You've done your job and done it well. If ever you come to Washington, let me know." Then he smiled. "That's if you come before next

227

Inauguration Day. After that I may be somewhere else. I read the editorial in Miss Barron's newspaper this morning. Even this early she thinks the election result is a foregone conclusion. She just wonders if the Democratic Vice-President, whoever he may be, will be an improvement on me."

"I haven't read this morning's paper yet," said Mc-Kechnie "I'll have a word with Lee, tell her bias is a bit obvious."

"Let her be. It's all part of the game, I've been used to it all my life." His smile broadened, became the famous Vanderhorn smile. "Ask her if she'd like to be taken over. The family own a chain of newspapers out west. We could do with a voice down here."

"I wouldn't be game." McKechnie returned the smile; the men were all at once old friends. "Good luck."

"You too, Jim."

## II

McKechnie and Roley Trubauer sat on chairs just to one side of each of the cabin's two windows. McKechnie looked down towards the lake and Trubauer looked out at the barn. If Clint Blamey came from the blind sides of the cabin he would still have to come within the view of at least one of the men to get to the barn. If he came at all . . . McKechnie wondered if this stake-out was going to be a waste of time. There was no reason why Blamey should come back here to the cabin except to change his own car for Molly Farquhar's and hope to get away in that. It was a long shot, but it was a day when all the odds had been as unpredictable as the weather.

He glanced out of his window at the sky. The weather had abruptly calmed again; the turbulent clouds of even twenty minutes ago had smoothed out into a dark grey bank that held no threat at all. The wind was still blowing, causing a few whitecaps at the edges of the lake, but even its force had decreased.

He sat slumped on the hard wooden chair, his feet propped up in front of him on the end of the double bunk. He was still trying to absorb what Vice-President Vander-horn had told him. It all fitted, explained a lot of things he had not understood. But he had had no experience of incestuous love. Incest yes, the sexual side of it: he had seen evidence of that in the New York ghettos. He did not condemn Gilbert Farquhar for what he had felt for his sister; he had always tried not to judge other men's failings. It was a philosophy that had its dangers for a policeman, but he had always been sensible enough to know where to draw the line. He had understood how junkies could become addicted to heroin; but, emotionally if not sensibly, he had drawn the line when the junkie had killed Paddy. He had no way of knowing, yet, what tragedy Gil Farquhar had caused; certainly, one way or another, directly or indirectly, he had caused his wife's death. But McKechnie couldn't see the lonely awkward man as a murderer. But then, looking back, he couldn't see him as a man who had held his agonizing secret for so long.

"My ass is beginning to ache," said Roley Trubauer.

"Sit a while longer. If he's watching the place and you move around inside here, he might see you."

Their cars were half a mile away, parked off the high-way in the scrub, and they had walked up through the timber to the cabin. The three young officers were hidden out in the woods and Bud Grierson was in one of the cars down by the road. McKechnie had brought a walkie-talkie with him and every five minutes he called Grierson to check on traffic down on the road. He and Trubauer had been in the cabin for fifteen minutes and the only sign of movement they had seen were flights of mallards taking off and landing on the lake. The ducks should be heading north at this time of year, but he guessed they had their own radar that told them the flight paths north of here were as stormy as those in Vista County. The afternoon was darkening and already McKechnie had begun to wonder whether he should not call it a day and take the men back to town. It had been a long hard day for all of them, particularly for himself and Roley Trubauer, and tomorrow was not going to postpone itself for them. If they got no twister today, they could still get one tomorrow.

"I used to fish a lake like that 'un when I was a boy, down near Clarkesville. Go out with my old man and we'd come home loaded down with bronzeback, bluegill, catfish, you name it. Never saw a lake with so many danged fish in it. We fed on fish all through the Depression. They say fish is a brain food, I oughta be the brainiest feller in the state. I ain't, so that disproves that theory. My old man used to take some of the catch up to the bootleggers in Joplin, fellers who were running liquor over the border into Kansas. They were the only guys had money to spend in them days. Joplin was a real busy town them days, you hadda keep your eye out crossing 7th Street, that's the one ran straight through into Kansas, or you might get run down by a bootlegger's truck. My old man'd sell 'em the fish and come back with enough money to keep us going a little while longer."

"I'm too young to know what the Depression was like."

"It was never too bad down heres, not like in the cities. Even so, my old man, he was alive today, he'd think he was in paradise or something. Maybe that's where he is anyways, though I doubt it. I doubt it." Trubauer put his feet up on one of the single bunks in front of him, took out a jack-knife and began to scrape the mud from his boots. "He used to wear split-leather boots, danged uncomfortable things. Coveralls, too—they were the uncomfortablest pants a man ever hadda get into. Used to get 'em by mail order from Sears Roebuck. Sometimes

230

they'd be stiffer'n the goddam boots, cut a man in half up through his crotch. Then J. C. Penney opened a store down our ways, brought out some coveralls had a softness to 'em. First time a working man felt comfortable going to work. Fellers got some feeling back into their crotch, it was like having your balls packed in feathers after them other ones." He looked out the window at the barn. "You really think Clint's gonna come out here?"

"I don't know. Maybe he's in Kansas City by now. Or Joplin, heading down 7th into Kansas like your old man's bootleggers. But we had to stake this place out, just in case."

"You ever do much staking-out in New York?"

"Once or twice." He wasn't going to talk about New York, not today; he hadn't the strength to bear another revival of memories of Paddy. He flicked on the walkie-talkie, kept his voice low. "Any movement down your way, Bud?"

"Nothing. One car's gone past on this road since you left. I think the storm's kept everyone at home today. How long we gonna sit this out, Jim?"

McKechnie looked at his watch. "Another fifteen minutes. I'll call you when we're coming in."

He switched off, put down his feet and straightened up in the hard uncomfortable chair. He wondered how many times Clint Blamey and Molly Farquhar had come out here to meet and make love. Had she become pregnant right there on the double bunk?

"She must of been danged unhappy."

"Who?"

"Molly Farquhar." Roley Trubauer, boots cleaned, put his feet down and looked about the cabin. "I used to see her there in church Wednesday nights, up there in the front pew, singing with her ass sorta moving in tune—I always admired her ass—"

"You told me that."

Trubauer nodded, sat for a moment lost in the reverie of an ass moving in tune to a hymn. McKechnie himself couldn't conjure up the same picture, but maybe they had different rhythms to their hymns in the First Baptist. None of the hymns he had ever learned from the nuns and priests had ever set any asses swinging, not even his own. But maybe things had changed: he had never been to a folk Mass and maybe there was a lot of swinging there . . . Suddenly he sat up absolutely straight. "She went to *your* church?"

"Sure. Every Wednesday night the past coupla months."

"I thought she was an Episcopalian. The Reverend Arber was up to their house this morning."

"Mebbe she went there Sundays, I dunno. I dunno. But she started coming to our church and nobody told her to stay away. Mebbe she figured that was the only way she was gonna meet Clint, if it was him she had her eye on. He used to be a real regular when his missus was alive. Then he sorta dropped off, but he started coming back again five, six months ago. Molly, she was regular once she started with us. I think she could of been lonely. Lonely. She was a joiner, ever I seen one. 'Bout the only thing in town she didn't belong to was the American Legion. I ain't thought 'bout it befores, but mebbe she was looking for someone just like Clint. Some widower feller she could run away with. She could of run away with me, some of the thoughts I had. Don't tell that to the missus." He looked around the cabin again. "This wasn't much of a place to run to."

"She was aiming further than here. California."

"That wouldn't be no better'n here," said Trubauer, unimpressed.

People dying under your very eyes, McKechnie thought, and you never see it. He wondered how many other people in town were as unhappy as Molly Farquhar had

232

been, were looking for escape. Friendship had never *appeared* an unhappy town; its peacefulness had seemed real enough to him to make him content. A police chief, along with the doctors and clergymen, was the one in any town who should recognize the unrest and melancholy among its citizens. But he had missed it in Molly Farquhar, at the time. Looking back now he saw the signs, but it was too late. He wondered if Dr Stenhouse, who had never had Molly as a patient but had known of Gil's impotence (had he also known of Gil's love for his sister? But that was something he couldn't ask the doctor), had recognized what had been happening to Molly?

"You were saying Mrs Farquhar and Wilma Mae went out to Clint's place last night." Trubauer stretched and yawned. "Jeez, I'm tired. Can't remember when I been outa bed this long. Mebbe that's why it slipped my mind."

McKechnie waited patiently, experienced in Roley Trubauer's way of getting to a point. Over on the other side of the lake he saw a flight of ducks take off, keeping low against the wind. Idly he wondered why any birds would choose to be aloft on a day like this.

"I was out along 86 this morning, 'bout four o'clock, four-fifteen, just cruising, you know. I saw a car pulling into Clint's place. I was about a quarter-mile down the road when I saw its lights swing in there . . . It must of switched off the lights, 'cause when I went past I couldn't see it."

"You didn't investigate?"

The ducks, giving up against the wind, had landed with a spatter of silver on the corrugated lake a couple of hundred yards from where they had taken off.

"Why would I? I just thought it was Clint coming home late from up in Joplin or somewheres. People coming home late Saturday night, Sunday morning early, ain't nothing unusual in that."

"So it could've been Clint and Molly?"

233

"Could of been. But where would they have gone? I mean, you said they were there at the farm when Mrs Farquhar and Wilma Mae were out there. Why would Clint and Molly go driving around the middle of the night, especially a night like last night? Don't make sense."

"Why were you out on 86 at four o'clock in the morning?"

"It's part of my beat." Trubauer looked around, jack-knife still open, as if seeking something to whittle.

"I know. But you were out there twice—four o'clock and again when you called me about the twister, around seven."

Trubauer ran the blade up and down the butt of his hand, then closed the jack-knife. "I was getting a bit of peace and quiet. Out there there's nobody to worry a man if he wants to snooze a little."

It was no crime for a cop to take a cat-nap when on duty: McKechnie had been guilty of it himself in New York. But he hadn't expected Roley Trubauer to drive out of town to do it, especially as far out as the Blamey place.

"Were you out that way earlier in the night? When Molly drove out there?"

"I didn't come on till midnight, you know that. What you getting at, Jim?"

*Jesus, I'm even beginning to suspect one of my own men!* Then a movement caught his eye and he stood up, peering out the window. "Here comes someone across the lake."

The rowboat had come out from the far shore where the mallards had taken off. When it had first left the shore it had been indistinguishable against the dark background of trees; now it was fifty yards out, rocking on the wind-chopped water. The man in it, pulling hard against the wind and water, head bent so that from the cabin he looked headless, was unrecognizable at the distance. But

234

McKechnie, his bones prosecuting him again, knew it was Clint Blamey.

McKechnie flicked on the walkie-talkie. "This is McKechnie. You hear me, everyone?" The three young policemen and Bud Grierson responded. "He's coming across the lake."

"I see him, chief," said Andy Lowther, the closest man to the lake shore. "Looks like he's gonna come in right below the cabin.

"Looks like that to me. Stay where you are, let him come ashore and up to the cabin or barn. You can come out behind him if he tries to make it back to the boat. No shooting, you understand? I want him alive."

"What if he starts shooting at us, chief?" said Gerry Hankesen.

"I want him alive," McKechnie repeated.

"Okay, chief." But even the static did not blur the chagrin in Hankesen's voice. What was a cop supposed to do, be a sitting target for every guy wanted to take a shot at him?

*You'll learn*, McKechnie told him silently. He switched off, looked across at Roley Trubauer. "You heard what I said."

Trubauer shrugged. "We'll get him okay. Clint's not the sorta guy is gonna start shooting down fellers he's been saying hello to all his life."

"He took a shot at Gil Farquhar this morning." But he was looking at the suddenly sullen Trubauer, another surprise in a day of surprises. The admirer of Molly's ass . . .

"That was something personal between him and Gil. You can ask him about that pretty soon. Here he comes. What you wanna do?" Trubauer had taken his pistol from its holster. "Let him come right into the cabin with us?"

"That'll surprise him the most."

McKechnie took his gun out of his holster, checked it,

released the safety catch. He had no intention of shooting Clint Blamey; he had not even thought of handling his gun till he had seen Trubauer with his. His weariness slid off him and he felt a surge of excitement. In a few minutes he might know the answer to all the questions that had plagued him since early morning. He glanced across at Trubauer, wondered if he was going to be part of the answer.

The rowboat slid into the shore. The man stood up and got out. It was Clint Blamey, all right. He was dressed in gaberdine trousers, a red-and-black checked mackinaw and a faded blue long-peaked cap; he could have been any man out for a Sunday's fishing on the lake. He looked around him, then pulled the rowboat further up in the mud at the water's edge. He straightened up, looked around again, then came up towards the cabin and the barn. He was still looking around him and McKechnie, watching him through the grimy window, hoped that Andy Lowther and the other two men were well out of sight in the timber.

Blamey came to a halt no more than five or six yards from the cabin porch. McKechnie, flattened against the wall inside, peering sideways through the window, everything outside distorted by the angle of sight through the cheap glass, suddenly lost him. Had Blamey seen them? Then he remembered: there would be their footprints in the wet earth below the porch. He raised his gun, was about to move, when, looking across at Trubauer, he saw Blamey pass beyond the other window.

McKechnie quickly crossed the room, stood beside Trubauer and watched Blamey go to the barn. He paused, looked down at the twist of tyre tracks in the mud. Then abruptly he snatched at the bolt on the barn doors, whipped it back and swung open the doors. He looked at the grey Dodge as if it might have been a tank or a

Conestoga wagon or a chariot, something wild and incredible.

McKechnie opened the cabin door, moved out to the end of the porch and levelled his gun. "Hold it, Blamey! Don't move! You're covered all around!"

## III

Blamey didn't move. He surrendered so readily that McKechnie felt ridiculous at the way he had levelled his gun at him. He submitted without any attempt to move even a pace. He held out his hands for Roley Trubauer to put the cuffs on them without being asked. He nodded to the two officers as they approached him, their guns still held ready; it was the same sort of nod McKechnie had got from him when they had passed each other in town on other days, in other circumstances. When the three young officers came out of the timber he nodded to them too, but still said nothing. All through the walk back down the track to the road he remained silent, making no answer whenever McKechnie or any of the others spoke to him.

"You drive my car, Roley," said McKechnie. "I'll ride in the back with Clint."

He and Blamey got into the back of the car, separated from Trubauer by the grille. Andy Lowther took over Trubauer's car. Gerry Hankesen took his car out in front to lead the small convoy. He set his siren going as they went down the road.

"Shoot," said Trubauer and looked over his shoulder at McKechnie. "We need that goddam thing going?"

"Tell him to shut it off. But keep the roof light on. We don't want someone running into us. It's getting pretty dark."

Trubauer reached for the microphone and a moment later the wail of the siren died away. The four cars went

237

down the highway, their spinning red lights a tiny galaxy in the darkening day. The wind had increased and it had begun to rain again. Lightning flashed, killing the world for a moment; everything was frozen in the blue-white light and rendered colourless; even the red lights disappeared. Then the grey rain, the blue cars, the red lights, the black-and-grey trees rushed back. Thunder broke immediately overhead, so loud the skull rang with it, and up ahead the lead car wavered on the road as if the sound had physically hit it. The convoy slowed, but almost at once the rain stopped and there was no more thunder and lightning. Hankesen speeded up again and the convoy drove on under a sky lightening from black to grey.

When they reached headquarters McKechnie helped Blamey out of the car but let the farmer, without man-handling him, walk ahead into the building. Blamey, he was sure now, had welcomed his capture.

Dorothy Kidmann looked at the prisoner with frank curiosity: she had never seen a murderer before, especially one she knew by name. McKechnie had to ask his question twice: "Dorothy, what's the weather situation?"

"Eh? Oh sorry, chief. Still the same, maybe a bit worse. They had a bad hailstorm down in Armaville twenty minutes ago."

Armaville was south-west, fifty miles away. Maybe the storms would by-pass them yet. He turned round and was blinded as Billy Greb shot off a globe right in his and Clint Blamey's faces. He swore and struck out a hand; it hit Greb's camera as the photographer stepped back hurriedly. McKechnie's gaze cleared and he looked at Lee as she stepped forward.

"When are you going to make a statement, chief?"

"I'll make you one now that'll be unprintable."

"Try me." Lee looked at Blamey. "Do you have anything to say, Mr Blamey?"

238

"If he has, he'll say it to us," said McKechnie. "Now get out of the way before I have you canned."

Lee stepped aside. "We'll wait here till you're ready with your statement."

"It's a free country," said McKechnie. "Unfortunately."

"Fascist," said Billy Greb.

McKechnie pushed the still-silent Blamey ahead of him into his office. He went in, sat down behind his desk and looked up to see Trubauer standing in the doorway.

"I thought you might need some help, chief."

"I'll call you if I need you."

Trubauer hesitated, then nodded and went down the hall to the off-duty back room. Bud Grierson took his place in the doorway with two cups of coffee.

"Coffee, Clint?" His tone was friendly. These two, McKechnie realized, had probably known each other all Blamey's life.

Blamey shook his head, saying nothing, but took the cup as Grierson pushed it into his manacled hands. Grierson handed the other cup to McKechnie. "You want me to come in and take down what Clint says?"

"Not yet, Bud."

Grierson nodded encouragingly to Blamey and went out of the room. McKechnie, sipping his coffee, looked across at his prisoner, wet, bedraggled, pitiful. The man had given up, but there was no way of knowing if he was ready for confession. Confession was good for the soul: McKechnie remembered that from his schooldays with the nuns and priests. But that was only so if you still had faith. And Clint Blamey looked as if he no longer had faith in anything.

"You want to talk, Clint? Before we get your lawyer here?"

Blamey suddenly gulped down his coffee, like a man dying of thirst. He reached across and put his cup on the desk, then sat back on the hard-backed chair, trying to compose himself. He was not a handsome man, particularly now with his face pale and strained beneath the long bill of his cap: exhaustion never did anything for anyone's looks, McKechnie thought, and wondered how he looked himself. Before he had got his detective's badge he had once been on duty at a track meet on Randall's Island in New York. He had admired some of the girl athletes, beautiful and sexy in their tight track shorts; the most beautiful of them had been a 400-metre runner and she had pulled up right in front of him after her race and she had looked like her just-exhumed grandmother. Clint Blamey was more accustomed to exhaustion than that girl had been, but he had probably never been through a night and day like the one he had just experienced. The flesh hung on his face like pale beige crepe and the dark eyes, which McKechnie remembered had once held a quiet humour, looked out with the hopelessness of a man who wouldn't have cared if he were blind.

"What's the use of talking?" He had a soft voice, the voice of a man who spent hours on his own in the fields. "You got me here in jail. I've done with running, chief."

McKechnie reached for the tape recorder on the shelf behind him; then changed his mind and turned back to face Blamey. Now was not the time to interrogate him properly; both of them were weary, the questions might be no sharper than the answers. And Blamey might give some answers that would be better if they were not taped. *I'm still protecting that house up on Forest View, damn it!*

But there was one question he had to put to Blamey: "Why did you kill Molly Farquhar?"

The hands folded together with a metallic clink. "You know I didn't do that, Jim. I loved her. Why would I want to kill her?"

McKechnie believed him at once. Blamey was too ex-

240

hausted, too despairing, to lie convincingly. "You did take a shot at Gil Farquhar, didn't you?"

Blamey nodded. "I must've been out of my head. I was, I guess. I've been that way ever since I got back home this morning and found Molly dead."

"You think he killed her?"

"I did. Now I don't know."

"Why would he have wanted to kill her? Because she was running away with you?"

"We weren't going to run away together."

McKechnie frowned. "She had two airline tickets for Los Angeles—?"

"They weren't for me and her. She came out to say goodbye, that was all. She was going to come out this morning, she said, early and say goodbye then. But then there was a big row at the Farquhar place last night and she came out to meet me at the cabin. She phoned me from somewhere in town and asked me to meet her there. Then I took her back to my place, tried to talk her into not running away."

"Did you know she was pregnant?"

"Not till last night. She told me then. Jesus God! Poor Molly." The dark hopeless eyes filled with tears; he raised his manacled hands and wiped his cheeks. "Everything went wrong for her."

"You said, *when you got back home this morning*. Did you leave her alone at your place?"

Blamey nodded. "About an hour, maybe less. We'd been arguing all night—the first time we'd ever done that." He dropped his head, made a sound that was half-sigh, half-sob. Still looking down at his manacled hands he said, "The argument started while we were out at the cabin. That's where we've been meeting the past, I dunno, four, five weeks. The cabin belongs to my brother-in-law up in Jefferson, he only uses it in the summer. We used to go there because we didn't want anyone to see her car at

241

my place. Roley Trubauer, for instance. I've seen him parked out along the highway from my place lots of times."

"Go on," McKechnie said as Blamey paused.

"When we were out at the cabin last night, that was when she said she was going away for good, that she wasn't ever going back to her place." He looked up. "Only she never called it her place. She used to call it the Farquhars', like it was some boarding house for her, that was all. So I took her back to my place and we continued to argue—I told her that maybe in a year or two, when things got better for me, I'd marry her if she got a divorce from Gil. That was when she told me she was pregnant."

McKechnie had a question about that; but he wanted to keep things in sequence. "When did Mrs Farquhar and Wilma Mae turn up?"

"I dunno. Just after we got back to the farm, not long, maybe ten minutes. I didn't say much to them, practically nothing. They accusing me of anything?"

"Not so far. Not Mrs Farquhar, anyhow."

"But Gil is, right? The son-of-a-bitch!" Blamey shook his head in despair. "I wish I'd shot him."

"Easy, Clint. You're making statements you may be sorry for later."

Blamey nodded. "Yeah. Thanks, Jim. Well . . . Well, Mrs Farquhar and Wilma Mae went home, leaving that danged gun there. Jesus God, if she hadn't left that—it was the one he killed her with, wasn't it?"

"Who?"

"Gil?" But it was a question now, not an accusation. He had been sitting hunched forward for the past minute, but now he slumped back. He lifted his hands as if to fold his arms, found he couldn't and let his hands drop back into his lap. He was like a man beginning to realize that terminal paralysis was setting in. He was still living, but his life was over. "I don't know. It was Wilma Mae brought the gun into the house. She had it wrapped in a scarf or something. I got scared she was going to use it, I dunno why or who she was going to shoot, but I took it off of her. She gave it to me without any trouble and I put it down on the table in the kitchen—that was where we all were. Then they must've forgotten it, they went off without it."

"What did Mrs Farquhar and Molly talk about?"

"I don't know. I got up a coupla times and went out of the kitchen. It got a bit het up one time—I heard Mrs Farquhar slap Molly's face."

"Did Molly ever tell you anything about her and Gil and his sister Rose?"

"No." Blamey looked surprised. "Why?"

Then the Farquhars' secret was still safe. "Nothing. Why did you go out on your own? Where'd you go?"

"I had to get out of the house, I couldn't stand fighting with her any more. I mean I didn't hate her or anything like that, it just hurt me, what she had told me about her being pregnant. I just walked out, telling her to sit down alone and think about what she was going to do."

"Where'd you go? Did you take your car?"

"No. When I walked out the door I didn't know where I was going, what I was gonna do. I just kept on walking right on down the road. Then I thought I'd walk right on out to the cabin, it's only five or six miles from my place, and I'd bring her car back and she could go home and nobody, I mean nobody in town, would know what she'd had in mind."

"That's a fair step out to the cabin."

"Only to someone who never goes anywhere without his car."

I should have taped that bit, thought McKechnie, let Jack Atcheson and the other men hear it.

"I like walking, always have. My wife—" He raised his hands, looked at them with a sudden puzzled frown,

243

as if wondering if his dead wife would believe what was happening to him now. "My wife and me, we used to go walking every Sunday in the woods."

"Did you get as far as the cabin?"

"No. The wind started to come up pretty strong and it was so dark I couldn't see a foot in front of me. And it started raining. So I turned back. When I got home there she was, lying on the floor beside the bed in the front room. I couldn't believe it. At first I thought she'd committed suicide—"

"She could have. I found the gun on the bed. She could've shot herself, then fallen on to the floor."

Blamey shook his head. "The gun was lying in the hallway, like someone had dropped it there. I kicked it when I came into the house and I picked it up and went into the bedroom with it. It was me dropped it on the bed. I just threw it there when I saw her—"

"Were you still there when the twister hit this morning?"

"No."

"Where were you?"

He looked at his hands again, clinked them together. Then he looked up. "I think I better have a lawyer, Jim."

McKechnie gazed at him steadily, trying to guess what else Blamey might have to tell. But the lean sad face told him nothing; there was no cunning in the hopeless eyes, just a shutting down. It seemed that Blamey had said all he was going to say for the time being. But McKechnie tried another question: "Did you see Roley Trubauer's car out there when you left this morning?"

"No."

"Why did Molly wait three months to tell you she was pregnant?"

"I don't know. Shame, maybe. She knew I was a religious man."

"That puzzled me. Why did she start going to the First Baptist?"

Blamey turned his head from side to side, as if embarrassed. He was, as he said, a religious man and conceit was not one of his sins. "She came because of me. She told me she'd picked me out as the father of her child, if things didn't work out as she hoped. She was a queer mixture, Jim, wicked at times. But I excused her because of the way things were up at the Farquhar place. She tempted me and I fell. Or almost did." He dropped his head like a man seeking penance.

"What do you mean by *almost*?"

"I couldn't bring myself to commit adultery. I wanted her, but she was still Gil's wife. I believe in the commandments—thou shalt not covet thy neighbor's wife . . ."

"But you got her pregnant."

Blamey lifted his head sharply. "I never went to bed with her. That's why she didn't tell me till last night about the baby. It was another man's, the feller she's been sleeping with for the past year!"

McKechnie sat back, all at once overwhelmed. It had been a long hard day and now he was back at taw. Unless . . . "Was it a man from around here? Someone else who might have gone to the First Baptist?"

"She never told me who he was. Only that she used to go up to St Louis to see him once a month, regularly. She'd fly up there and he'd drive up."

McKechnie suddenly stopped thinking of Roley Trubauer. Every officer on the roster had to leave notice with headquarters where he could be found. Trubauer could not have gone to St Louis once a month for a weekend. He might take cat-naps out on Route 86 when he was supposed to be patrolling elsewhere, but he had never missed a call to return to emergency duty.

"Did she say anything else about him?"

"Just one thing." Blamey leaned back, lifted his manacled hands in front of him; the fingers were steepled together, as if he were praying. He closed his eyes and for a moment McKechnie thought he was indeed praying. Perhaps he was: for the soul of Molly Farquhar: "She said something vicious, wicked, that I wish I'd never heard. She said she had got her revenge on Rose Farquhar. She'd got herself pregnant by the only man in Friendship that Rose had ever loved."

# *Chapter Eight*

Perhaps the National Severe Storms Forecast Center in Kansas City had erred in maintaining its warning bulletins throughout the day. For several periods it did reduce the cautionary messages to a Tornado Watch, but then it went back to issuing the more serious Tornado Warning. Its own radar screens and those of the various Weather Service Offices throughout the Central Region kept showing "hook echoes", the weather men's trade name for embryo tornado formations on their screens. Looking like a drunk's scrawl of the number six, it hangs below the larger, shapeless mass of a severe storm system. The hook echo signifies a whirling tail of moisture or hail, and weather men, seeing it on their screens, take it as a warning that a tornado is developing. Such a development may peter out before it becomes dangerous, but the radar screens of the Central Weather Region were that day plagued with hook echoes.

So the Tornado Warnings were renewed and eventually, like bad static, became only an irritant to the radio listeners and television viewers. It is of the nature of a great many people to be suspicious of warnings of disaster, especially when issued by a government department; they take heed of the astrology columns in their newspapers, willingly part with money for a session with a clairvoyant, shudder when they break a mirror; but they are sceptical of any warning a government department gives them. Especially if the warning isn't immediately followed by the predicted disaster. But the weather circumstances that Low Sunday warranted the intermittent warnings and the Center had to take the risk that the people in the threatened region would not be lulled into thinking that the boys up in Kansas City were crying *Wolf*!

Not all the populace of the Central Region ignored the warnings. Those who had already been hit by twisters in the morning phoned relatives and friends further north and the word spread. The wise and cautious prepared to go to their storm cellars or, if they did not have a cellar of their own, marked down some safe place to retreat to as soon as they saw the awesome funnel approaching. They went about their Sunday business, but every time they passed a window they looked out; some husbands remarked that the windows were not as clean as they might be and domestic storms blew up as to whose job it was to keep them clean. Even most of the cautious were convinced that no tornado would hit their place. The more mathematical-minded of them remembered figures they had seen: that the probability of a twister striking a given point in the area most frequently subject to the storms was once in 250 years. No town in their region was more than 150, 160 years old at the most: so . . . There is no proof in history that fools have been proved wrong more often than wise men.

The warm air coming up from the Gulf of Mexico finally arrived at a stand-off with the cold front over northeast Oklahoma and south-west Missouri. The cold heavy air covered the region, stationary now like an occupying army. The warm moisture-saturated air arrived, found its path blocked and tried to climb above the cold cover. It pushed at the front above it, much like thermal springs

248

come to life and trying to break through the crust of the earth. It succeeded in certain weak spots, rising and drawing the cooler air into a high-speed spin. The spinning motion began to form a hollow column, as a potter's wheel forms a bowl. The column, unable to rise further against the cold cover, turned and reached downwards. It went down through the lower cover of cloud, taking some of the cloud with it. It was white at first, because it was only air and moisture and so far had not sucked up any debris to darken it. It began to darken at once as it hit the ground ten miles south of Friendship.

# I

McKechnie grabbed his cap, went out of his office and down the hall to Bud Grierson's room. "Lock Clint up. Don't worry about the charges just yet. Get him his lawyer if he wants one. I'll be back in ten minutes."

"Where you going?"

"The Farquhars'." He went back to his own office, hurrying to get there ahead of the slow-moving Grierson. "Clint, answer no more questions till I get back—it'll be for your own good. You understand? Just say nothing!"

Blamey was puzzled. "You on my side or what, Jim?"

But McKechnie didn't answer that. Grierson was already behind him in the doorway; and anyway he had committed himself too much today. He wanted no more weights around his neck; already he could feel the burden of another one coming up. He nodded to Grierson to take over Blamey, pushed past him and went out through the front office. He told Dorothy Kidmann he would be back in ten minutes, that he was going up to the Farquhar house, and went on out to his car.

Lee ran out after him. "What are you going up there for?"

He had forgotten she and Billy Greb were still at headquarters. "It's none of your business! You shouldn't have been eavesdropping—"

"Oh, come off it! I wasn't eavesdropping—you could be heard all over the office. What are you going up to the Farquhars' for? Has Clint Blamey made a confession? Given you some new information?"

He hesitated, then snapped, "Get in! The car, dammit —get in!"

She looked surprised, but there was no hesitation on her part; she was in the car as quickly as he was. He took the car out of the parking lot with a screech of tyres, swinging it out into the street in front of a pick-up that had to brake sharply. He went round the square, which was one-way, with tyres still screeching and slowed only fractionally as he went straight through the red light on the north-west corner.

"Hadn't you better use your siren if you're going to drive like that? I haven't written either of our obituaries yet."

His hand went towards the switch, then he pulled it away. "No. We don't need it."

"I hope you're right. What's the hurry, anyway?"

"I'll tell you later. Have you made up your mind whether you'll take the V-P over to Springfield?" He slowed as he came to the curve that led up to Forest View; he didn't want people rushing out of their houses to see why he had arrived in such a hurry. "I need to know *now*."

She said nothing till they had climbed the curve and straightened up into Forest View Drive itself. "I'm sorry, darling. I can't. Not now you've got Clint Blamey down there at headquarters. That's my story now—his murdering Molly Farquhar. I can't leave that—"

He slowed the car, pulled it up at the entrance to the Farquhar driveway. There was no police car guarding the house; he hadn't sent Jack Atcheson back up here. The old blue Cadillac stood at the bottom of the front steps. The big house, the copper cupola on its tower looking greener than he remembered it, as if it had been newly painted, appeared as solid and secure as it had ever been. It was difficult to imagine the storms that had gone on behind its windows and doors.

"I need you, Lee. Really. I've got to get the Vice-President out of town *now*—and you're the only one who can do it for me."

She shook her head. "I'm sorry. I won't write a word about him and Rose Farquhar, but that's all I can promise you. But I've got to stay here and write up everything that breaks on Clint Blamey and the murder of Molly."

"You've got other reporters."

"I'm the *editor*. As police chief, do you run off when something big breaks down at headquarters? I don't see you offering to drive the V-P over to Springfield."

He had wanted to keep this information to himself a while longer, but it was a card he was forced to play: "Clint had nothing to do with Molly's murder."

"But you've arrested him—" She looked at him suspiciously. "What are you holding him for, if he didn't kill her?"

"He was the one took a pot shot at the house—he was trying to kill Gil. But he didn't kill Molly."

"Then who did kill her?"

He had no proof yet; but his bones were right this time. "This is off the record till I clear you on it—" He stared at her and after a moment she nodded agreement. "I think Doc Stenhouse killed her."

She was shocked, but she kept cool. "Why?"

"That's what I've got to find out. Just over an hour ago he volunteered to drive Vanderhorn over to Springfield. I can't let him do that now. But I've got to get Vanderhorn out of town before I arrest Stenhouse, before all hell breaks loose. That's why I need you to take him over to Springfield."

She considered for a moment, then at last she shook her head again. "I'm sorry, the answer's still no. If Russell Stenhouse murdered Molly, that's an even bigger story than if Clint did it. You'll have to get someone else." She looked up at the house. "Get someone in there to do it. He's their responsibility, not yours or mine."

He knew her well enough to know when she was adamant about a decision. He was angry with her, but later he would concede he had been unreasonable. Her duty was to her newspaper and her readers. All day he had been telling himself he owed the Vice-President nothing in these circumstances. He could not blame Lee if she felt the same way.

He got out of the car without saying anything further. He was halfway up the driveway before he became aware of the change in the atmosphere. The air had turned humid, was almost mid-summer air; and it was still, absolutely so. He stopped and looked up and about him. The maples were as unmoving as they might have been on an August day; they looked even stiller because there were no leaves to catch the moving light. The light itself had changed, had taken on a greenish tinge; that explained the heightened colour of the copper cupola. There was not even a whisper of wind; he heard the sound of a car starting up and he would not have been surprised if it had been on the other side of town. He looked towards the west, saw the long thin break in the clouds: that was the source of the greenish light. Then he looked down towards the south and saw the black boil of clouds.

He ran up the steps and rang the doorbell, cursing under his breath as Wilma Mae seemed to take forever to open the door. When she did he pushed in past her.

"Where's the Vice-President? Quick—I can't waste time—"

"Don't talk to Wilma Mae like that, Mr McKechnie," Adele Farquhar said from the doorway of the drawing-room. "She is upset enough as it is."

Only then did he see that Wilma Mae was weeping, her dark cheeks shining with tears. Suddenly he felt awkward, brutal; and put out a hand to touch the black woman's arm. "I'm sorry, Wilma Mae. I didn't mean—"

"Come in here, Mr McKechnie. Go and make us some tea, Wilma Mae." Then Adele Farquhar added softly, like a comforting pat of the hand, "We'll all feel better if we have something to occupy our minds."

Wilma Mae, wiping her eyes, went down the hallway and McKechnie impatiently followed Adele Farquhar into the drawing-room. "I don't want tea, Mrs—"

"Neither do I, but it gives Wilma Mae something to do. My daughter is dead, Mr McKechnie. Rose died almost an hour ago, just after you left."

"I'm sorry." He knew the inadequacy of words in such a situation; he had knocked on too many doors bearing tragic news. As he had told Vanderhorn, they gave you no citations for such missions; but he wished some police speech-writer would give him something more to say than the banal *I'm sorry*. "I wouldn't have barked at Wilma Mae like that—"

"I know." She sat down in her straight-backed chair; it now made her look curved-back and crumpled. A lamp on a side table had been turned on and it struck her face, marking the years there like scars. "You have been under a burden, Mr McKechnie, and I do appreciate it. But it is all over now."

"Not quite," he said as kindly as he could.

She looked up at him. "You mean the funeral? No, that of course—"

"No, I mean your daughter-in-law's death."

She shook her head from side to side. It was difficult to tell whether she was denying that Molly's death should be discussed in the same breath as that of her daughter or whether she was ashamed that she had forgotten all about her daughter-in-law. She made an effort to straighten up, but it seemed beyond her now.

"Of course, of course. There will have to be a double funeral—No, we can't have that. It wouldn't be fair to Rose. Not after—" Her voice trailed off.

The room grew suddenly dark. She turned her face away from the light and he found it impossible to read her expression.

"There's more than just the funeral—" But she wasn't listening to him and, suddenly impatient again, one eye now on the black sky beyond the windows, he said, "Where's your son?"

"I'm here." Gilbert Farquhar stood in the doorway. "What is it now?"

"Your mother has told me about your sister's death. I'm sorry to hear it. But there is something else—" The wind had begun to rise, rattling the windows; the maple branches once again scratched the walls of the house. "Where is Mr Vanderhorn? Is he upstairs?"

"He's gone," said Farquhar. "He left here about ten minutes ago with Dr Stenhouse."

"For Springfield?"

Farquhar nodded. "I understood you had arranged it—"

McKechnie left them, was running before he was out of the house. He wrenched open the front door and was almost blown back into the hall. The wind, like a gale now, slammed at the house. His cap blew off and flew back into the hall; he shut his eyes as dust and grit hit his face. Then he opened them and looked down to the south.

The twister was there, a huge dark frayed rope whirling beneath the rump of a black cloud that covered the whole of the southern sky but for a bright strip on the horizon against which the tornado funnel was clearly silhouetted. McKechnie had seen several tornadoes at a distance, but never one as big as this. The black cloud above it was immense, space itself exploding.

He yelled back into the hall, "Tornado's coming!"

He didn't stop to see whether the Farquhars had paid him any heed. He dragged the door shut against the howling wind. He almost fell down the steps of the porch, running against the wind that tried to sweep him off his feet. He saw Lee's frightened face behind the wound-up window of the police car, then he had run round the car, wrenched open the door and scrambled in. He had to use both hands to pull the door to against the force of the wind.

He grabbed the microphone. "Headquarters—this is PD-One! We've got a twister on the way, south of town. All units out—*immediate*! Sirens and horns—tell 'em to warn everyone! Divide the town into quarters from the square. I'll take the south-west quarter. Move!"

"Ten-four, PD-One!" Lucy Chapley was back on duty; and for once he was glad. Whatever her other faults, Lucy wouldn't panic. "I'll alert the Fire Department. Over and out!"

He hung the microphone back on the dashboard, started up the car and swung it out into the street, turning left. "I'll take you home—"

"You won't! Turn around—do whatever you've got to do! I'll take my chances with you!"

He didn't argue. He bounced the car up into a driveway; Gwen Stenhouse stared at him from the front window of her house. He grabbed the microphone of the loud-hailer, shouted his first warning of the coming twister. At the same time he was backing into the street, turning the car round and heading down towards the main section of town. In his driving mirror he saw Gwen Stenhouse come out her front door, blonde hair blowing wildly in the wind, and run round the side of the house.

He turned on his red roof-light, sounded the siren, then switched it off and continued shouting into the microphone. He slowed as he came to the Farquhar house, sounded the siren again and shouted another warning. But he couldn't stop to see whether the Farquhars had heeded him or were too locked into their grief to hear him. He had fulfilled his commitment to them. Now he had the whole town to protect.

As they came down the curve below the bluff they could see the tornado moving steadily up from the south. Already the air ahead of it was faintly clouded with debris, as if the funnel were hurling in advance of it a sample of what it could do. The black cloud above it had thickened even more and had spread; dark, lightning-jagged night was coming up out of the south, as if the compass points had been swung through a 90-degree angle. Then they saw the second funnel forming beside the first, merging into it at the top. The twin tornadoes were approaching the town at the same speed as McKechnie was driving through the streets to warn its citizens.

He went straight across the western end of the square, going the wrong way against the traffic lanes; but there was no traffic now, only the other squad cars taking off from headquarters to quarter the rest of the town. He saw their red lights, faintly heard their sirens above the wind. He had his window wound down against the possibility of running right into the vacuum created by the tornadoes; he didn't want the car, yielding to pressure, to explode outwards from around him and Lee. Yet a spark of logic, still alive in his confused mind, told him that if he and Lee did drive right into the middle of a funnel their chances of survival would be practically nil, whether the car windows were wound down or not.

Lee was hunched down in her seat, frightened but not so

much so that she was powerless: she was scribbling furiously with a shaky hand in her notebook. The car was bucking into the increasing wind as McKechnie took it down McKinney Street past the fire house; he was having difficulty in holding it on the road. He saw the firemen standing in the doorway of the building, helmeted and ready; he was about to shout to them to get under cover when he saw the figure of Al Boatswain. The fire chief wouldn't appreciate the police chief telling his men what to do for their own safety. McKechnie had time for a flash of wry amusement: there always had to be protocol, even on the brink of disaster.

"We're heading right into it." Lee's voice was faint but calm: or trying to be. "What are you going to do—tell it to turn back?"

"I wish to Christ I could!" But he managed a grin. "You're right—I'm not thinking very straight."

The tornado funnels looked less than a mile away now. McKechnie grabbed the microphone, but at once had to put both hands back on the wheel as the car tried to turn itself round. Lee took the microphone, held it in front of McKechnie's mouth as he called headquarters again, describing the path of the tornadoes. The air was thick with flying debris now; stone, pieces of wood, a saucepan smacked against the car. Miraculously the windshield remained unsmashed. The noise was deafening, a medley of sounds. They could hear one sound, a constant series of screeches, that puzzled McKechnie; then he realized it was the shriek of thousands of nails being pulled out as pieces of lumber parted company. But above all the other noises there was the roar of the funnels themselves, an armada of a thousand jets flying at ground level. He swung the car to the right, had to battle so that the wind didn't sweep it into a U-turn, and went down Oak Street across the face of the storm. As he turned right again at Taft, heading north again, the funnels came up level with him on *his* right, the nearest of them only two blocks away.

The wind was hitting them sideways and from the rear now, an immense invisible surf that threatened to whip the car over on to its side. The air was thick with debris, a whirling cloud of it that reached from the ground into the blackness overhead. Tree branches, a glassless window-frame, a section of picket fence, a motor mower: all were sailing through the thick, dirt-filled air as if weightless. Something hit the car with a terrible thump; McKechnie felt it rather than heard it. His ears were paining him dreadfully, cracking and cracking again, as if something in his skull wanted to blow them out. He glanced at Lee and saw that she had both hands over her ears and her face was screwed up with pain; in one hand she still held the micro-phone and he realized he had been talking into the empty air in front of him for perhaps the last twenty seconds. Or ten or five: there was no way of measuring time. It didn't matter anyway: if everyone in town hadn't taken cover by now there was no warning in the world that was going to help them.

The car was trying to run off the road to the left and he had to keep holding the wheel down to the right; it was like running against a swift side current, shooting rapids of wind. Muck was still smashing against the car; the rear window and one of the side windows just suddenly disap-peared. But the windshield was still intact, protecting them from what was coming at them from the front. He drove on, not really knowing why, as if the tornadoes were suck-ing him into their vortices by awe rather than the power of the vacuum they were creating.

In the immediate path of the storm he could see that part of the town literally being torn apart. Houses were exploding outwards like so many trick boxes; entire roofs lifted and sailed away, cone-shaped magic carpets; the contents of one house followed a roof, sucked up and drawn away, a cornucopia in reverse. A car, on a perfectly even keel, rode through the air forty feet above the ground. He saw a man rise up into the air, arms waving frantically, as if he had been hurled upwards from a giant trampoline. Poles were snapped off and whirled aloft, cabers tossed by some giant; snapped power lines filled the darkness with their own blue lightning. McKechnie saw all this but it only registered on his eye, memories photographed to be recognized later: his mind took in none of it. He knew now he had done the wrong thing in trying to follow the tornadoes. He should have turned, driven away from them, tried to save himself and Lee and left everyone to their fates. There was nothing any man could do against the terrible fury of the storm.

Then the outer edge of the nearest funnel hit them as the tornadoes suddenly veered to the left. The car slewed sideways and he had no hope of controlling it; the steering wheel almost broke his wrists as it spun round. The windshield abruptly disappeared, gone as if it were no more than a film of dust suddenly wiped away. The car went into a spin, whirling round and round in the middle of the road as if on an oil slick. It was only a small part of a great spinning mass of debris in the eye of the funnel. They were surrounded by a whirling stew of what had once been a section of Friendship: parts of houses, a church steeple, furniture, toys, bodies. A dead man, eyes plucked from their sockets, clung to the hood of the police car and stared in at them.

McKechnie blindly reached out a hand and clutched Lee's arm. The seat-belt was trying to cut him in half. Something told him that if it sliced through him he would go out of the car in two halves; but it neither carved him up nor snapped and later he would realize that it was probably all that saved him. He was hunkered down in the seat as far as he could bend his long body and legs, in the foetal position in the womb of destruction. He had his eyes shut tightly, but he would have seen nothing had he had them open; total blackness now surrounded him and Lee. He had his arms wrapped across his head, his shoulders hunched against his piercingly painful ears. It seemed that every hair on his body was standing up, trying to pluck itself out of his skin; the skin itself was being stretched till he knew it was going to split and everything, his whole self, was going to spill out of it like an over-ripe fruit. His lungs felt empty, yet were trying to burst out of his chest; his stomach was forcing its way up out through his gullet. And his bones, the barometer of the day, their case proven, were trying to tear themselves out of him at every joint.

His mind had no comprehension of what was happening to him and Lee. Pain registered, but that was all; it required no intelligence to know that death was next. Without opening his mouth he yelled a silent prayer that had no words . . .

Then the terrible clamour suddenly stopped. The car was lifted off the ground, stood on end, then crashed down on its side. In the moment before he blacked out McKechnie wondered where all the noise had gone.

## II

"The first man she loved and the last," said Russell Stenhouse. "In a way I guess you could say we were the bookends of Rose's adult life."

It was not the sort of image Vanderhorn would have seen for himself and he wondered at Stenhouse's flight of fancy. The man seemed nervous, as if suddenly embarrassed at being alone with the Vice-President in his own car; on his tours Vanderhorn had met many people who had suddenly become awkward when they were left alone with him. Yet Stenhouse's remark suggested a certain confident intimacy.

Vanderhorn said agreeably, "I suppose so. I wonder if she thought about the coincidence of our meeting. I mean before she died."

"She didn't mention me to you? I mean towards the end?"

Was the man fishing for some kind of compliment? He was the second one today who had asked if Rose had talked about him: but somehow he didn't sound as sadly pleading as Gil Farquhar had. Yet Farquhar had also sounded a little afraid—and so did Stenhouse.

"No, not at all. Does that upset you?"

"No. It's better to let bygones be bygones. I used to collect clichés—like other people collect stamps," he added, seemingly irrelevantly.

Yet Vanderhorn knew the doctor was talking to cover something. Grief, perhaps. Well, why not? He could feel his own grief within him, bitter and heavy as a grave illness. He was accustomed to the hard facts of life; yet he still couldn't bring himself to believe that Rose was dead. Even the sight of her, pale and stiff and shrunken in the bed, her cheek cold against his farewell kiss, had not convinced him. He was afraid of when the truth would strike him and he thought with trepidation of tomorrow and the speech he had to give at the United Nations in New York. He closed his mind against the sour irony of the speech. A vote catcher, aimed at the national scene as much as the international: Women's Rights in the Political World . . .

The green Rover reached the edge of town, picked up speed as it went out along the highway. Vanderhorn saw the route sign, US 60; then the distance signs. They would be in Springfield in less than an hour and three to four hours after that he would be home in Georgetown. He would be alone there but for his servants; today, more than ever, he was glad that Carolyn came to Washington only when it was imperative. He turned in his seat to look

261

back at Friendship, but it made no impression on him. The heart of the town, he had seen as they had driven through it, was pretty; but out here it was tatty, forgettable. They were on the edges of it and the outskirts of every town looked the same. Used car lots, gas stations, motels, a McDonalds, a tacos hut: the homogeneity of America. He wanted something more than that as a memory of Rose's last resting place. He was about to face forward again when he saw the black sky to the south and the whirling tail beginning to appear out of it.

"That looks bad."

Stenhouse had slowed down, was looking back towards the south. "It's a twister. I'm afraid that alters our plans."

"What do you mean?"

"You've lost your priority. I've got to turn back. In another ten minutes me and every other doctor in the county is going to be needed back there." He slid the car into the side of the road, brought it to a halt. "I can leave you here and you can take your chances on getting a lift to Springfield. You've got your dark glasses, maybe you won't be recognized."

The Vice-President of the United States standing beside a Federal highway thumbing a lift: the man in the White House would have a heart attack at the thought. "What if the tornado comes up this way, along this highway?"

Stenhouse was watching the approaching storm. "That's another of the chances you'll have to take." He looked quickly around, up and down both sides of the highway. "None of those places looks as if they've got a basement or a storm cellar. Maybe you'd better come back with me. But you'll be taking your chances there, too."

Vanderhorn turned round, looked back at the storm. He was surprised at the speed of its approach; the tail had now become a white funnel that reached to the ground. Even as he watched it the funnel started to darken; the immense turbulent cloud above it had spread right across the sky. He felt suddenly afraid as he had never felt before.

"You think I *should* go back with you, don't you?"

"It doesn't matter what I think. I just wonder what Rose would have thought."

"You must wield a pretty savage scalpel."

"I've never believed in mincing words."

"Another goddam cliché!" Vanderhorn could feel his temper rising. "All right, turn around. I'll go back with you!"

Stenhouse nodded, as if he had taken it for granted that Vanderhorn had no other course. He watched the sparse traffic coming along the highway, then he did an abrupt U-turn and accelerated the Rover swiftly as he headed it back towards town. They were driving through a bright green light, but darkness lay ahead of them. Cars were pulling up beside the highway and people were coming out of the motels and gas stations and diners to stare at the storm. Wind was hitting the car side-on but Stenhouse kept it steady.

"You're not going to drive right into it!"

Stenhouse eased the speed of the car, dropped it to no more than 30 miles an hour: they drove leisurely towards what looked like the end of the world. "No. There's nothing you or I or anybody can do about that son-of-a-bitch up ahead. They don't have preventive medicine for twisters. We'll get there when it's all over and I'll try to patch up the injured and the dying. You're going to see something you've probably been protected from all your life. Human misery."

"You must have been a different man when you were young. I mean, for Rose to have fallen in love with you."

"I probably was. I had reason to be."

The wind was stronger now and Stenhouse's arms were braced to hold the wheel steady. The air was thick with swirling dirt and light debris; small objects thumped against the car. He slowed the car to a crawl and they watched the tornadoes, two of them now, strike the southern edge of town and begin to carve their way north.

"We might as well wait." He brought the car to a halt, but kept the engine running. Still looking towards the storm and the town erupting beneath it, he said, "I did you a favour last night. I killed Molly Farquhar."

*I've never experienced a day like this nor ever will again.* Vanderhorn had a feeling of being totally apart from himself. One half of him was taking in all the buffeting he was being subjected to, but the other half was absolutely remote, objectively disbelieving everything Stenhouse was telling him. None of it was possible, Stenhouse was making it all up out of jealousy.

"She has been my—my mistress, if you like. For just over a year now. Not in the same way you and Rose were together. With me it was just sex—my wife and I stopped sleeping together about three years ago. It was the same with Molly at first—all she wanted was the sex she wasn't getting from Gil. Then some months ago she found out about Rose and me, how close we'd been all those years ago. I don't know how she found out, but she did. She changed, though I didn't realize it right away. She started to talk about us going away together, for good—" He laughed, a sour cough of mirth. "I didn't think she was serious at first. Christ, why would I want to give up all I've got here? Would you?"

"I don't know what you have here." Beyond the windshield, less than a mile down the highway, a wide swathe of the town was being sucked up into the black cloud. "Perhaps after today you won't have much."

"I can always build another house, if that's what you mean. Or do you mean something else?"

"Go on," Vanderhorn said. "Tell me about you and Molly."

Stenhouse looked at him carefully, then went on, "She

wanted us to go out to California—that's where you came from originally, isn't it? A month ago, when Rose came home, I started to realize Molly was a bit crazy. Or anyway unhinged. I'm no psychiatrist, I don't really know what crazy means any more. It's a crazy goddam world anyway. Just like what we're looking at down the road there."

He paused and Vanderhorn waited impatiently. But he said nothing, remembering what his grandfather had once told him. *Never interrupt a man who thinks he's done you a good turn; if you do, you'll never find out how to get out of his debt.* He wondered how that cynical, ruthless old man would have handled this situation.

Stenhouse said, "She told me she'd let herself get pregnant, that she'd stopped taking the Pill. I had to marry her or else."

"What about this man—Blamey, is that his name?"

The twin funnels seemed to have veered away from them, were moving north-west across the town. Vanderhorn was seeing incredible things: whole roof-tops whirling up into the air, a car airborne as if on an invisible elevated expressway. The green light had darkened as the black boiling sky moved on over them.

"Blamey meant nothing to her. He was just a front—I don't know what she intended doing with him. The poor bastard—"

Stenhouse paused again, looked towards the town as if wondering if now was the time to start going into it. Vanderhorn thought he saw the figure of a man sucked up into the air, but that was too bizarre a thought, despite the bizarre day, and he dismissed it.

"It all came to a head last night. I went to their house to have a look at Rose before I went to a dance out at the country club. That was when I knew she wasn't going to live another twenty-four hours and I told them so. I guess that was when they decided to call you?"

265

Vanderhorn nodded, deciding not to interrupt. Stenhouse was going to tell him everything, perhaps more than he wanted to know. Yet he knew he had to know.

"On my way out of the house Molly took me aside and told me I had to go away with her today—she'd bought the airplane tickets. She said she would wait for me out at Clint Blamey's place and we'd drive up to Joplin this morning. I don't know what Blamey was going to think about being made a sucker like that, us using his place for a rendezvous. I don't think Molly cared. She was really off her rocker last night."

Everyone is off his rocker, Vanderhorn thought. How did I ever get involved in all this? Through love, he thought: and wanted to weep for Rose.

"She said if I didn't go away with her, she was going to spill the beans. Another cliché," Stenhouse said drily. He was talking dispassionately, or anyway in a dispassionate voice: a doctor discussing an operation he had performed. "The beans about all of us. Her, me, me and Rose, you and Rose. Even Gil and Rose. She was going to destroy everything, she said. Tear the town apart, make you and Rose and Gil suffer along with her. I had a dreadful time out at the country club. I just sat at the bar all night—I can hold my liquor, but I've never poured as much into myself as I did last night. But I was still stone cold sober when I left. I went back to the Farquhars' on my way home. Gil was still up, sitting with Rose—" He looked sideways at Vanderhorn. "He's a poor son-of-a-bitch. I feel sorry for him. What do you do when you fall in love with your sister? You and I should understand him. We fell in love with the same girl."

"He drove Rose out of this town," said Vanderhorn and at once sounded pompous and prudish in his own ears.

"If he hadn't, you wouldn't have met her."

*True.* The storm was up in the north-west corner of

266

the town now, over Forest View Drive. Please God, thought Vanderhorn, who hadn't talked to God in more years than he could remember, don't harm Rose.

"I told Gil it was just a routine visit, that I'd called in to see how Rose was. He told me then that Molly had gone. I asked where she'd gone to, and he told me he guessed she was out at Clint Blamey's. He must've known about her and Blamey."

The wind had gone and the worst of the storm seemed to have passed. But Vanderhorn could still see the whirling funnels.

"I drove out to the highway near Blamey's farm. I was going to go in and see Molly, but I didn't know what the hell I was going to say to her in front of him. For all I knew he might take her side and get violent with me. I'm a coward when it comes to physical violence. I sat in the woods off the other side of the road and then Blamey came out and went walking off into the darkness. Christ knows why. I sat there a while longer waiting for him to come back. But he didn't. So I drove up to his house and went in and had it out with Molly. She was really crazy by then, making a noise like that storm over there. I hadn't intended harming her, I hadn't gone there with anything like that in mind. But when she started screaming about you and me and Rose, that was it. I blew my top. She had a gun, one of her father-in-law's, I'd seen it in the Farquhars' study when I'd gone to their house to look at Gil—he was the only one of them who was my patient. She must've brought it out to Blamey's with her—Christ knows what she intended doing with it. Shooting herself, shooting me, I don't know. We fought for it and I took it from her and, Christ help me, I shot her."

The tornadoes had passed on beyond the town. Stenhouse moved the gear-lever from *Park* to *Drive* and the car started to move forward.

"Why are you telling me all this?" Vanderhorn said. "Aren't you afraid I'll tell Jim McKechnie?"

"You won't tell him or anyone else. If you did it would all come out in the wash about you and Rose. And that's the last thing you want. It's something I don't want, either. I'm telling you because sooner or later I'd have to get it off my chest to someone. I've never done anything like that in my whole life. I've never even put a dying patient of mine out of his misery, though I've often felt like it. I told you because I think I've got you figured correctly— you're the only one who'll never be able to tell anyone else. Not if you still love Rose."

They had reached the edge of the devastation. It started on one side of a street running north: the roadway was a clean-cut boundary between the town as it had been and the chaos that had been visited on it. Vanderhorn had never seen destruction like it. He had spent his wartime service on a carrier in the Pacific and you never saw total devastation like this out at sea. The storm, only two blocks wide, had gone right through the town from south to north. Its path was a curving sweep of flattened lumber, strewn bricks, twisted iron: the eastern and western sections of town were separated by a junkyard of homes, cars, trailers, stores. Power cables lay everywhere like giant intestines, crackling and sizzling a deadly discharge of blue and yellow sparks. Natural gas lines were ripped apart, hissing evilly. A water main had burst and a fountain sprayed over a metal garden of wreckage from a car that had exploded apart under pressure. Despite the crackling and the hissing and the spatter of water, the town seemed to be utterly silent, dead.

Then people began to appear, dazed zombies. Stenhouse wound down his window and shouted out to the first group they passed, "You all right? Anyone hurt?"

They shook their heads dumbly: it was impossible to know which question they were saying *no* to. But Stenhouse drove on, avoiding fallen power poles, driving over cables where the insulation still covered them; once he had to drive up on to the sidewalk to get round a pile-up of four cars in the middle of the road. It began to rain, a steady downpour falling straight down: there was no wind now to slant it. Then he and Vanderhorn simultaneously saw the blue police car on its side in the middle of the road, the power pole lying across it.

Stenhouse jerked the Rover to a stop. "Watch out for those cables!"

Vanderhorn felt the weakness in his legs as soon as he got out of the car. He clutched at the side of the Rover, then instantly drew his hands away. What if the car was standing on an open power cable? Then he remembered: how would the electricity get through the rubber of the tyres? And he would be dead now, anyhow, if it had. But he didn't relax his caution. For him to die here in the middle of this carnage would be a fitting end to the day.

Then he cursed for thinking only of himself. He followed Stenhouse across to the wrecked police car. The doctor had already checked that the car was free of any electrical charge, was trying to open the uppermost rear door. The power pole lay across the passenger's front door and Vanderhorn knew he and Stenhouse were never going to be able to move it on their own.

"Is it Jim McKechnie?"

"Him and Lee Barron. They look okay—they don't look smashed-up or anything. Here, help me with this goddam door."

Between them they managed to force open the rear door. Even as Stenhouse clambered into the rear of the car Vanderhorn, looking down past him, saw both McKechnie and Lee Barron stir. The grille dividing the two sections of the car had broken away from its struts, but Stenhouse was having difficulty in pulling it down so that McKechnie could struggle out of the front seat.

On the edge of his vision Vanderhorn was aware of more and more people appearing; he was glad of the dark glasses he was wearing but he didn't know how long they would disguise him. Then again he cursed himself for his selfishness. These people were too dazed, too shocked by their own tragedy, to care to know who was the stranger working with Dr Stenhouse on freeing the police chief and his girl-friend from their car. He put the battered, bewildered people out of his mind, reached into the car and helped McKechnie clamber out of it. Then he did the same with Lee. Both of them were bruised and cut, blinking and shaking their heads as they tried to throw off the effects of having been knocked out. But neither of them appeared seriously injured and Stenhouse, checking them quickly, assured them that they weren't.

McKechnie looked from one to the other of the two men. "I thought you were on your way to Springfield."

"Dr Stenhouse decided he had better come back when he saw the storm."

"The Vice-President thought the same. It was a joint decision. A Republican one," Stenhouse added with a thin smile.

How can he joke at a time like this? Vanderhorn wondered. The silence of the town had gone now. They could hear weeping, shouts, cries of joy: the sounds of grief, relief, reunion. There was the wail of sirens and in the distance Vanderhorn could see the flashing red lights of police cars and fire engines. People were clambering over the wreckage of their houses, looking for loved ones, pets, prized possessions. The town was coming alive again. Some faces were turned up to the rain as if for baptism. A man and a woman stood outside their flattened house, their heads bent in prayer.

"You'll have to get out of here, sir," McKechnie said. "I can't be responsible for you—"

"You don't have to be," said Vanderhorn. "I came back to do what I can to help."

"There's nothing you can do. Please go, sir. I don't have time to argue with you."

Vanderhorn felt useless, unwanted. "How do I get to Springfield? Will Miss Barron take me?"

"No," said Lee. Vanderhorn felt she wasn't really interested in him any more. She was looking about her, already writing her story in her mind. "I've got too much to do here."

"Take my car, drive yourself," said Stenhouse. "I won't need it the rest of today. Leave it at the airport in Springfield, I'll get someone to pick it up. Go back to Highway 60, that'll take you right through to Springfield. The airport's on the north side of town."

Vanderhorn could see that no one had the time to argue with him. His name was synonymous with charity; the Vanderhorn Foundation had given away more than what this whole town was worth. It had been created to help people: and now when his help could be personal, came from the heart and not the cheque-book, he was being told to get out of town. But he knew they were right: he would do more good by leaving than by staying.

He nodded to Stenhouse. "Thank you. For everything."

"My pleasure," said Stenhouse, but his voice was drier than usual. He took his medical bag out of the Rover. "I'll need my tool kit."

Vanderhorn got into the car, started it up. "Goodbye again, Jim. I'll be in touch. I can't do much here, but maybe I can in Washington."

"It'll be appreciated sir. And I'm sorry about Miss Rose."

Vanderhorn nodded. "I'm going up there before I leave town. Just to make sure everything's all right."

"She's dead, sir. Whatever's happened to the Farquhar

271

place, there's nothing you can do for her. Just keep on going."

Vanderhorn looked out at the cut, bruised and earnest face. There were lesser men than this one in higher places in Washington. He owed McKechnie the solution to the Molly Farquhar murder, but he would never be able to tell what he knew. Stenhouse, the unlikely murderer, medical bag in hand, was already walking away through the steadily falling rain, not even looking back, certain his secret was safe.

"I'll be in touch, Jim."

He drove carefully out of the devastated area. Nobody seemed to take any notice of the fact that a stranger was driving Dr Stenhouse's car; he realized that such a car must be distinctive in this town. He wondered if some police officer would pull him up as a suspected car thief. But nobody took any notice of him, they had far too much else to occupy them.

He climbed the curve of the bluff up into Forest View, his hopes rising as he saw that the path of the tornadoes appeared to have changed direction at the last moment. The woods below the bluff had been flattened as if a giant bulldozer had gone through them; hundred-foot trees had been reduced to kindling. He came out on top of the bluff, saw the blue Cadillac in the driveway and behind it the old house standing as solid and secure as ever. Some windows had been smashed and the copper cupola had a dent in it, but the house, he felt, would stand for another hundred years. He knew, however, that the three living people in it, Adele Farquhar, Gil, Wilma Mae, were finished, as dead in spirit as Rose was in fact. He could do nothing for Rose, McKechnie had said. And he could do nothing for them.

He drove on. A blonde woman came out of a ranch-house next door to the Farquhars' and waved frantically to him, as if she knew him. He kept his face averted, glad

272

once again of the dark glasses. He drove on down Forest View, found a side road, skirted the town and picked up Route 60. The rain was falling heavily and it took him an hour and a half to reach Springfield and find the airport.

"I'd almost given up, sir," said his pilot. "I heard the news on the radio about the tornadoes over there at Friendship. I've been out of my mind wondering what the heck to do."

"Thanks, Roy. For worrying, I mean. But everything's all right now."

"What about Miss Farquhar, sir?"

"She died, Roy." She had travelled with him in this plane; but all his travelling from now on would be alone. "Let's get back to Washington."

### III

The Vice-President drove away, but Lee paid virtually no attention to his going. Instead she looked after Russell Stenhouse as he walked up the street, looking as she had seen him look so many times: raincoat buttoned to his neck, old golf cap pulled down on his head, medical bag hanging from his hand. "What are you going to do about him?"

"I don't know yet," said McKechnie. "We need him for now."

"You'll have to do something about him sooner or later."

"Christ, don't you think I know that!" Then he gestured apologetically, but was still choked with angry frustration. "Are you all right? I've got to leave you."

"I'm all right. I'll see you later. I'll be at my office."

She left him quickly, walking away through the havoc towards a group of people coming down the block. But she went by the group and then he saw her break into a run. He looked after her, concerned for her; then it came

273

back to him that he had a wider concern, the whole town. He turned and ran after Stenhouse, caught up with him as they came into the square.

They both stopped. "Jesus!" said Stenhouse.

The tornadoes had gone right through the middle of the square. It had no clear-cut southern or northern boundary. On the south side the *News* plant and all the stores were flattened; on the north side the First Citizens' Bank, the picture theatre, the drugstore and J. C. Penney's were just a wasteland. In the centre of the square police headquarters and the city hall were total wrecks. Trees lay like jagged grey skeletons on their sides and the flagpole was just a shattered stump. Only the Confederate soldier still stood. He had been torn from his plinth and hurled against one of the fallen trees. He stood leaning back against it, facing south, the true direction of his faith. But he still looked bewildered and he could have been watching for another storm.

McKechnie looked towards the south-west corner, saw Lee standing staring at her demolished plant. He wanted to run down to console her, but again the wider concern took hold of him. He ran across the square, careful to avoid the crackling power cables, to police headquarters. Lucy Chapley and Dorothy Kidmann, dazed and bleeding, were sitting on the ground in the rain while Jack Atcheson fussed over them. It suddenly struck McKechnie that he had been warning all the citizens to go to their storm cellars, yet police headquarters had no basement or cellar.

"It hit us before we could do anything—" Atcheson was shaking, but was more exercised about the women than about himself. He had a large dark lump on his forehead and blood was running from a cut on the back of his neck. "Lucy and Dorothy were still on the air—God Almighty, how they survived, I dunno—"

"Look after the girls, doc," McKechnie said. "Come with me, Jack. Who's still inside?"

"Bud. Oh, and Clint Blamey."

The town was starting to swarm with recuers, the fortunate ones who had not been hit coming down to help rescue those who had. Sirens were wailing and McKechnie saw Zeke Norval go down the eastern side of the square, driving flat out as if he had a clear road. There was a strong smell of gas and McKechnie wondered how long it would be before the utilities men cut off the gas and electricity.

It took him and Atcheson only two minutes to find Bud Grierson and Clint Blamey. They could be left in the wreckage for the time being: they were both dead. Atcheson sat down suddenly without looking where he was going to sit; his legs just folded under him and he thumped down in the middle of what had been McKechnie's office. McKechnie squatted down beside him.

"Jack—"

Atcheson looked at him dazedly: he reminded McKechnie of far-gone junkies he had seen in New York. The power cables into headquarters must have been undamaged; several lights glowed eerily under the piles of masonry. The communications console was still working: static-blurred voices crackled from beneath a fallen wall. Atcheson kept glancing towards it, as if he felt he should answer the calls but couldn't move.

McKechnie slapped him hard across the face. "Jack—" Atcheson's eyes cleared and he peered at his chief like a man suddenly being wakened. "Jack, go home and see if your wife and kids are okay. Then come back here on the double. That's if they're okay, I mean."

Atcheson stood up without a word and, stiff-legged, walked out of the wreckage and across the square towards the section of town where there would be an undamaged car that he could borrow to drive home. He would be back in ten minutes, recovered, with the news that his family was safe.

The square was busy with people now, like a Saturday shopping crowd. McKechnie suddenly realized he was not being much of a police chief; he still hadn't widened his concern beyond himself and his immediate staff. He was as shocked as Jack Atcheson by the deaths of Grierson and Blamey, but so far no reaction had set in.

He would have to set up a temporary command post somewhere. He knew that, under the emergency plan the town had approved some years ago, the city manager, Dave Herakles, would run the command post. But it was his job to see that it was established.

Stenhouse, raincoat already smeared with blood, came up to him. "I'm going over to the hospital. I can do a better job in a central place instead of wandering around like bloody Florence Nightingale."

McKechnie wondered where he had picked up *bloody*: from some golfer on the courses in Scotland and England? He said, "Where did you play golf in St Louis, doc? Forest Park or one of the country clubs?"

Stenhouse's expression didn't change. "I haven't been in St Louis since I was there as a replacement. I didn't play golf in those days. You want me, you'll know where to find me."

He walked off without looking back and Lucy Chapley, on her feet now, said, "He's a wonderful man. I bet he just works right through the night tonight. He'll be needed, too."

McKechnie just nodded. "You better go home, Lucy, check that your boys are okay."

"They're up in Joplin. I better get back to work." She stared at the wreckage atop her console, was frustrated that she couldn't answer the voices coming from it. Then she suddenly looked lost, an expression McKechnie would come to see time and again over the next few days. "Where will I go, chief?"

"Over to the fire house." McKechnie could see it still

276

standing down on McKinney. "We'll set up the command post there."

The rain stopped as darkness fell and the mocking stars came out in a cloudless sky. By that time the Civil Defence, National Guard, Red Cross and other emergency units had arrived. McKechnie stayed on duty but gradually he saw other men taking over from him and he didn't mind; he was too tired to fight to preserve an authority that would revert to him when the others had all gone. He had done a good job and he knew it; he would be pleased if others knew it and remembered it. But he wouldn't pine if they didn't. At 3 a.m., having been up for 24 hours, he went looking for Lee, found her at home on Forest View. She had turned her house into her office and all her staff were working with her. She had arranged for the newspaper plant over in Vista to print her Monday edition and she was just phoning in the last of her copy. Her production manager was already over in Vista making up the paper. The news will out, thought McKechnie, whatever.

He sat down in his favourite chair in the living-room, the one that he hoped would some day be his permanently, said, "Wake me in two hours," and fell asleep.

Lee let him sleep an extra hour, woke him at six o'clock with coffee and toast. "It looks like a fine day."

"A fine day for what?" He got up and looked out the window, but could see little damage from here. A few branches had been stripped from trees, but Forest View seemed to have escaped unharmed. He went out to the back of the house, saw that his favourite elm was safe, and came back into the living-room. "Did you get your paper to bed?"

"It'll be on the streets by nine o'clock. There's only one story in it, the twister. I've had to junk a lot of other stories."

He kissed her on the cheek, watched smilingly by her

staff, and left her. He had no car, but he welcomed the opportunity to walk: it gave him time to prepare himself for meeting Stenhouse. He passed the big house at the end of the street and was surprised to see Adele Farquhar standing in the side garden looking down over the town. He hesitated, then went up the driveway.

"You're up early, Mrs Farquhar. Is everyone all right?"

"At my age, Mr McKechnie, one doesn't need much sleep. Yes, we are all all right, thank you. But there seem to be a lot of unfortunate people down there in the town."

"The latest count is seventeen dead and ninety injured." He had got the figures from Lee, but he knew they weren't complete. "It's going to be a sad town for a long time."

"Yes. It may help to put things into perspective for us. Though not entirely, I suppose. Will you be coming back to see us about my daughter-in-law?"

"Eventually. But not for a day or two."

Wilma Mae came out of the house, bringing McKechnie's cap with her. "You left this yesterday, chief. You gonna need it."

He thanked her, then looked at the two women. He glanced up at the old house, but there was no sign of Gil Farquhar and he wondered if the sad, pitiful man was still sitting beside his dead sister. Finally he said, "The Vice-President got away okay. He should be safe in Washington now."

"Rose would be pleased," said Adele Farquhar.

He left them and went down into the town. He reported in to the command post, told them he was going over to the hospital and left again. He walked through the town, nodding to the greetings of rescuers still working among the havoc, and came to the hospital. He asked the whereabouts of Dr Stenhouse and was told that the doctor had been in the operating theatre all night, had just come out and could be found in the staff commissary. He went there and met Stenhouse as the latter, haggard, exhausted, came out through the swing doors.

"Just going off, chief. You want to see me?"

"You finished for a while?"

"There's a new team coming on, there's fellers coming from all over. I'm going home and I'm going to sleep till tomorrow morning. We've been working with emergency power all night and the light wasn't very strong. My eyes feel like I've been rubbing 'em with sand."

"The power company says it's got all the cables in town fixed. There are some lines down outside town, but they'll fix those later. They're switching on power again at seven-thirty."

"Glad to hear it. We can do with it."

They walked out into the narrow strip of garden that fronted the hospital. The tornadoes had missed the medical centre by four blocks and the only signs of damage were a few bent television aerials on the houses on the opposite side of the street and the tops lopped off a few of the taller trees. Stenhouse was wearing his raincoat, the bloodstains on it now a dark brown, and carried his golf cap in his hand. He looked old and tired: too old, McKechnie thought, to have to bear what I'm going to put on him.

"Doc, this is a hell of a time to ask it, but I've got to ask it sooner or later. Why did you kill Molly Farquhar?"

Stenhouse ran a thumb along his moustache, stood looking down at his feet as if debating whether he should answer the question. Then he looked up.

"I don't think I want to tell you that, Jim. I've been thinking about it ever since you mentioned St Louis yesterday afternoon over there in the square. I guessed then that you knew, that you were telling me you knew. I've been working all night, sewing up people, saving some, losing some. After a while, in wholesale carnage like we had last night, you start to work automatically, your hands do the job for you, and you can let your mind run anywhere it wants. I knew you'd be back asking questions and I decided I'd tell you the bare minimum. The bare minimum is yes, I killed Molly. As to why—I'm not going to tell you that. You going to lock me up now?"

"I don't have a jail. If you told me *why* you killed her—"

"Are you trying to help me, Jim? Trying to find some extenuating circumstances?" He looked steadily at McKechnie and after a moment the latter nodded. Stenhouse shook his head. "It wouldn't work, Jim. There were no extenuating circumstances, none the law would recognize. I'm sorry I've got to make it hard for you, but you'll have to arrest me and prove your case without any help from me. Come to think of it, that may not be easy."

McKechnie thought of Clint Blamey, his only witness and then only a circumstantial one, lying dead in the temporary morgue in the high school gymnasium.

"I can't let you get away with it, doc. You know that."

They had left the hospital and were walking along the street. On the opposite side people were cleaning up the debris in their front gardens; a man was up on the roof of his house trying to straighten his television aerial. They waved to the police chief and the doctor, friendly greetings that, to McKechnie's acute eye, had a new respect for himself and Stenhouse. *What are they going to think of me when I haul him off to jail on a murder rap?*

"Give me time to think about it, Jim. All I want to do now is go home and sleep—if I can. I won't run away. If I was going to do that, I had plenty of opportunity to do it during the night."

They had come to a cross-street. One way it led up to Forest View; the other went towards the town square. McKechnie put out his hand. "Call me when you're ready, doc. And I'm sorry it's got to be the way it is."

"A goddam awful lot will come out if I have to tell the truth."

"I guessed that. But if I turn a blind eye to it all, where do I draw the line?"

Stenhouse pondered a while, looked at his watch, then nodded. "You're not a bad son-of-a-bitch, Jim. There's worse than you around."

They shook hands and went their separate ways, McKechnie towards the centre of town, Stenhouse up the hill towards Forest View. Neither of them looked back at the other.

## IV

Jack Atcheson had gone home for a well-earned rest and McKechnie had taken over his car. The clock on the dashboard showed 7.53 when the radio crackled and Roley Trubauer came on the air: "This is PD-Four out on Route 86. You there, chief?"

"Come in, Roley. What is it?"

"Doc Stenhouse. He's out here, down the road a piece from Clint Blamey's place, laying beside his wife's car. Dead."

"Dead? How?"

"He's got a-hold of a power line. He must of picked it up just when they were gonna switch the power on. Didn't he know they were gonna switch it on at seven-thirty? We put it out on the radio so's everyone would know. It's a goddam shame, chief. What puzzles me, what the hell was he doing out here this time of morning alone? Alone."

# *Chapter Nine*

The tornadoes continued north, touching down in four more areas, causing more destruction, more deaths. They went on over Illinois, swung east through Indiana, turned north again over the Great Lakes and petered out just over the Canadian border. But they would come again during the summer and again the following year and again and again, would still be as powerful and devastating as ever when the storms of men had dwindled to whispering echoes in eternity . . .

Willis Vanderhorn went to New York and made his speech to the United Nations on Monday afternoon. It got no reaction from the majority of delegates, who came from countries where women didn't know they had any rights, political or otherwise; it got very little space in the domestic newspapers whose editors, all men, recognized it for the political speech it was. He returned Monday evening to Washington.

He went to see the President and the two men had half an hour alone in the Oval Office. The President gave his condolences on the death of Rose Farquhar and succeeded in hiding his relief that any chance of a scandal now looked remote. Then he said, "I'm leaving tomorrow morning for that junket out in the Mid West. I'm going to stop off at a couple of places where those tornadoes hit, tell them we're going to declare them Federal disaster areas. You want me to go down to that place, what's it called, Friendship?"

"It would be a nice gesture, John, but I don't think it would be wise. I got the word on the extent of the damage down there. I think you could safely declare them a disaster area. It won't win us any votes, but I'd like it done anyway."

"I suppose you'd like to go back there yourself?"

"No, John. That's all behind me. Have a nice trip."

The Vice-President went back to his office on the second floor of the Executive Office Building. His staff had gone home and he went in through the deserted outer office to his own room. He was sitting there in the dark staring out through the window when there was a tap on his door. He switched on his desk lamp and said, "Come in."

The door was pushed open and a woman's figure was silhouetted against the light from the outer office. For a moment he thought it was his wife and he felt a sour welling of irritation that she had followed him down from New York to talk to him. They were beyond reconciliation and he had avoided calling her while he had been in New York this afternoon. But he wondered how she knew so soon that Rose was dead.

Then Miss Delamaide said, "May I have a word with you, Mr Vice-President?"

He recovered, sat up in his chair. "Switch the light on—the switch is there beside the door." He blinked in the sudden glare as the lights went on. "Is it something from the President?"

"No, sir, it's personal. I understand Miss Hallstrom, your secretary, is leaving to get married. I wonder if you'd consider me as her replacement? I'm sure the President would recommend me—"

"How did you know Miss Hallstrom is getting married? I know she's been keeping it secret—"

"I know that, sir. The man she's marrying is still waiting on his divorce, but I understand it will be through very soon. But there are no secrets in Washington, isn't that what they say?"

She knows, too, that the assistant personal secretary to an ex-President doesn't amount to a row of beans in Washington. She's been reading the opinion polls . . .

"I'll think about it, Natalie."

"Thank you, Mr Vanderhorn. I think I could make myself indispensable to you."

She smiled, good-looking, sexy and as sure of herself as the Chief Clerk of the Senate. She said good night and closed the door and he sat there and wondered how secure the phone calls from Friendship had been.

# BESTSELLERS

| | | |
|---|---|---|
| ☐ THE SIBYL CIPHER—Simmel | 04395-4 | $2.25 |
| ☐ CROWN IN CANDLELIGHT<br>—Rosemary Hawley Jarman | 04396-2 | $2.25 |
| ☐ VENOM—Alan Scholefield | 04378-4 | $2.25 |
| ☐ WOMEN WHO WAIT—Elaine Bissell | 04415-2 | $1.95 |
| ☐ FAT CITY—Leonard Gardner | 04388-1 | $2.25 |
| ☐ LOVE STORIES—Martin Levin, editor | 04172-2 | $2.50 |
| ☐ THE MANNER MUSIC—Charles Reznikoff | 04337-7 | $2.25 |
| ☐ THE ICE AGE—Margaret Drabble | 04300-8 | $2.25 |
| ☐ DEATH OF AN EXPERT WITNESS—P. D. James | 04301-6 | $1.95 |
| ☐ ALWAYS IS NOT FOREVER—Van Slyke | 04271-0 | $2.25 |
| ☐ TIM—C. McCullough | 08545-2 | $1.75 |
| ☐ MIDNIGHT EXPRESS—B. Hayes<br>with W. Hoffer | 04302-4 | $2.25 |
| ☐ A BRIDGE TOO FAR—Cornelius Ryan | 08373-5 | $2.50 |
| ☐ CHILD OF THE MORNING—Paulene Gedge | 04227-3 | $2.25 |
| ☐ A CORONARY EVENT<br>—Michael Halberstam, M.D. & Stephen Lesher | 04213-3 | $1.95 |
| ☐ DO BLACK PATENT LEATHER SHOES<br>REALLY REFLECT UP?—John R. Powers | 08490-1 | $1.75 |
| ☐ EARTHLY POSSESSIONS—Anne Tyler | 04214-1 | $1.95 |
| ☐ THE HEART LISTENS—Helen Van Slyke | 08520-7 | $1.95 |

Buy them at your local bookstore or use this handy coupon for ordering:

---

**POPULAR LIBRARY**
P.O. Box C730, 524 Myrtle Ave., Pratt Station, Brooklyn, N.Y. 11205

Please send me the books I have checked above. Orders for less than 5 books must include 75¢ for the first book and 25¢ for each additional book to cover mailing and handling. I enclose $_____ in check or money order.

Name_____

Address_____

City_____ State/Zip_____

Please allow 4 to 5 weeks for delivery.

# FREE
# Fawcett Books Listing

There is Romance, Mystery, Suspense, and Adventure waiting for you inside the Fawcett Books Order Form. And it's yours to browse through and use to get all the books you've been wanting . . . but possibly couldn't find in your bookstore.

This easy-to-use order form is divided into categories and contains over 1500 titles by your favorite authors.

So don't delay—take advantage of this special opportunity to increase your reading pleasure.

Just send us your name and address and 35¢ (to help defray postage and handling costs).

**FAWCETT BOOKS GROUP**
P.O. Box C730, 524 Myrtle Ave., Pratt Station, Brooklyn, N.Y. 11205

Name_____
(please print)

Address_____
City _____ State _____ Zip_____

Do you know someone who enjoys books? Just give us their names and addresses and we'll send them an order form too!

Name_____
Address_____
City _____ State _____ Zip_____

Name_____
Address_____
City _____ State _____ Zip_____